Also by Jane Shemilt

Daughter
The Drowning Lesson
How Far We Fall
Little Friends
The Patient

JANE SHEMILT

ALL
HER
SECRETS

HarperCollins*Publishers*

HarperCollins*Publishers*
1 London Bridge Street
London, SE1 9GF

www.harpercollins.co.uk

HarperCollins*Publishers*
Macken House, 39/40 Mayor Street Upper
Dublin 1, D01 C9W8, Ireland

Published by HarperCollins*Publishers* 2023

1

A catalogue record for this book
is available from the British Library

ISBN: 978-0-00-852455-5

Set in Sabon LT Std by
Palimpsest Book Production Limited, Falkirk, Stirlingshire

Printed and Bound in the UK using
100% Renewable Electricity at CPI Group (UK) Ltd

MIX
Paper | Supporting
responsible forestry
FSC™ C007454

This book is produced from independently certified FSC™ paper
to ensure responsible forest management.

For more information visit: www.harpercollins.co.uk/green

To my family

Chapter 1

Paxos 2003

Sofie

The visitors were shocked into silence. The first glimpse of the ocean through the pine trees was always shocking. That blue came at you hard. Close up there were other colours: the crimson of Babas's boat, black shadows under the cliff, silvery fish in the shallows, but at a distance the sea was as unbroken and garish as one of Nico's wax drawings.

Sofie watched from the shade of the olive tree by the back door, the cat on her lap, his claws kneading her thighs. The old man climbed stiffly down from the driver's seat of his black Mercedes. His wife emerged from the other side. Peter and Jane, names that were the same as the children's in the books that Athena used to teach her English. Those children wore

1

clothes like the ones Athena made her wear: shirts with collars, bunchy skirts, and brown sandals, clothes from an England that no longer existed.

Real Peter and Jane were old and very rich. They wore expensive clothes. Her silky dress was patterned with red squares; he wore a soft white shirt, a biscuit-coloured suit, and a Panama hat. Jane's shoes were made of straps, they looked as though they'd never walked on a dusty path or even a pavement. Peter was head of an investment company in England, with branches all over the world. He put money into property and newspapers, books and films as well as alcohol, guns, and toothpaste. Sofie tried to work out how these things were connected; it seemed a jumble to her. Christos said that was the point, putting money into lots of different things meant one of them was bound to work. He must be right. Christos was clever, he studied engineering at university in Athens. He was saving to go to America after his degree, which was why he was here, working in Paxos for the summer. He wrote down how much he was earning each night in a notebook and added it up week by week. He said it made him feel better about being a slave.

'Peter earns a lot of money. A lot,' Athena said in a whisper, though she was in the kitchen at the time and no one else was there apart from Sofie and Christos. It was as though it was shameful to mention it. You weren't supposed to notice when people had money, though it was obvious that the renovation of the old mill had cost millions of euros. Sofie wasn't to talk about it. She mustn't let the guests know she had given up a month of the summer to help, either. A month of no friends, no trips to Monodendri beach, no picnics at Lakka. No ice cream sundaes at Capriccios with Gabriella. It was worse this year. There was more to miss, Gabriella had whispered, things might happen. She meant boys. Sofie didn't care about boys, but the ice creams and picnics were a loss.

Peter and Jane tipped their faces to the sun, drinking it in through their pale northern skin, absorbing the heat and the scent of thyme. They needn't hurry, they could stand here all afternoon if they wanted. Everything here belonged to them: the buildings, the fields of silvery olive trees, the beach, and the yacht bobbing in the sea. *Thalassa* was written on its side in gold; it was the name of their house too. *Thalassa*, for the sea.

Athena came to greet them, smiling her wide-open smile and wiping her hands on her apron; sizzling aubergines in preparation for supper, she had missed the sound of the car. Nico followed, holding fast to her skirt in his small fist. Sofie pushed Aries off her lap and got up. She'd made a friendship bracelet for the couple's daughter. 'Julia' was written in blue, letter by letter, on shells from the beach, strung together with Papa's fishing twine. She touched it in her pocket, feeling the shells' sharp edges with her fingertips.

But no young girl descended from the car. Sofie waited, her throat tightening. Julia hadn't come after all, stupid to think she might have done. She'd be nineteen by now; she would be travelling with a boyfriend to Thailand or India, one of those kinds of places. Why return to Paxos with the rest of the world to explore?

There were handshakes, exclamations over Nico's four-year-old size, how tall he was these days and Sophia, how grown-up for thirteen! What excellent English!

Sofie tried to smile but her mouth twisted awkwardly. She hated people calling her Sophia though that was her given name, after Babas's aunt, a complaining old woman who had died years ago. Nico had called her Sofie as soon as he could speak and now everyone did. She liked it better; it sounded more like her.

She had to pretend to be pleased to see the owners, but she wasn't. Peter and Jane weren't really interested in them, it was obvious they were only pretending and that her family were just caretakers to them, workers paid to do a job. The pretence would fade as the holiday wore on, it always did, she was used to that. Already Peter was inspecting his watch, though he said to his friends when they arrived, turning to indicate the house and the gardens with a grand sweep

4

of his arm, that this was a place where time ceased to exist.

That wasn't true for them of course, the workers. Babas was fishing by four in the morning. Athena rose at five to make breakfast, though you wouldn't guess that from the way she smiled at the guests. She told them their room was ready and that Dimitrios would bring up their bags. It was obvious they were tired, Jane more than Peter. Jane moved slowly; the journey had exhausted her. Kolena, the baker's mother, in her eighties, gathered olives and clambered along the cliffs for wild sage, but Jane would spend most of the holiday lying down.

Athena went back to the kitchen, still smiling as she tucked a strand of black hair behind her ear. She liked it when guests came, or she liked it at first. She enjoyed cooking and didn't mind that no one ever said thank you, but when they left at the end of summer, she would walk in the garden, admiring everything Dimitrios had done. She would go to the beach in the evenings or out in the boat with Babas. She looked younger then, she sang more.

The kettle was put on the stove for mint tea. Sofie had picked the mint earlier and arranged *kourabiedes* biscuits on the plate with the olive tree pattern. She thought the biscuits had been meant for their own Christmas and tried not to mind.

Nico stayed with Athena in the kitchen to help her make the loaves for supper. He stood on a stool to knead the dough for *eliopsoma*, special bread made with olives, rosemary, and oregano, Sofie's favourite. She retreated to the olive tree to shell peas and watch the drive for Peter's guests who would shortly arrive. It was mid-afternoon and searingly hot. The cicadas were screaming. The peas hit the side of the pot with a noise like tiny bullets from a gun.

Peter and Jane would be in their bedroom now, the biggest one, with long windows and a balcony that faced the sea. The shutters had been closed against the sun earlier in the day. New lemon soap was in the dish by the basin, she had put it there herself, along with a lemon leaf; afterwards her hands smelt of lemons all day. A bottle of wine had been placed in the fridge, two bottles on second thoughts. Jane liked wine.

There was a new mosaic of horses in the courtyard, and a fountain with the statue of a naked girl bought from a museum and delivered last week. Peter chose what he wanted very carefully. The house was famous, there were photographs in magazines that Athena kept in a scrapbook.

Dimitrios and Christos moved from where they had been standing in the shade by the wall near the car. They were the sons of Athena's two older sisters. Dimitrios had a ponytail and wore red trainers; Christos had short hair and was thinner – at least, that was how the guests would tell them apart. They wouldn't know Dimitrios was kind, soft, as Babas called him, or that he was in love with Roxana, who worked in a bar in Gaios. Roxana had short black hair and sloping eyes; she loved reading and lent Sofie her books when she'd finished with them. Dimitrios was saving money to buy land for a house so they could get married. Christos didn't have time for a girlfriend; he studied late at night. He'd go far, Babas said. Christos dreamt of getting rich in America, but Sofie thought that was much too far. She looked forward to the arrival of her cousins every year for weeks and felt sorry that Peter always stared at them as if they were strangers he'd never seen before.

Dimitrios opened the boot of the Mercedes and reached for the cases at the same moment that the back door swung open and a girl stepped out, blonde hair swinging, one tanned hand holding a red phone. Julia, here after all. She had changed almost beyond recognition, though she still had that way of holding her head sideways, as though listening to something, or the echo of something. The boys stared.

She was taller, that was to be expected, but also much thinner, so thin it could be ill thin rather than diet thin. She was film star lovely. It was difficult to tell if her beauty was connected to her thinness, because or in spite of it. Her features were symmetrical as if placed on the smooth surface of her face by a

7

craftsman. One of Sofie's eyes was slightly higher than the other, her mouth too wide, her hair too wild. Julia's hair was smooth and blonder than it used to be, lighter in stripes. She wore torn denim shorts, and her thighs didn't touch at the top. There were leather bangles around her wrists and her nails were a shiny red. Two years ago, seventeen years to Sofie's eleven, she had allowed Sofie into her room and let her try out her make-up. It was obvious that wouldn't happen now.

Julia didn't look happy but other things might be more important to her than happiness, admiration perhaps, or her father's approval. She had admitted as much when painting Sofie's nails. It hadn't mattered that Sofie was shy, words had poured from Julia in a thick stream, like the yellow stuff that burst out of the boil on Sofie's foot when Babas had removed the sea urchin spike she got on Osaka beach.

'My father,' Julia spat. 'Christ. What a fucking pervert. He watches me constantly. He wants his friends to like me, touch me. Does yours do that?'

Sofie hadn't known what to say. Sometimes Babas patted her head or said she would make him proud, but mostly he was silent, tired out from working. Everyone knew his rules, they were simple: to help Athena, work hard, and go to church on Sundays and saints' days. He met his friends in the quiet season for a drink in the bar or when they came to help with the olive harvest. They were hard-working types like him, with leathery faces and big families.

Julia hadn't needed an answer anyway. She bent lower over Sofie's foot as she painted each nail. Her hair tickled the skin of Sofie's leg.

'He wants me to flirt with them, so they'll get hooked in and then feel guilty. It's a bit like blackmail. I slept with Paul two years ago. I was fifteen. It was okay actually, I quite liked it.'

Julia inspected the nails she'd done, then tapped hard on that ankle to let Sofie know to put that foot down, she wanted the other one.

'Daddy likes power over his friends. That's why he invites them. It's what my mother says anyway, though she doesn't know the half of it. Or pretends she doesn't.'

Sofie still didn't know what to say but Julia's words kept gushing out.

'Men are so fucking stupid.' She had said fucking like it was a word that made her feel grown up. 'I like making them beg. I'm cleverer than any of them but no one cares, not even my father. I came top in my class last term, and he didn't give a fuck.'

Now, today, she ignored everyone and walked down the steps to the pool, slouching a little. There was a pot on each step containing jasmine, lavender, and roses that Athena had planted and watered for months. You could smell the scent as you passed, but Julia was looking at her phone and didn't glance at them once.

Sofie picked up a towel from the pile in the box by the back door and followed at a distance. The friendship bracelet was cupped in her hand. Julia was already lying on a sun lounger, having discarded her clothes in a heap. Her body in a black bikini was angles and bones, long limbs, and unmarked skin.

Athena told Sofie she was too thin but that wasn't true; she wasn't thin like Julia, not glamorously, dangerously thin. Julia's toenails gleamed and her body glistened. Sofie's toenails were lined with dirt, there was a faint fuzz of hair on her legs. She had scratches on her arms from Aries, and her right thigh was bruised where she had fallen against a rock on the beach, pulling in the boat for Babas.

She put the towel on the table next to Julia and the friendship bracelet on top, but Julia didn't even look. Sofie turned for the steps, cheeks burning, when Julia made a sound, and something flew from her hand to land with a splash in the pool. For one long moment, Sofie thought it was the bracelet, but it was a green lizard, legs grappling in the water. She cupped her hands and lifted him out. The tiny body twitched once against her palm. Julia's sunglasses had slipped, her gaze levelled on Sofie, the stare was defiant. Sofie saw she was recognized and dismissed.

The gravel from the drive crunched, more cars were

arriving. Sofie hurried back up the steps, past the Mercedes. A red sports car and a blue van had arrived. She placed the lizard in the sun on the table by the back door, out of Aries's reach. It lay very still. She wouldn't think about it now: she was good at not thinking about things; Babas had taught her that. When *Yia-yia* died, Babas was all right in a week. You go on, he said, keeping steady, same as usual. It worked, at least it had so far. Her mind touched her grandmother sometimes. *Yia-yia* had smelt of lavender, her face had been crumpled and kind. She had given Sofie her precious necklace, a little chain made of gold. And then Sofie made herself think about something else, like how to persuade Athena to buy her jeans like Gabriella's or the taste of lemon ice cream at Capriccios and *Yia-yia's* image would fade.

A large woman with long white hair and a creased dress got out of the sports car. Her face drooped one side. She'd had one of those operations, Julia told her, to make her face smoother and it was worse than if she hadn't bothered at all. Her fault, Julia had said, smiling. The woman was a writer who won a prize for her book last year, the news coming through at supper when all the guests were here. Peter was pleased but the others had seemed downcast.

A man with a shaven head jumped out of the van; he had the look of a boxer but was something important to do with films. His name was Paul, he'd been coming for years. He knew everyone in America, Julia said. He had a different woman with him each year. The new one struggled out of the passenger seat; she wore a ring and was carrying a squirming toddler that she put down on the drive.

A guy with thin grey hair stepped down from the back seat of the van, blinking in the light. He'd been before too. Christos said he was head of a big company that made phones and was incredibly rich. He was pale and tall like the plants Sofie grew at school without light, as an experiment. Three boys got out of the back, clambering down awkwardly. One was his teenage son, Steven, pale like his father. Last year he had hunched at the table, playing games on his phone. This time he had friends: a dark-haired skinny boy with spots, and a shorter, fatter one whose curly orange mop looked wet with sweat.

Everyone stood there silently like the start of the play she'd seen with Mama. The actors had been on stage when the curtains went up, but no one had said anything for a while. Sofie was afraid they'd forgotten their words. Mama explained afterwards that the pause was important, it was a sign of danger, a warning to watch out. A few moments later, as if an invisible director had whispered start, everything happened at once. The men laughed and shook hands with each other; Paul kissed the white-haired woman on the cheek. The three boys swarmed down the steps, there

12

was a splash then shouts and laughter. They must have dived into the pool with their clothes on, hoping to impress Julia, though Sofie imagined her getting up and walking away with that slouchy new walk of hers.

The toddler staggered across the drive to the steps. The mother didn't notice; she was holding Paul's arm as if he was an expensive handbag that might get stolen if she dared put it down. Sofie ran, bent to the child, and encircled him with her arms. She didn't touch him, she knew better than that. A moment later, the mother was there, shrieking and lifting him high as though Sofie was a disease he might catch. The child began crying. The woman was new, she didn't understand the rules; you had to pretend to be nice to the servants, nicer than was natural. It was sham of course, a show. Everyone knew that too.

Sofie walked back to her olive tree and sat down. She would be asked to baby sit, sooner or later. She hugged her knees, inhaling the traces of earth and salt on her skin. They would take her help for granted, in the same way they accepted the silky sheets and the thick white towels, the food, the flowers, and the sparkling water in the pool. Did they think these things appeared by magic? Christos said it was more complicated than that; they knew the family worked hard, but it was easier to pretend they had no idea.

Peter allowed the family to live on the estate year-round in a converted olive store near the donkey sheds. They didn't pay rent, but they worked instead, looking after the guests in the summer, taking care of the garden and the yacht, harvesting olives in the winter, and repairing things. The money they earned in the summer had to last them until next year, together with the cash from Babas's fishing. Money in exchange for effort. Equations were supposed to balance but this one didn't, at least not for her. She was needed all the time, in the kitchen, in the house, and in the guests' cabins for cleaning and for laundering the sheets. She helped serve the meals. There were some good things: Christos taught her backgammon in the afternoons and Dimitrios took her round the fields on his motorbike if everyone was out. At night she watched nature programmes with Babas or picked out films from Dimitrios's DVD collection. Then there was her secret place where she could sometimes escape: the shed at the back of the beach where the old boat was stored. The hull was perfect to rest against, and the shafts of sun that came through the gaps in the roof gave just enough light for reading. No one else ever went there, it was hidden by trees. It smelt of creosote and diesel oil and it was very quiet, with only the noise of the sea and the birds, the scratchy sounds of mice and lizards to keep her company.

There wasn't time to go today, already the light had deepened. The smells of dry soil and rope from the hammock folded themselves inside the scent of wine and fish from the kitchen, the cigarette smoke from the men round the table and, when the women joined them, the sharper scent of perfume.

It was Nico's bedtime; this was Mama's busiest hour, so Sofie watched him while he cleaned his teeth, then read him a story from Mama's *Legends of Greece and Rome*, she had read them so often, they both knew them by heart. She stroked his hair till he went to sleep, then changed into a fresh shirt, though it didn't really matter what she wore. None of the guests looked at her, most of the time they didn't notice she was there. They didn't notice the fish stew either, though it had taken Babas hours to catch the fish and Mama more time to simmer it with fennel, capers, and ouzo. The guests swerved to avoid the plates as Sofie set them down; it felt as if they were swerving to avoid her. Athena walked back to the kitchen. She was limping a little. Her feet in her best shoes were starting to swell. Once the food had been set out, Sofie sat on the low wall circling the terrace, half hidden among the red bougainvillea, watching as Athena had told her to do.

Peter served everyone. Julia didn't even glance at the food on her plate. Paul arrived late and sat beside her, his wife and child on his other side. His head bent towards Julia, while his wife tried to talk to the pale grey-haired guy who was smoking and shovelling in food at the same time. Jane watched her daughter and sipped her drink. She hardly touched her food.

The younger boys sat on the opposite side of the table from Julia; the pale guy's son was still looking at his phone; the spotty boy, now in a blue shirt, talked loudly; and the ginger one in pink linen laughed with a noise like the pig on Syrios's farm. He knocked his wine over. Sofie picked up the spare tablecloth next to her on the wall, but the woman with white hair said it was an offering to Bacchus and waved her away.

Peter's mouth was smiling but his eyes were everywhere, darting to the spilt wine, Julia's plate, her face, Paul's face. Paul's hand touched Julia's as he filled her glass, her hair swung as she turned towards him, and Peter watched it all. Gabriella talked about sex a lot; it sounded disgusting to Sofie, but even she could tell that sex, the possibility of sex was being traded around the table. All the time the woman with white hair talked non-stop, a wrinkled hand on Peter's arm. The stream of conversation reminded Sofie of oil, the green-gold oil from Peter's trees, coating everything in a smooth layer, disguising the taste of what was underneath.

The shadows from the trees were very dark. The child began crying. His mother left the table with him, her mouth was angry, so was her walk. She might have thought a baby would bind his father closer to her, but before she was out of sight, Paul had moved even nearer to Julia. Jane left the table, carrying her glass of wine, and walked unsteadily to the house. The boys stopped talking altogether. The dark-haired boy pushed his seat back, scraping the stones. He and his friends were frowning though no one seemed to notice. Sofie recognized the moment from those nature programmes when the young males began to turn away from the group, looking elsewhere.

Her feet tingled and stung and, looking down, she saw little red ants were running over them, sending pinpricks up her legs like darts.

Chapter 2

London 2023

Julia

We are a perfect family.

That's what you might think, it's what James would want you to think, one of those perfect families you see in an upmarket Sunday newspaper supplement. People want role models: it seems we fit the bill. A headmaster in his thirties and his lovely family, youth, brains, and beauty wrapped in a package. We were in *GQ* this week: Charlotte, my beautiful Lottie, fifteen years old, surfing in Cornwall, blonde hair flying; James, on the lawn with a Labrador, borrowed specially; me, in our Westminster kitchen, homemade focaccia on the island.

My husband has the important job and salary. I am the wife and mother, though not of his child. I am the cook for school events; chef sounds better but, all the same, a job that doesn't threaten his. Never mind that I am the cleverer of us two, I needed the marriage and accepted the trade-off. You wouldn't think that from the wedding photos of seven years ago. I look radiant, slim as a knife in backless ivory at the door of Chelsea Registry Office.

Father was dead by then. Mother was there, ravaged but making an effort. No one dreamt she'd outlast him. Lottie was eight, angelic in a white frock with her ringlets, it was impossible to tell how much she disliked James, even then.

Perfect lives you might say, looking at the magazine, perfect daughter, homes, clothes, hair, and teeth. You would have trusted in those images, they have power, which is what my story is really about: truth and power, how it's traded and how lost.

A headmaster's life is marked out in bells: assembly and lesson bells, lunchtime and prep time; they ring out across the narrow streets between the main school buildings and our house, louder and more insistent than the chimes from Big Ben, though we hear those too. Even if the bells didn't echo in every room, I would still hear them. Even now I hear them in my sleep.

Back to the present, because this is a story that needs to be told as it unfolds.

Today is the first day of the autumn term. The London sky at dawn is clear, tinged tenderly with pink. It will be hot. In a couple of hours, the school children will dress in their thick winter uniforms, ties, and blazers. The doors of school will close behind them, shutting out the woods, the sandy beaches, and the sea.

James sits at the island in the kitchen, the lowest of the four storeys of our narrow terraced house which stands in a street of identical Georgian homes with dark brick walls and sash windows, three streets from the school. James is hungry after his work-out; he eats a mix of oats and seeds, yoghurt. Fruit. Two eggs. I eat almost nothing. Usually, nothing.

The kitchen looks over an enclosed and shady court-yard where the stems of a passionflower climb the walls, leaves yellowing, tendrils seeking the sun in vain. The plant is a long way from its sisters in Mexico, where we saw them on our honeymoon. It's supposed to climb and sprawl in the heat, to throw up flowers and then fruit, but it's struggling. I should root it out but it's still alive.

It isn't the first day of term for us. We've been back a month. A headmaster needs to set the course and steer the ship, never mind that it sails with a momentum of its own, piloted by others. With his hand barely resting on the wheel, James can focus on what he does best, charm. He charms the parents, especially future ones. He murmurs, with a self-deprecating smile, that he's like a GP. He knows enough to diagnose and refer, though, here his voice dips in sincerity, the buck stops with him. You wouldn't think that to look at him this morning: his face is calm. He knows the day ahead will be full of challenges, but he is confident others will meet them. Others, like me.

I sit opposite, reading his diary on my tablet, adjusting as I go, tapping in additions with comments for Libby, his PA. I keep abreast of the educational news, especially the current topics, sexualized bullying in private schools and paedophile teachers. We talked about it last night, but James is confident neither are problems here. James is always confident, it's part of his charm.

He smiles when I pour coffee, but I doubt he sees me clearly, though he would if I wasn't perfect: if my hair wasn't shining with highlights and cut so it swings; if my body were not slim; if I didn't smell of Chanel No. 5 or wear beautiful clothes. He pays for whatever I want, he's generous like that. I represent the school and therefore him. Appearances are everything. Luckily, he can't see inside. I hide my anxiety well. I make lists.

There are twenty items today. I've ticked off the first five already. The dawn run. Tick. James's clothes laid out ready. Tick. The muffins with which to greet the staff preparing the food for the evening event. Emails sent to Libby. Diary updated. Tick. Tick. Tick.

The list frees my thoughts, which return to Lottie. She went back last night. Boarding was James's idea, he thought it best she separate herself from us when she turned thirteen; after all he explained, he was her headmaster as well as stepfather; it could be tricky for her and in any case she needed independence. Anthony, her father, my first husband, was tracked down and consulted. He agreed as long as he didn't have to pay the fees. Lottie was happy, she wanted to be with her friends and, I suspect, away from James, but I miss her. The boarding house is a mere six streets away; the kind of distance I could run in ten minutes, but all the same, I miss the late-night confidences, the random jokes and passing hugs, her sleepy freckled face at breakfast. I miss the stomping way she ran upstairs, the music, the scent of bubble bath. I even miss the mess, the games kit by the door, her scattered shoes. The toast crumbs and dropped butter knives, the empty biscuit packets in the cupboard. I'd wondered if moving out might make us closer still, but she's more distant these days, she shares less. It's her age, James says. He tells me not to worry but he can't police my thoughts any more than I can. I can't stop the background ache of missing her all the time.

James turns to the leaders, then skims the education pages. He has ten minutes left. He knows I'll tell him when it's time to slip on his jacket and walk the narrow streets that bring him to the school, through the stone archway and along the sides of the grassy square to his office. Libby will be waiting with a list of the day's academic events, aligned with the social ones sent by me. I know the outline of his days before he does, and that today will end with the parents' evening for future pupils.

You would think that the first parents' evening would concern the current children, but you would be wrong. School life is about business: the next step, the cash flow. The first day of term is always about the future.

James is fine with that. James is fine with anything his team suggests, which is why everyone loves him. He trusts people, they trust him back. The mothers adore him. It doesn't matter what the school children think of him, he is not someone they are expected to have opinions about, which makes him a little like God; they take him for granted as they do God. They feel safe, as I do. I doubt the pupils love him, though I did. I do. We are talking in the present tense, and in the present, I tell myself quite often we are deeply in love.

When we first compared notes, it was obvious my dreams had been brighter than his. I'd planned to set up a language school after university, but by the time I met James that dream had faded. I was thirty-two, a single parent, teaching part-time, tutoring at night, clinging on by my fingertips. James's dreams had never been dreams; they were ambitions. My dreams had won a student award but look where I am now and look where he is. Ambition wins every time.

The bell goes, the one that wakes the boarders. A few streets away, Lottie will be waking, wandering into the bathroom in her new pyjamas, yawning and greeting her friends. James stands up, tall, and broad-shouldered, his looks catch at my heart, still. I smile and hold out his jacket and he puts it on. He tells me I'm on edge today, and that's not a good image to project, especially at parents' evening. I need to be calm, and I promise to try. We kiss, my tongue in his mouth and his hand on my arse. I push my pelvis into his. I want him to remember this moment. I want him to remember the sex last night. I need him to think of that when he is with Libby or walking to lunch with a young student teacher. The equation balances: sex and cooking in exchange for a home and Lottie's education. Money matters since I have so little of my own. It's more than that of course, there's his kindness, he's always been a generous man. His looks count too. I want him to think of us standing in the hall, the bunch of dahlias to our right on the polished table. Our reflections in the large eighteenth-century mirror look like the cover of a book. Not a love story as it turns out, but you would have to be clever to guess that. The blood red dahlias would give you a clue.

Chapter 3

Paxos 2003

Sofie

Ants swarmed over Sofie; their bodies crawled between her legs. They crept to her abdomen and then to her chest in their thousands. Some trickled along her arms, up her neck and into her ears. She heard a voice shouting; her eyes snapped open. It was a dream. She was in her bed, in the room she shared with Nico. It was her voice.

Nico's wide brown eyes were level with hers. He was running a small Lego car over her arm. She forgot to close the shutters last night and the bright light must have woken him. The room was warm, he was wearing his swimming trunks. She wanted to stay in bed, but this was his promised time. He would spend the rest of the day with Mama in the kitchen or hanging around with Dimitrios, who might allow him to pull up weeds or pick tomatoes, but no one had time to play.

It was no use protesting she was still in her pyjamas, a thin top and thinner shorts, as soon as her feet were on the ground, he began tugging her out of the door. He was strong for a four-year-old, unrelenting when he wanted something. They had to be quiet: they weren't allowed on the beach when the guests were here, and they shouldn't go into the sea. Neither of them could swim.

It took ten minutes to hurry down the path and through the trees on the headland, crunching on pine needles, jumping down narrow stone ledges to the beach. The air was mint fresh. They avoided the easier steps leading from the garden path through a gate to the quay on the other side of the cove, too exposed. Babas might spot them, or one of the guests. Nico ran over the pebbles and straight into the sea, while Sofie walked to the edge of the water and stood ankle deep, ready to wade in and pluck him back.

This was the year she should learn to swim. Christos would teach her: he offered every year, but she was scared. What if there was something hiding beneath the water that no one could see, like the shark in that film? She stepped further, a little deeper, shivering with fear. Most people plunged in and swam, emerging with a grin, as if they had shed something they didn't want in the water. She made herself go forward and now she was up to her knees.

She heard the boys before she saw them, two figures emerging from the dazzle, walking slowly at the water's edge, footsteps crunching in shingle: the two new boys without their friend. Even at a distance they looked tired. They were wearing what they wore last night but their shirts were crumpled, the pink linen stained. They were smoking, blue-grey fumes drifted in the air.

Nico was still in the water; he hadn't noticed the boys approaching. Would they be angry that she and her brother were on the beach? They were new, perhaps they didn't know the rules. Sofie faced away from the shore, that way they might walk on by, but the crunching stopped. She stepped further, the water creeping higher, reaching to the divide between her legs.

'Nico,' she whispered. He carried on jumping up and down, his hands slapping the water, and took no notice at all.

'Hey.' The new voice was English, it had an unfamiliar, twangy accent and sounded amused. Could they see through her thin clothes? Was that funny? She didn't dare turn round.

'Hey there.' There were two voices this time, they sounded impatient. What if they reported her for being rude?

She turned around. Both boys were taking off their shirts and their trousers. The ginger one had rolls of fat on his front, the dark one was scrawny. She saw him notice her glance and smile. She looked away quickly, her skin prickling.

'Nico, come back,' she whispered, hoarsely this time.

He was muttering to himself in that fast way he had and still hadn't noticed the boys. She wanted him closer, much closer, for herself as much as for him. The next moment, she was up to her waist.

The boys splashed up to her, one on each side. 'Had a swim then?'

She shook her head, not looking at either of them. 'Why not?'

'*Fovos.*' Unnoticed, Nico had come near. He spoke so rarely to strangers that she stared at him, surprised. The boys seemed to know what that word meant. Fear.

'Aha.' The dark one gripped her arm with his thin fingers, his clasp surprisingly strong. The cold shivered to her shoulder.

'For God's sake, Jay,' his friend said, laughter feathering his voice.

'Fuck off, Ginger.'

Jay bent so his mouth was level with Sofie's ear. 'Would you like me to teach you?' he whispered. The words were warm and wet in her ear.

She stood very still, excitement swelling alongside surprise. He had heard what Nico said, and he wanted to help her. No one usually noticed her. She wanted to close her eyes as she did when the sun was too bright; she wanted to bask in the moment.

'I'll take care of you.' His breath moved her hair.

Ginger was grinning but she didn't look at him. This kind of thing didn't happen, not to her, not when guests were here, when all the days were the same, with lists of jobs to do and no time to spare. This was a moment to hold close and examine later, to share with Gabriella who would be jealous.

She nodded, her heart fluttering.

'Trust me,' Jay whispered.

He took hold of her by the waist and tipped her body forward, his arm pressed under her abdomen like a clamp as her face dipped into the water. She could hear Ginger's grunting laugh.

'Kick,' Jay said.

There was a little block of stained concrete among the pebbles on the seabed beneath her; she had never seen the bottom of the sea like this. She felt weightless and very strong. A quicksilver pulse of excitement, of triumph coursed through her body. Jay told her to kick again, and she felt her feet break the water into shards. For those moments she was someone else, someone different, with power and daring.

And then her lungs were bursting, so she put her

feet on the ground. Jay's arm slid away, and she was standing, gasping for breath. Jay was grinning but now she felt awkward. She was in the sea with a guest against all the rules and her clothes were clinging to her like wet paper. She turned and ran, kicking through the water to the beach. Nico followed more slowly, picking up stones for his collection. They scrambled up the cliff to the wood, the boys' voices following them into the trees. She reached the path and Nico caught up and raced her back, both gasping with laughter, though she wasn't sure why.

Nico showered first. Sofie threw him a towel when he'd finished and showered quickly, dried and dressed. A clean skirt, her tight shirt. Gabriella had a bra, a lacey one with a pink satin bow, but Athena hadn't noticed Sofie was growing and changing, that her breasts were swelling. They felt sore, especially the nipples. There was no point in asking Athena for a bra, she couldn't spare the time to take her daughter to the shops while the guests were there. She would just have to wait. Sofie tucked her curls behind her ears, shoved her feet into plimsolls and hurried outside.

It was hot now. The cicadas had started. The males had tiny drums hidden under their bodies; the noise attracted females, Dimitrios told her, though Sofie thought that couldn't be right, surely it would scare them away. Dimitrios was already in the vegetable patch, watering the lettuces. She waved, and he grinned back with a thumbs-up sign. Even if her eyes were closed, she would know exactly where she was in the garden, the dark odour of wet earth mixed with the sharp smell of tomatoes and the bitter scent of lettuce. She rounded the stand of lemon trees and hurried through the courtyard at the back of the house with its beds of sage, thyme, and peppery basil. The kitchen door was wide open.

Athena was walking back and forth, slippers slapping against the soles of her feet. The radio was playing the Bouzouki music that Athena loved. She danced to it sometimes in the kitchen at night, but mornings were busy. She was throwing away the shells from the oranges she'd just juiced. Sofie was late, squeezing the oranges was her job. Athena didn't say anything, there wasn't time to talk, though a swirl of words from the guests outside flowed into the kitchen. Babas said talk in the morning was a luxury you had to be rich to afford.

Athena's eyes were shadowed with tiredness, but she looked as calm as she always did. It seemed impossible that her mother had ever had thoughts like Sofie's, multitudes of wordless ideas, frightened and hopeful, fluttering together like birds in a cage. Athena must have let those kinds of thoughts escape a long time ago, she seemed so peaceful, her movements so certain. How did you get to that stage?

Athena handed Sofie the basket of bread and the jug of orange juice. Sofie carried them both to the terrace outside where the family was sitting. Jane took a slice of bread from the basket before Sofie had put it on the table and placed it on Julia's plate, but Julia ignored it completely.

Sofie ran back and brought out slices of thin pink ham and hard-boiled eggs, Athena's fig jam. Her stomach growled as she hurried back and forth, bringing a cake studded with apricots and almonds, peaches, and bowls of creamy yoghurt.

Christos was cleaning the swimming pool beneath the terrace; she could hear his footsteps and the splashy sound as he dragged the net through the water. When Sofie looked over the wall, a fragment of blue gleamed from the pile of old leaves and cigarette stubs by his feet. The friendship bracelet. It would be swept up and dumped with the rest of the rubbish in the bin for collection. She ran down the steps, picked it up, put it in her pocket and ran back again, eyes stinging.

More guests arrived at the table one by one: Paul arguing with his wife in an undertone, the baby whining in her arms; the pale guy was yawning, his grey hair stragglier than ever. By the time Sofie came back with the coffee, Jay and Ginger were sprawled in their chairs, ignoring everyone including the friend who'd invited them, already hunched over his phone. Would they give her away? She needn't have worried, they gave no sign of having seen her before. Ginger seemed half asleep, his red curls falling over his face, while Jay leant across the table, holding out the butter to Julia. She ignored him, turning to Paul. Jay's face flushed pink, he withdrew his hand abruptly, knocking over the jug of juice. Orange juice soaked into the cake, some dripped onto the blonde wife's lap. Peter was furious, shouting for cloths, snatching them from Sofie. Later she took the wrecked cake away.

After breakfast, Peter asked Athena to lay a separate table for the boys for future meals. That evening at supper the boys talked and laughed louder than ever, though Sofie saw Jay glancing at Julia across the gap between the tables, his face sullen.

After the meal, everyone went back to their rooms apart from Peter, Julia, and Paul. Julia sat by the pool; her legs hanging down in the floodlit water looked like sea creatures in an aquarium, the toenails were little red eyes. She was smoking and leant against Paul's shoulder, laughing and talking with a slurred voice. When she had cleaned Paul's room last year, Sofie had seen a little pile of white powder on his bedside table. Dimitrios had come to see; he said it was cocaine, she was not to touch and not to say anything. Perhaps Paul had given Julia some of that. Peter sat at the table on his own, watching Paul with his daughter. His expression was remote but intent, like the emperor watching wild animals circling the prisoners in Dimitrios's film about gladiators. After a while Peter got up and stumped off to his bedroom, as though he already knew how this would end.

Sofie was wearing her swimming costume the next morning when the boys came to the beach for the second time. She was holding hands with Nico in the water, and her heart began to pound when she heard footsteps on the shingle. Jay came close and smiled and she smiled back; she imagined Gabriella telling her not to grin like a child, but she couldn't help it. She put her hand to her mouth to try to disguise the way her lips were stretching in case it made her look ugly.

'So, you want to do it again?'

She nodded and, slipping his arm around her waist, he tipped her forward and told her to kick hard. She was conscious of the grip of his arm and hands, his high-pitched laugh. He half pulled and half dragged her fast through the water, more roughly than yesterday. It was exciting but frightening at the same time. She squirmed away after a few moments and ran out of the water, taking Nico's hand and hurrying him up the beach. They clambered up the cliff together, and ran through the wood to their home. Later, sweeping the terrace and making beds she found herself smiling for no particular reason. That evening when she brought out the lamb *kleftiko*, she was aware that his gaze swung briefly from Julia to her and then back again. He wasn't smiling though.

She wanted to tell her mother she'd had a swimming lesson with a guest, but she didn't. It was one of those things that were forbidden for reasons never properly explained. Excitement and guilt bubbled inside; it was as if she had pushed at the boundary between her and the guests and, for a few seconds, it had seemed to give.

Chapter 4

London 2023

Julia

The great hall is full of parents. James stands on the stage; through the mullioned window behind him the autumn evening darkens. Heads turn towards him, voices hush. My face might have the same expression as other parents. I am interested in what my husband has to say as he so seldom says it to me.

The tables at the back of the hall are laden with the food I prepared: pieces of curried lobster on sticks, boar sausages, mini avocado toasts with caviar, bruschetta with tomato jam and mozzarella. Tiny portions of smoked salmon quiche. Macarons and strawberry tarts. Not much has been eaten, the audience is focused on information for now, not food. They want to know what they might be buying into.

James stands at the podium, head high and shoulders square, hair swept back, all part of the performance, as are the Armani suit and Louboutin shoes. Good taste and reliability, like the school. He looks good this evening, and I feel proud of him, proud of the attention he commands. Big Ben sounds the hour with seven deep notes which echo in the room, and James begins to speak. The silence of the audience grows deeper. Who is he really, they might be asking themselves as they listen. What is he like? The answer would be surprising. He doesn't exist, not in the way they imagine. He is a symbol of power and success, albeit younger than most, one in a line of appointed rulers whose picture lines up with the others that hang in the hall. He talks about success. He doesn't mention failure or the issue of boys' behaviour towards the girls and certainly not paedophilia. They want to believe their children will triumph and the success that they crave can be bought; they take safety for granted.

James talks about opportunities, class sizes, Oxbridge entrance and pastoral care, sports facilities. His tone becomes sonorous like church bells on a Sunday evening, gathering in the faithful.

There is little new in his speech, that's not what parents want, they are after reassurance and promises they can believe. They listen, absorbed; most don't notice that someone has come in, though the people nearest the door are whispering and looking. The hairs on the back of my neck rise. Last year there was a disruption at this very meeting. Arron Mitchell had stormed in, shouting. His daughter, Angel, had accused the art professor of assault. By the time of the disturbance, the complaint had been dismissed and Angel had left. Her father couldn't accept the verdict, he had come to rage and threaten. Police were called to the meeting and Mitchell was swiftly removed, but it cast a pall and affected the numbers signing up. James had been worried, an accusation could harm the school's reputation, including his. It was a dangerous time to be a teacher he told me quietly, especially a male one, a teacher's innocence is hard to prove if a child decides to lie. As it was, the complaint had reached the press. Cosmo was lucky to have escaped unscathed, as was the school. Angel had been Lottie's best friend, her mother, Grace, had been mine. Lottie stayed in touch with Angel, but she didn't call round any more, and Grace refused to take my calls.

But it's not Arron Mitchell this time, it's a woman. She stands by the door at the point where the wave of attention crested then retreated. Now I can see her, I understand the flurry of attention. She is dressed in crimson and has the starry beauty of a young Elizabeth Taylor. I watch her watching James before the crowd shifts again, hiding her from view.

I needn't have panicked, a late arriving parent, that's all, albeit an attractive one. James was right, I'm on edge.

The speech ends and the crowds surge towards the table. As I hand out plates and pass food, I hear a fruity cough behind me.

'You have excelled yourself, my dear.' My elbow is touched with damp fingers; Cosmo, the teacher accused then cleared of misconduct, famous for his photographic portraits and one of the draws of the school. James said we might have guessed he'd attract blackmail. His soft voice is at odds with his bulk, disguised in an untucked black shirt. His bald head shines. He jumbles sausages onto his plate, along with lobster on sticks, and bruschetta. Strange that an obese man should be so publicly greedy, you might have thought he'd be ashamed. It's hard to believe he's in his mid-thirties like James, he looks decades older, but no one minds, he's a celebrity. His exhibitions draw crowds. His photographs are usually of bodies, sometimes famous ones, with perfect skin, curves that could be breasts or buttocks, smooth outlines of flesh from the inside of a wrist or thigh. Privately I think his work lacks compassion, he is more of a spectator, a voyeur, though he wouldn't use that word. On second thoughts, he wouldn't care. As we talk, a musky scent floats between us: the woman in red has approached and is standing near Cosmo, as if waiting to talk. I could tell her she'd be wasting her time, Cosmo dislikes parents. A sharp-faced man jogs my arm, he wants to talk about scholarships. His stream of words seems to need no answer, and I try to hear what is being said on my other side.

'. . . proven to reduce stress.' The woman's voice is lightly accented, Italian at a guess. Cosmo's glance flickers over her and then away.

'What makes you think I'm stressed?' He posts a sausage into his mouth. His eyes are hostile.

'Teaching is stressful, all teachers deserve the chance to reflect and set achievable goals for themselves.' Her smile seems effortless, though it must cost something in the face of his rudeness. 'I could help.'

He shrugs plump shoulders, turns away and is claimed by a couple who all but genuflect. The man beside me has disappeared. Before I have a chance to excuse Cosmo's behaviour, James appears and leans across me to take a slice of salmon quiche.

'Okay, darling?' He has come for praise about the speech, though the truth is, I wrote much of it myself. He won't thank me, someone might overhear.

'You spoke beautifully.'

'Almost as well as you cook.' He swallows his slice and kisses me.

I tread down irritation; he doesn't mean to be

patronizing, though he knows I gained a starred first in languages to his 2.2. Making canapes is not my career, teaching was. I have to remember I made this privileged bed for myself, it suited me to lie on it at the time. An impoverished single mother wants a secure home for her child or at least I did. James had arrived like a godsend.

As he lifts his head from the kiss, the woman who had talked to Cosmo steps nearer, almost between us. She smiles up at him; the dark hair is smoothly gathered, her make-up flawless. James smiles back; he likes women who are well-presented, and she is immaculate.

'I'm Laurel Rossi,' she says, and her voice is quiet, the kind of quiet that draws you in.

'How can I help?' James's tone is gentle as if she were shy, though I can see already that's a misconception. 'Your daughter or son wishes to join us?'

I know the answer to that too, even before she shakes her head. Close up, she has the fresh look of a woman with no children. Her eyes sparkle, her skin is dewy.

'I wanted to offer you something.' Her body tilts towards him. It seems primitive to me but James stills as if at a command.

'I'm a therapist. I have a track record of helping those in top-level jobs to greater success.'

It's as if she has studied him carefully and knows exactly what to say. It works, he looks interested.

'You think I need helping?'

'Teaching is tough. I should know, my husband is a teacher.'

'Really? Where?'

'Rome.' She moves closer still. 'Worries lessen if you talk them through.'

'So, you think you can lighten the load?' He smiles again, an edge of mockery has crept into his voice.

'I could help you carry it more easily.' She is taking this seriously. I want to warn her that James is stringing her along. Later, with me, he will make fun of her.

'Anxiety and stress make it difficult to cope,' she continues, her dark eyes are serious. 'It's hard to imagine a more stressful job than being head of a school. I can offer a way of coping.'

'I'm lucky.' James's smile glimmers with cruelty. He puts his arm around me, and I watch her, hoping she won't be hurt.

'Very lucky.' His voice is as silky as the wine. 'I'm never anxious. There's no need to be, my wife is anxious enough for two.'

I'm wrong. It isn't the therapist who's the victim, it's me. He knows the anxiety that laps at my life like sour milk: Lottie, the catering, writing his speeches, and keeping the diary. My volunteering job. My looks and my weight; but he doesn't usually mock me, at least not in public.

Laurel doesn't smile; she is not colluding in the joke, if that's what it was.

'My card.' She hands him a small, blue-edged card. She looks professional in her sleek red dress and matching lipstick, a necklace gleams half hidden by the neckline. Her fingers are ringless despite the husband she mentioned. James puts the card in his pocket and steps back, glancing round. His instincts tell him he has been talking to this beautiful stranger for long enough, though his wife is at his side. Parents might notice, it doesn't take much.

Laurel looks at me with compassion rather than judgement, a brown-eyed glance that's steeped in warmth. I could swear I've seen eyes like hers somewhere before, and then it comes to me, not Elizabeth Taylor, her eyes were famously blue, but Penelope Cruz or Rachel Weisz, deep brown eyes with the power to pull you in.

James begins to talk to a Chinese couple. He smiles, listens, leans in to murmur quietly, touching the man on the back, a seduction that's compelling to watch. I am compelled. I assume Laurel is watching too, though when I turn to make some face-saving joke about his quip, she has gone, leaving only a trace of scent in the air. I see her making her way to the door through the crowd. People stand back as she passes and turn to watch. I know how that feels, I felt it once. It doesn't happen so often these days.

The crowd thins. James and Cosmo chat, sipping wine, old friends from way back. There are no old friends for me. There's been scant time, my father saw off my child-hood companions; work, children, my second marriage, and James's career have kept them away.

As if I have sent out a signal, Maud Hatch comes over. She is the director of art, sixty-ish with the unmarked face of a nun. Her clothes are plain, her hair in a grey plait, and feet in sandals. James and Cosmo privately mock her appearance, even as they take for granted her unfussy air of coping and her excellent way with children.

'Oh Maud, I'm sorry. There isn't much left to eat.'

'I didn't come over to eat, I wanted to see how you are.'

'I'm fine.' Though I'm not, I feel shaky. I could cry at her kindness.

'Good.'

'Everything's perfect.' How easily I lie, but then I'm used to it. I tell James I'm fine all the time.

'Cosmo behaving himself?' Maud asks abruptly.

'I hope so.'

Why would she ask this? Maud is loyal. She refused to talk to the press after Angel complained about Cosmo, but she supported Angel too. She accompanied her to the police station albeit to no avail. Cosmo would have resented that, I imagined he could behave very badly.

'There's the drinks party for the scholars' evening soon,' she murmurs.

'I'll talk to Cosmo, see what he has in mind.'

'When you do, come and see me afterwards. We'll have a cup of tea.'

Maud walks away, her square shape and brown cardigan standing out in the crowd of elegantly dressed parents. I let myself imagine what might happen if I ran after her, if I told her that I wasn't fine at all, that my anxiety was worse and that I'm lonely. She might invite me to her home. We would make our way by underground to a small flat in a suburb. There'd be a cat on the chair. It might be messy, perhaps a little cold, but that wouldn't matter. Over tea I'd explain that my marriage worked as an equation: a home and safety in exchange for sex and cooking. It would sound primitive to her though I have a feeling she wouldn't be shocked. I would mention James's generosity but not his tendency to control.

Later, in our bedroom, James closes the window and draws the curtains. The room feels claustrophobic, but he likes it like that, he finds it sexy. He is smiling to himself. I can see he is thinking about the evening, the applause, the handshakes, and the admiring glances. He has probably forgotten about the therapist unless she is providing an image that feeds his desire. He turns me around and I let him. He runs his hands up my legs, pausing at the suspenders, his breath comes more harshly, he is in a hurry now and wrenches my dress up, the silk tears. He unzips himself and pushes into me grunting with pleasure, his open mouth on my neck.

See Maud? This is what I mean. This is how the equation balances.

Chapter 5

Paxos 2003

Sofie

Sofie's skin tingled as she cleared the table and then made the beds, an electric thrill as if the touch of Jay's hands was imprinted at her waist. The early mornings were exciting now. She yanked the sheets off the woman writer's bed, smiling to herself. There were long white hairs on the pillow and biscuit crumbs on the floor, several dirty pants shoved under the bed. Sofie didn't care, not today. She bundled it all up, then swept the floor. Once the guests had gone back to England, she would show Christos her strokes, but she didn't want to think about the guests going home though usually she couldn't wait.

The heat was at record levels even for Greece in August. There were deep cracks in the earth, the grass had withered to dust. Dogs lay by the wayside. Babas said old people in Athens were dying in their houses. Aries slept all day, stretched out in the sun. The heat didn't bother cats, but there were lines of dead fish strung along the edge of the sea. They'd started to stink. Dimitrios watered the garden twice a day, but the vegetables still split and shrank. It was hotter every year, he said. It's going to get hotter still, we'll all go up in smoke in the end. It was hard to tell if he was joking.

Nico kept to the shade, making Lego towns under the olive tree or lying on the floor of the kitchen under the table, humming. It was his favourite place. He watched Athena's feet as she journeyed back and forth, waiting for a slice of *spanakopita* or a *souvlaki* from the pile she'd prepared for the evening.

The guests lay about the pool, the blue water glittering in the dry garden like a jewel in the dust. Julia spent hours dozing on a lounger, Paul next to her while his child and wife splashed in the pool. The baby was fretful, the wife looked defeated. Jane sat in the shade sipping wine and talking little. Ginger took pictures on his phone of everyone close up, though they asked him not to.

Peter was restless. He decided on a sailing expedition, although as Christos muttered, it was motoring, not sailing. Peter hadn't the patience for sailing.

'We'll have a simple picnic,' Peter told his guests, 'and eat it on deck.'

The picnic wasn't a picnic either, but a feast put together by Athena over days, much more work than an ordinary lunch. She made *tyropita* and meatballs in a spicy tomato sauce, *dolmathes*, salad with calamari, chicken threaded on sticks and scented with thyme. Loaves of bread. *Eliopsoma*. Baklava. Christos bought those special white grapes. Crates of beer and wine were requested.

'They'll get drunk and fall overboard,' Athena muttered. They were in the kitchen with the hampers and cool bags, waiting for the guests to organize themselves. 'Christos will get the blame. Can they even swim, those boys?'

Sofie wanted to blurt out of course they could swim. I can too, Jay is teaching me, she longed to tell them but Athena would be worried and Babas furious. She shouldn't be in the sea, Athena would scold and she shouldn't let Nico go in either, it wasn't safe. Babas would growl that Jay was a boy as well as a guest. A teenage boy. The lessons would be stopped, and she had begun to look forward to them more than anything she could remember, more than the motorbike rides with Dimitrios or watching his DVDs. She liked the way she moved in the water, the way Jay's arms felt when pressed against her body, the glimpse of the sea floor. She liked it when he grinned at her.

'Christos will keep them safe. He's a sensible boy,'

Babas said as he glanced at his wife from under his shaggy eyebrows. He was worried about her. Athena had a bad headache yesterday. There had been sparkles in front of her eyes. She'd dropped a pile of plates in the evening.

'The heat,' he muttered. 'It's the damn heat. There'll be a storm tomorrow night, you'll feel better then.' He looked fierce as if the weather was an enemy to be defeated, although it made no difference to him. He might be the oldest in the family but he was tougher than any of them.

'He's all boiled down to muscle,' Christos told Sofie one evening as they stood on the cliff top, watching him pull in his nets. 'Any softness got burnt away years ago.'

He'd sounded jealous. Christos craved hard muscles; he ran around the olive fields and did press-ups in the courtyard when no one was looking. He kept track of his fitness by writing down what he did in the book where he totted up his earnings. He told Sofie the summers were for getting fitter and richer.

After breakfast, Sofie cleaned Peter and Jane's room. She rinsed the smeared wine glasses on Jane's bedside, stripped the bed then watched from the balcony as the guests made their way through the garden to the jetty. Peter led the procession wearing his Panama hat, followed by Jane in a white kaftan, the pale guy now red with sunburn, the white-haired woman, and then Julia in a bikini with Paul close behind her. His wife and child must have stayed in their cabin. Jay and his friend followed, Ginger waddling along in the rear.

Julia looked up at the house, sunglasses flashing. She seemed to be looking straight at her. Sofie moved back behind the curtain feeling guilty and jealous at the same time. The guests would have a wonderful day: the piles of towels, binoculars, goggles, flip-flops, and spare hats were on board already. The food and drink would be stashed in the fridge. They would lie on cushions as the yacht cut silently through the water, the wind cooling their faces. Babas's fishing boat had splintery planks to sit on, the engine coughed continually. Christos would anchor the yacht off the cliffs on the west coast or in one of the bays on Antipaxos. The guests would dive into the turquoise water and then sit under the striped awning, eating *dolmathes* gleaming with oil. She hoped Christos would eat the same food, but she wasn't sure if it worked like that.

Sofie was hungry already, sweat trickled down her back. Her arms stretched around a pile of sheets; they had to make the most of a day without guests. The plan was to do all the laundry and clean every room. Dimitrios's voice startled her and she dropped a pillowcase. He was calling up to the balcony from the garden, eyes half-closed against the smoke from the cigarette in his mouth.

'Athena's been sick. Babas is taking her to see the doctor. You've got to clean Julia's room and the boys' as well. And for God's sake, buck up with those sheets.'

It's just this heat, Sofie whispered to herself, though the day seemed duller now, its brilliance tarnished. Mama's sick because it's the hottest August we've ever had, Babas said so. She ran to the laundry room, tripping over the sheets, thrust the bundle at Dimitrios and hurried to Julia's cabin by the bed of peonies in the garden. Mama's been sick with migraines before, she told herself as she opened the door. The doctor will give her something and she'll be fine by the time she gets back.

Julia's bedroom was shockingly untidy, the clothes scattered over the floor were muddled up with books. Sofie picked up dresses, kaftans, and wraps but it was difficult to make them neat, they slipped through her hands like live snakes. The books were about other languages as far as Sofie could tell, French and Spanish; when she looked inside, there were notes in tiny hand-writing in the margins. Julia must have brought them along to study, though it didn't seem as if she was doing anything other than sleeping. There was a pamphlet under the bed about applying to university, which Sofie would have liked to read, but there wasn't time. She changed the sheets, inhaling their musky scent.

In the steamy bathroom, there were fair hairs

wrapped in the plughole which she pulled out with the little hook on a hanger. A tube of lipstick lay on its side on the marble shelf under the mirror. Sofie stared at it, then pulled off the outer tube; it gave with a little sucking noise. She stroked it on her lips, the colour sliding on like soft plastic. Her mouth felt coated. In the mirror, she had become older, prettier. She stared. Was that all it took then? Lipstick?

Encouraged, she stepped into the shower and directed the nozzle at her feet; the dust and dirt swirled in a brown stream down the plughole. Afterwards, she stamped her feet dry on the towels lying on the floor, they had to be washed anyway. A stripey sponge bag lay open by the basin. Heart beating fast, she drew out a little bottle of red nail varnish. She stroked some onto each toenail, re-capped the bottle, replaced it in the bag then put the lipstick on the shelf in the same position as she'd found it, as carefully as if someone had taught her how to cover her traces after a crime. She cleaned the shower, polished the glass, then put fresh towels on the rack and new soap in the dish.

'It's okay,' she told the new reflection in the mirror. 'Julia will never know.'

The heat punched her face like a fist when she stepped outside with the towels and sheets, but now there was a line of dark clouds at the horizon. No one had believed Babas when he said a storm was coming but he was usually right. Dimitrios was outside the laundry shed, leaning against the door, eyes half closed, ear plugs in, smoking. She swung her bundle, so it thumped against his hips. He opened his eyes and looked down at her.

'You took your time.'

'Her room was a mess.'

'Whose room?'

'Julia's.'

He looked closely at her. 'Christ, Sofie. Did you nick her lipstick? Don't let Athena see you.' He ground the roll-up in the dust, picked up the bundle of dirty linen and disappeared inside.

He didn't say she looked pretty or even different, and now she had to work fast to make up the time, picking clothes off the floor in the boys' bedroom in a rush. She held Jay's blue shirt to her face; it smelt of his skin. She put it down quickly as if stung by a wasp. In the bathroom there were scattered boxer shorts and trodden towels, the mess dirtier but less complicated than Julia's. She scrubbed the lipstick off her lips using toilet paper, wiping hard until her lips felt torn.

Dimitrios was ironing when she dumped the last of the linen at the entrance of the shed, the sweat staining his back in a dark triangle. He didn't turn round but raised one hand in acknowledgement. Nico was there too, playing by his feet, absorbed in the

Lego garage he'd made. Sofie picked up the pile of ironed linen on the table and took it to the kitchen to stack by the stove. A spray of cicadas scattered from the tops of the lavender bushes as her skirt brushed past. The heat was fiercer still, thudding in her head like a drumbeat. The air felt heavy. The dark clouds were lower in the sky. It would be cool on the yacht. Julia would be stretched out on the cushions or swimming, her tanned arms flashing. The boys would be staring at her, all of them. Stupid to think lipstick would make any difference when you had to be beautiful, thin and rich for boys to like you.

The air in the kitchen was stifling as if someone had covered her face with a hot flannel. It was very quiet. A fly crawled over the white icing of a cake that Mama had made before she went to the hospital. Sofie flicked it away. Mama's flowery apron hung behind the door, and her old shoes with their trodden backs and dark soles were placed neatly side by side beneath it.

Sofie sat down, her hands felt clammy. What if the doctor found something wrong? What if Athena never came back? Minutes ticked past. She was trying not to look at the clock when the familiar chugging of the engine came through the open door. Sofie sat very still, her heart beating fast. In a minute she'd find out what the doctor said. The truck door slammed, and footsteps sounded on the paving outside, then Athena

59

walked into the kitchen, put a package of coffee and a box of strawberries on the table and patted Sofie's head as she passed. She picked up the cake, put it in the fridge and switched on the kettle. Babas came in for coffee, grumbling about parking in Gaios. No one said anything about the doctor, and the day started up again.

The guests came back mid-afternoon, earlier than expected, walking slowly and saying little. Most went to their rooms to rest, although the boys slept in hammocks slung between the trees. Jay's body made a thin curved shape; Ginger's was rounder and denser, his bottom hung almost to the ground.

The cake turned out to be for Jay. It was his birthday. Sofie put on her yellow shirt, the one Athena had made for Gabriella's party a year ago. It was far too tight, but *Yia-yias's* embroidery was on the collar. Jay would be at the centre of laughter and presents, but he might glance over and see she was wearing something pretty. He wouldn't say anything but he'd know she'd bothered, and he might be pleased. He wouldn't smile either, but that didn't matter; tomorrow, when he came to the beach, he'd be smiling.

She was wrong. There was no laughing at supper, the atmosphere was subdued. No one was pleased about anything. The woman with white hair was sunburnt and seemed cross. Jane was almost asleep. Julia wasn't even there, and Paul seemed downcast though his wife was smiling. Ginger had put on a flowery shirt which Peter stared at scornfully. Christos whispered that Peter had made them come back earlier than planned. The boys had been a nuisance; they'd surrounded Julia in the sea, pretending to be killer whales closing round a seal. Sofie remembered how frightening that looked on television, though Julia hadn't appeared scared as she ran up the path past Sofie earlier. She'd looked determined, her eyes had gleamed. Christos said she'd left with her luggage in a taxi soon after. Sofie felt bereft, though that was stupid, it wasn't as if Julia was her friend. She'd hardly glanced at her once but then she'd hardly glanced at anyone except for Paul.

After supper, Athena brought out the cake she'd made, now with a crown of strawberries. She put it in front of Jay and lit candles for him, sixteen of them, but no one clapped or cheered. When Athena left, Ginger flicked two strawberries off the top, and they landed on the tablecloth. He pushed them with a finger, and they left wet, pink trails. Jay cut a cave into the side with a spoon, swallowing a mouthful of sponge, but no one else ate any of it. Sofie watched, breathless with dismay. It was lucky Athena had gone to bed, tired out with her headache, and wouldn't see this. Dimitrios said something would happen very soon, he meant a storm, but the dark air felt full of danger as if wild animals were hiding in the bushes

61

near the pool, waiting to pounce. Sofie imagined the body of a lion crouched low, his mate alongside, panting in the heat.

She and the cousins finished washing the dishes, then she tidied the kitchen and refilled Aries's water bowl as Mama usually did. Dimitrios left to visit Roxana in her bar. Christos took his notebook and went off to his room. All the guests disappeared, Peter supporting Jane. Sofie found Athena's cake on the wall outside, pushed under the edge of the bushes. Ants were swarming all over it. She took it to the kitchen and, ignoring the ants, tipped the whole cake into a bag. She had to get rid of it somehow. Athena mustn't know her efforts had been wasted. She put the bag in the waste bin and then took it out again, it could be discovered there, and that's when she thought of the sea.

The air was still hot at the beach, but the waves were higher than normal, the moon appearing and disappearing as clouds raced across the sky. Sofie slipped off her shirt and skirt, put them on a rock with a handful of pebbles on top and slid the cake from the bag. She stepped into the water in her pants, walking to waist height, tearing the sponge into pieces and throwing them into the waves. The fish would make quick work of the crumbs. She rinsed her hands in the water and, on impulse, dipped down to her neck, but the waves were stronger than she'd thought and almost tipped her over. She scrambled to her feet with a jolt of fear and ran splashing towards the shore where she left her clothes.

But her clothes weren't there.

She tried to see if they could have blown along the beach, but they couldn't have, they had been held down with pebbles. The moon vanished behind a cloud and the night became pitch black.

She could hear breathing sounds which made her think of lions again, crouching low in the dark. Her skin stung as if ants were swarming all over, the biting kind. A low laugh came out of the dark.

'Julia?' she whispered, crossing her arms over her naked chest. 'Is that you?'

Chapter 6

London 2023

Julia

James wants more sex these days, or perhaps I want less so it just seems that way.

I'm tired this morning. Sore. He likes to try new things in new locations; today it was the bathroom floor. He's started to want it quick, rough.

I pretend to enjoy it; he thinks I do. I used to. I used to be drawn in, a willing accomplice but not now. He's changed. Sex has tipped into something darker, more painful. Punishing. I ache all over when he's finished, and now I'm bleeding. Today, I wouldn't care if we never had sex again, but I won't tell him that. He might mention my age, thirty-nine to his thirty-six, which he does, from time to time, implying I can't keep up. He might tell me how fortunate I am.

It's true that my life is privileged compared to the folk around me at St Jude's. If sex is the price to pay for what I have, I'm lucky. I still think I'm lucky.

The kitchen in the crypt of St Jude's Parish Church in Vauxhall is small, a slice of a room for tea-making at Women's Institute gatherings and Alcoholics Anonymous meetings. It wasn't built to accommodate three women, a stove, and large containers of food. The water runs cold after an hour and we must boil it in the kettle and spare pans, tricky when the stove is crowded with pots of food keeping warm.

The faces crowding the other side of the hatch are reddened with weather. The folk here don't look at us, they look at the food. There are more men than women. Most are young, a few very old, though rough living might make them seem older than they are. One or two thin dogs have been sneaked in; Joanna is on the door, she has a soft spot for dogs. Neither of the languages I perfected at university are of any use here, but then hardly anyone says a word, words aren't needed.

Zoe and I ladle scoop after scoop of coconut and lentil dahl. Her glasses steam up repeatedly, and she wipes them on her tee shirt, shoves her brown curls back with a forearm, and carries on. Ruth refills the pans. She is small, which is just as well in this kitchen, her blonde hair is scraped into a ponytail, a packet of cigarettes is squashed into the top pocket of her dungarees.

The plates are taken quickly; there are about sixty guests. My back and wrists ache. I had stopped looking up, or at least looking properly, when a voice says, 'Thank you.'

'You are welcome.' I reach for another plate off the stack.

'It is extremely kind of you.'

I glance up, encountering a young face with narrow eyes that look closely at mine, and a ragged scar near the right temple. The accent is difficult to place. He looks Middle Eastern, possibly Syrian, but I've learnt not to guess and never to ask.

He nods and moves away unsmiling, two plates in his hands. No one smiles here. I rest my ladle on a plate and watch him. He looks different from the others, neither thin nor bloated. His hands and face are a normal colour. He doesn't seem tired, though from the guarded expression in his eyes, he looks like someone to whom much life has happened, a lot of it difficult. He sits down next to an older man, gives him one of the plates of food, and eats but not fast. This pleases me, not many take their time to savour the food.

There is silence in the hall, the silence of people who are eating hungrily. Zoe takes cups of tea round in trays and, today, eclairs at their sell-by date, given by Marks and Spencer's. She places the eclairs and the tea by each elbow, then steps back swiftly. It wouldn't be difficult to guess she has an abusive husband, currently in jail.

After a while, chairs scrape and people get up, though some have gone to sleep, leaning back in the chairs or slumping forward, resting their heads on their arms. The sleeping ones are gently woken by Ruth, and they look up dazed, before stumbling to their feet. Unusually for a guest, the young man clears the tables. Washing up absorbs us then, the difficulty of cleaning plates and cutlery in cooling, greasy water.

'A good meal.' The same guy leans into the hatch.

'I'm glad. My name is Julia.' I hold out my hand. He shakes it firmly.

'I'm Rasul. I could help you.' The voice is serious with an edge of determination. 'I can cook.'

'We prepare most of the food off-site but maybe—'

His name is shouted by another refugee, and he is gone. I stare after the tall figure weaving between others, until he disappears. I could accept his offer of help. Lottie would want me to, she thinks I should do more. I've invited refugees who can cook to our house before, to assess them and help build their skills. I paid the fees for a City & Guilds Diploma in Professional Cookery for Fahdil last year and Kassim the year before. James thinks it's a waste of effort. He says they won't succeed in the long run: their experiences make it too difficult. I think that's precisely why they will succeed.

Rasul comes to the crypt again several times. He hands food to other refugees, brings back their plates, and asks for a cloth to wipe the tables.

The fifth time it's just Zoe and me in the kitchen, Ruth is away. We sweat in the heat, arms straining with the heavy pots, stirring, serving, wiping up spills. Rasul leans into the hatch again and asks if we want help. I glance at Zoe who nods warily and steps back when he enters the kitchen, but Rasul moves carefully around us. He cleans the pans until they shine, mops the floor, and scrubs the oven. Afterwards, we make coffee. Zoe pushes her glasses back up her nose and squeezes past on her way to fetch her children from school, her carefully bland expression hiding the fact she's impressed.

'You seem to know your way around a kitchen.' I nod at the tidy rows of pots, the shining floor.

'I learnt when I was young.'

'Your mother?'

He nods, then leaves. I shouldn't have asked. Refugees don't tell their stories, at least not to us. There could be horror behind his silence, a woman hurrying to the shops despite the risks, an earth-shattering explosion and when the dust settled, blood on the pavements, scattered clothes. Body parts in the trees, rubble everywhere. A kitchen could be his way of safeguarding the good memories, the warmth of a stove, the smell of the food, his mother's hand on his shoulder.

The next time Rasul cleans the entire kitchen and takes out the rubbish.

'I cook,' he tells me again over a cup of tea. His hands are broad and capable looking, there is a mark on the back of one, like a burn. 'Maybe you can train me like the others.'

He's done his research then. There is an appeal behind his words, but he doesn't want to beg. There is something separating this young man from the rest, he hasn't lost everything. He has the look of a survivor.

I know nothing about his past but then I didn't with the other lads that I helped, there can never be references to hand. He hasn't told me where he's from though I doubt that would make any difference. I have to go on instinct, on what I see and feel. I've seen that he handles himself with dignity, I've seen his kindness. He has a reserve that seems natural, resilience that would have come from childhood. He must have been loved. Ridiculously I am envious, and find myself driving to Richmond afterwards, instead of going home.

My mother's nursing home is a large Victorian mansion built by a wealthy industrialist, red brick and gabled, grandiose enough to satisfy my father. He liked the immaculate lawn and the fact that the cars in the drive were Bentleys like his. He probably made up his mind before they went inside. My mother would have approved of the expensive curtains, the thick carpets, and chandeliers. There was no protest on leaving her home; if she realized what was happening, she disguised it well. Maybe it was a relief to escape my father. He always encouraged her to join in the activities. How little he knew her. I could have told him the very word made her shudder, but as he died soon after her admission, there hadn't been the chance.

She is asleep in her chair when I get there. I didn't phone ahead, the nurse tells me reprovingly. She leaves us together, and I watch her sleeping: the coiffed hair, the painted nails, the fragile body in a designer bed jacket; it's as if she is still pleasing my father. There's little point in waking her but I take her hand in mine; even in sleep, she pulls it away, muttering. Odd that it still hurts.

I've never known what she does all day, the room gives me little to go on: a large television set, books neatly arranged on a shelf, photograph albums, and a silver framed photo of Lottie, her freckled face beaming against a background of the sea. A framed image of the Cornish house is next to that but there are none of the Greek one; it's twenty years since they left Paxos for the last time. She's never fully explained why that was, and now it's too late to ask. Dementia has put her beyond my reach. I kiss her sunken cheek and leave.

*   *   *

Cosmo is visiting when I return home: a crumpled linen jacket is over the banisters and the house smells of cigarette smoke. He and James are walking in the garden, Cosmo smoking, gesticulating, James watching his face closely, nodding. They are in their own world, oblivious. When I go out to greet them, they stop talking abruptly. Cosmo leaves soon after, frowning like a child as though I'd disrupted their boys' club. It would be almost endearing if I liked him more.

After supper I sew name tapes on Lottie's netball socks while James listens to a Bach cantata. He has Thomas Hardy's poems on his lap and a glass of red wine at his elbow. His face is smooth, his hair shining. He looks like an advertisement for some food supplement that brings health and happiness. He glances at himself in the mirror from time to time, then smiles at me. He's in an affectionate mood. I smile back. I don't want him to guess how trapped I feel, he might lecture me about anxiety. I begin to tell him about Rasul, but Lottie calls round to collect some clothes.

'Where's my blue jersey, Mum?' she calls from her bedroom, searching through her wardrobe, tossing clothes on the floor. 'I promised it to Angel. Why is nothing ever where I leave it in this house?' She looks more tired than usual.

The blue jersey is on the back of her chair. She takes it from me silently.

'How's Angel? I'd love to see her—'

'I wouldn't dream of bringing her here.' Lottie is shovelling clothes back in the cupboard and doesn't look at me. 'She might bump into James.'

'You seem tired, sweetheart.'

'So would you if you had as much art coursework as I do. He does it on purpose.'

'Who does?'

'Cosmo. Who else?' She sounds exasperated as she bundles up her jersey.

I hand over her socks and hug her; she smells the same as always: bubble bath, apples and faintly, of ink. I give her the tin full of brownies I made for a governors' meeting, and she leaves in a hurry without acknowledging James. It will take her ten minutes to get back to her boarding house, but I feel as bereft as if she'd departed on a journey abroad.

'Lottie's a bit of a rebel,' James says, sipping wine and stretching his feet to the fire. 'She gets that from me.' A little smile as he wriggles more comfortably in his seat.

'How, exactly?'

'As her father—'

'Stepfather.'

'The tendency to push at boundaries is bound to rub off.'

I stare at him. James likes boundaries or, at least, he likes me to set them for him, leaving him free to take risks. He tries to set them for Lottie but without success. He complains she avoids him now she's older, but the truth is she's never liked him. I don't tell him that of course, I say that she is missing her father, which is only partly correct. She regards Anthony as a wayward older brother, loved but unreliable.

'She's becoming quite the loner,' James continues, glancing at me. 'I saw her today on her own, lost in thought.'

'Lottie's not a loner.' I shouldn't rise to the bait, but I can't help it. 'She has lots of friends.'

He shrugs. 'She used to be part of a gang, now she's more on her own.'

She didn't tell me that. Worry sweeps me, it doesn't take much. 'What gang was this?'

'Does it matter?'

'Have they been bullying her?' Anxiety rachets up. 'She might be avoiding them if they are. You know what it said in *The Times*, boys of this age can be predators—'

'The papers exaggerate, they always do.' His face becomes smooth. 'What they suggest is vanishingly rare, certainly here. The boys she was friends with are some of the best in the school. She probably just needs some space.'

'Best in the school?'

'Their fathers are politicians, CEOs, top players in industry.'

'That's the problem right there.' I stare at his calm face, mine is growing hot. 'Entitlement. I expect the boys feel they can behave as they like.'

'Just because bullying has been found in some schools, doesn't mean it's in ours.'

'It doesn't mean it's not.'

He finishes his glass of wine and then smiles. 'Calm down, my darling, this is your anxiety speaking. We trained up extra pastoral care officers, and they make sure we run a tight ship. I think you should leave it to us.' He gets out of his chair and drops a kiss on my head on his way to fetch another bottle of wine from the rack in the kitchen.

He is being kind, I tell myself, not patronizing. He's always been kind; it tips the balance. He could also be right. Lottie might need space, or it could be as simple as tiredness.

'You were telling me about your refugee.' James pours another glass of wine and settles back in the chair. 'Why him?'

'He's helpful and polite. Zoe likes him. He's keen and he knows how to cook.'

'Background?'

'I'm guessing his family ran a restaurant. I could train him up like the others.'

'Where does he come from?'

'There's been a big intake from the Middle East recently, Syria especially. Does it matter?'

'A little, yes.' He sips his wine and sighs, but he doesn't really care. This is a game, it's all about power. 'I'd prefer references, but I can see that would be tricky. If you think we can trust him, I don't think there's anything to lose. I'd like to meet him first, bring him here one evening.'

'Thank you.'

James nods and returns to his poetry. I'm seeing Cosmo then Maud tomorrow, Rasul could come after that. I text him with a time and he texts back immediately to accept.

The art department is a sprawling building, with high ceilings and stone stairs; the smell of clay is caught in the hallway. On the way up to Cosmo's room, I narrowly miss a young girl running down. She clutches a portfolio and swings hard around the banisters with barely an inch between us.

Cosmo's office is an internal room with no windows, carved from the landing. The door is open, and he is sitting in the dark, his face and head bathed with the blueish glow from the computer. His pudgy cheeks shine, a leg bounces up and down. He is frowning as he taps on his keyboard with one hand, a cigarette between the fingers of the other.

He looks up and a smile switches on. He stubs out

the cigarette, unconcerned that I've caught him smoking, which is strictly against the rules.

'Hello, beautiful.'

I wish he wouldn't call me beautiful: he doesn't mean it, he doesn't even like me. He gets to his feet and lumbers towards me. Close up his face is lined with wrinkles; his breath is fetid. I step sideways. He smiles to himself and sits on the edge of his desk, one thigh overlapping the edge.

'How is the delightful Charlotte?'

He is playing a game. He takes Lottie for the photography module of her art GCSE, so he knows how she is better than I do.

'Fine, thank you.'

'It never ceases to amaze me . . . ' He shakes his head. The sentence remains unfinished.

'What never ceases to amaze you, Cosmo?' He has some card to play but nothing he says can surprise me.

'James having brought her up as his own, he's hardly the paternal type. He had to, I guess, her actual father having flaked out.' He grins.

He has surprised me after all. I turn to his photos on the wall, framed studies of young bodies in black and white. James didn't bring Lottie up, I did. He didn't meet her till she was seven. She's mine, Anthony's and mine. Cosmo returns to his desk, bored of baiting me. I pretend to study his photos, but I'm seeing my

77

first husband, the boy who appeared on the boat from Paxos to Corfu, twenty years ago. He was barefoot and strumming a guitar, the antidote to everything I'd left behind. It didn't take us long to fall in love. He followed me back to England and lived in my flat, busking in Waterloo while I studied languages at University College. He was peaceful and easy to please, for once I felt less anxious. My father threatened to cut me off; Anthony was a lower-class wastrel, he said, pointing out he was living for free. I didn't care. I was pregnant by then, old enough to know my mind, or so I thought. We married. I was disinherited but we didn't care, we were thrilled to be having a child. Anthony had changed by the time Lottie arrived; he began to steal cash from my bag and started sleeping all day. I was relieved when he finally left. I couldn't afford him any more.

Time passed in a haze of exhaustion and love, ambitions on hold. Lottie became the centre of my life. I trained as a teacher then took a part-time job, teaching French and tutoring pupils in the evening, employing au pairs. Lottie and I slept squashed in my bed, leaving the second room for the au pair. Anthony showed up from time to time, but mostly it was just us. We had holidays in Cornwall; hot summer days when we ran barefoot down fern-lined paths to the sea, splashed in the shallows and had picnics on the beach. We painted together in the garden and I read her stories all the time. I would have done anything for her, wondering how it was possible that my father used me as he did, and how my mother had turned a blind eye.

The university reunion took place the day after my thirty-first birthday. Lottie stayed with Angel, who had been her best friend since play group days. Grace paid for my haircut and highlights. I was tired and nervous, quickly tipsy; when a tall guy called James sat next to me and began to flirt, I flirted back. He smelt male. I'd missed that smell. I watched his hand on the table between us, the tanned fingers curved on the cloth. I stopped listening to what he was saying and imagined them on my skin.

That was the beginning; he gave me things: jewellery, clothes, shoes. He still does. I must remember that. He was amusing company and kind to Lottie. After six months he asked me to marry him; whoever says you shouldn't marry for security hasn't had years of trying to make a small salary stretch to pay gas bills, council tax, and school clothes, hasn't cried with exhaustion late at night.

It was a tiny wedding. I was thirty-two, James almost twenty-nine. My father and his parents were dead. Lottie and Angel were bridesmaids. James's best man was a large guy with a shining bald head, who became very drunk. My introduction to Cosmo. Mother, memory wavering, stared at James with a question in her eyes. Father's ghost hovered, disapproving. He'd died of a heart attack a month before the wedding and never met James, but had lined up a hedge fund manager for me, an older man of obscene wealth. I had disappointed him for the second time, and he never forgave me. His will was read two weeks after the wedding. I'd inherited nothing. James was more dismayed than I was, if anything I felt freed.

'About the food for the sixth-form evening.' I turn back to Cosmo, trying again.

'Food? Oh God, Jules, I don't give a fuck. Ask Maud.' He is tapping on his keyboard and doesn't look up.

Maud's room is light filled, the walls covered with art from all age groups, wild splashes of oils, pale watercolours, and precise pen and ink sketches. She is leafing through timetables but puts them aside to make me tea. I count ten moth holes in the sleeves of her cardigan and wonder what she makes of my Armani jacket and Hermes scarf. James expects me to wear these things, I want to tell her, they're headmaster's wife kind of clothes, at least in his eyes. They are not my choice, but we don't talk about clothes, we discuss food. There should be cakes and tea at the sixth-form evening we decide, as well as wine and canapes.

'I saw a young girl just now, we almost collided on the stairs. She seemed upset.'

'Cosmo is interviewing for our scholar placements; he probably doesn't make it easy.' Her face is difficult to read. Cosmo probably doesn't make it easy for Maud either. 'Have you considered sending Lottie away to art school for the sixth form?'

I stare at her, surprised; what have I missed?

'Cosmo is careless with language, but Lottie wouldn't mind as long as she's taught by the best. Are you worried?'

'I'm sure she can stand up for herself, but a change can be good, especially for someone as talented as she is.' Maud opens a folder and starts pulling out sheets of photographs. 'Have you seen her work recently?'

They are studies in black and white, Cosmo's influence maybe, but the contents are very different: these are close-up shots of faces, Angel's among them; intimate and tender. There is one of me, asleep in a deck chair in Cornwall last year, another of waves churning in a storm against dark cliffs, and an empty Minack theatre at dusk, stone seats shining in the rain.

'She couldn't produce work like this if she wasn't settled, surely?' I glance at Maud, but a bell rings and she stands with a sigh, she has a meeting to attend. There is a new photograph of feet on the wall by the door that I notice on my way out. Each toe is half shadowed. They look defenceless, unblemished against the rough wood grain of floorboards. I see with a shock the little toe is curved in, the big toe on the right has a band across the nail. Lottie's feet.

'Who took this?'

'Cosmo, as a matter of fact. He wanted a subject for a lecture about light and shadow.'

The composition is compelling, the man has talent. Little wonder that Lottie put up with him.

'May I have this when you've finished with it?'

'She gave it to me.' Maud's cheeks stain pink. 'I wouldn't want her to think I didn't value it.'

'Of course.' Now I am the one who is embarrassed. 'I didn't realize.'

'How could you have?' Maud pats my arm. 'She comes in to chat sometimes. She misses Angel, they used to be together all the time.'

I know Lottie was close to Angel, but I hadn't realized how much she missed her.

'Thank you for being here for her.'

'It's always a pleasure.'

The revolving front door of the art department is heavy. I am trapped in panels of metal and glass. Anxiety begins to swell: it doesn't take much. Outside the girl who brushed past me on the stairs earlier is texting furiously. She stares at me when I emerge.

'Hi there.' I smile at her, relieved to be free. 'Good luck with the scholarship.'

'Fuck off.' She pockets her mobile and runs down the street.

I envy that defiance even as it stings; if I'd had the courage to tell my father to fuck off, my life would have been very different.

Another bell rings and the large school courtyard is flooded with teenagers, boys in groups that spread over the pavements, untucked shirts flapping and raucous laughter, the girls hanging back behind them. A group of boys follow a couple of girls, staring at them, turning their heads to each other, grinning. The girls are hurrying, heads down. Are they worried by the boys behind them or simply late? I look for Lottie, as I always do, but she isn't among these teenagers. A small knot of teachers walk past on the far side of the square, a slim figure in red walking with them. I glimpse piled dark hair. Laurel? Here? The teachers stand talking together, before they split up to go in different directions. The dark-haired woman is no longer among them. I must be imagining things. I'm tired, anxious as James says, or perhaps it's as simple as loneliness. Laurel must be in my mind, her glance had warmed me at the time, she'd seemed like a friend.

Rasul is waiting on the pavement outside our house. He stands against the black railings, staring at the potted olive trees either side of the door; they've done well in our sheltered little street. The green leaves are glossy, dagger-like.

83

'Hi there, Rasul.'

He swings round, his eyes clouded as if the trees had taken him back home, to a ruined garden where olive trees stand amidst the rubble. He bows.

I unlock the door and push it wide open, ignoring the voice in my head that tells me not to let strangers into the house. It's James's voice at its most dictatorial and I take no notice; how can I help the homeless, yet not invite a homeless man into my house?

'Come right in.'

Chapter 7

Paxos 2003

Sofie

Sofie stood still, her skin crawling with fear. Muted sounds like breathing came through the darkness. The waves moved softly behind her. Was that what it was, the sea breathing in and out?

A flash of light punched through the night and another, as sudden and shocking as lightning. There was a click, several clicks. Her legs trembled, poised to run.

Trespassers? People coming by boat from Gaios or Corfu, stealing in at night? They've had them before. Christos would need to know, the yacht might be a target. Unless it was Christos himself, checking up on the boat, and that could be worse. What if he saw her without her top? What if he told Babas she'd been in the sea on her own?

Laughter came bellowing out of the darkness, shockingly loud. She could smell alcohol and, beneath that, the warmer scent of tobacco. Jay stepped in front of her, a cigarette in his mouth and her clothes in his hands. Ginger was next to him holding a bottle of wine.

Jay and Ginger. She felt sick with relief.

'Julia's done a runner. It's just us,' Jay said through his laughter.

Later it would be strange to think that at this precise moment she was glad it was them, not thieves and not Christos, though her face burned with shame. At least she was wearing her pants. The boys collapsed on the pebbles, laughing like children. Jay reached up and tugged her elbow so she stumbled and sat down, quickly re-crossing her arms over her chest.

She should have known right then. When they were watching those nature programmes, Babas always said that if lions got their prey on the ground, that was it. They were finished, but she didn't think of Babas or lions, not for one second. Instead, she was trying to imagine how Gabriella might behave. She would have told her to stay cool though Sofie had never been sure what that meant.

Jay put her shirt on her shoulders, and she flinched at his touch, which made him laugh again. She turned away to slip her arms in the sleeves, buttoning it up to the neck. Her skirt had been dumped near the waves which had soaked it. She grabbed it awkwardly and wriggled into it. The boys watched every moment, chuckling all the time. They'd drunk too much, that's all it was, happy laughter as Dimitrios said when he was drunk. It didn't mean a thing.

Ginger handed her the bottle of wine, and she took it because that seemed to be expected. Jay leant over and held it to her lips, tipping it so she was forced to swallow. It burnt her throat and dribbled out of her mouth.

'Oops!' Jay's voice was amused. He took the bottle away and gave it to Ginger, then wiped her lips with his fingers, sending a buzz through her skin, an electric shock that seemed to end between her legs, making her tremble.

'You need to take it slowly,' he told her, even though he was the one who had tipped it.

Ginger leant over and put the bottle in the pebbles by her feet, using his phone as a torch, then peered closely at her toes. 'You stole that varnish from Julia!'

She was surprised he noticed but he was the one who'd taken photos of the guests close up. He must like detail. She dug her toes into the pebbles, but it was too late.

'Thief,' Ginger said. 'You need to be punished.' He sounded angry. 'Drink the rest up if you don't want us to tell Julia.' He sat down on her other side, plucked the bottle from the pebbles and handed it back to her.

Jay was so close the hairs on his arm brushed against her skin sending another warm rush through her, jostling with shame and guilt. They were waiting. It seemed a small price to pay. The wine was sour. She took a gulp, coughed and put the bottle down.

'All of it.' There was something hard at the back of Ginger's voice.

She closed her eyes and drank. The wine spilt around her mouth, but Ginger tipped the bottle more and she had to swallow the last dregs. She put it down, feeling sick.

Jay gently put his arm around her shoulders. 'You're pretty, aren't you?' He whispered, 'I bet you didn't know that.' He kissed her neck.

No one had called her pretty before except Athena. No one, outside the family, had kissed her. Her mind was spinning so fast that nothing felt real. Jay stood up and held out his hand. She stood too, but the world tipped sideways. She staggered and clung to his hand.

'There's no need to be scared. It's fun.' They burst out laughing again. She must remember all of this and write about it in her diary. She'll tell Gabriella, though Gabriella may not believe her. He said I was pretty. He kissed me, she will say, on my neck. He held my hand. Gabriella's face will get that bored look as it does whenever she's jealous.

'I want to go somewhere where we can be private,'

Jay whispered. His mouth was so near her face that his breath moved her hair. 'Do you know where we could go?'

She shook her head. Jay looked disappointed. He dropped her hand. Ginger rolled his eyes.

'Let's go,' he said to Jay. They turned as if to leave.

It was her fault. She was stupid. She must have done something wrong. She hadn't been cool enough. She had spoilt it all and now they were going to go. In a panic, she gave it up, her precious, secret place.

'The shed,' she whispered, 'where we store the boat. No one goes there except me.'

'Tell the phone. Say "It's quiet in the shed, we can be private there".' Ginger held his phone close to her mouth, staring at her intently. Jay was giggling.

'We can be private in the shed,' she said, tripping over her words. She wasn't sure why she had to say it, but Jay smiled warmly at her as though she had done something very clever.

'Show me,' he said.

They walked together over the beach although she tripped and fell once, scraping her knee on a rock. Jay knelt beside her and pressed his mouth to the sore place; the lick was hot and wet. It felt wrong.

'*Ochi*. No.' She jerked her leg away.

'Ungrateful little bitch.' Ginger's voice sounded hostile. Had she ruined everything again? The air felt cold. She shivered; her clothes were still wet. There was a deep rumble of thunder, Babas's storm was arriving at last.

'Let's find that shed.' Jay's breath was melting something low down in her body.

After he helped her up, she led them both through the trees which grew tightly together at the back of the beach. The shape of the hut was just visible in its small clearing.

'How is that a boat house?' There was scorn in Ginger's voice. 'You couldn't get boats to the sea from here.'

She hadn't explained properly. It wasn't a boat house, not a house specially for boats like Peter's grand yacht. Babas just stored his old trawler here; he was going to break it up for wood one day. In the meantime, she sat against it to read, and Nico climbed inside when they played hide and seek. She could have explained all that, if she had been able to find the right words, if her mind could stop whirling.

Quite suddenly it began to rain. If she had been in her bedroom, she would have woken Nico. They would have leant out of the window together to feel the rain on their faces. She could smell the damp earth already and the scent of wet thyme. She wanted to listen to the ground drinking it in, but Ginger was trying to open the door of the shed and the rattle tore the silence like an angry voice.

'Wait,' she whispered.

A tiny owl lived in one of the trees; his cry floated into the bedroom keeping her company on nights she couldn't sleep. Ginger's rattling might frighten him away.

'Wait a minute.'

The key was under a shell by the door; such an obvious place for a key but no one had ever found it. She tried to turn it in the lock, but her fingers were trembling too much. Jay slid it from her hand, unlocked the door and put the key in his pocket.

Give it back! That key belongs to me! Her mind was crying in protest, but she couldn't say it out loud, it wasn't even true. It didn't belong to her or even her family, it just felt as though it did. It belonged to Peter and Jane and probably the guests while they were here. Nothing in the house or grounds belonged to her or her family, she should remember that. Nothing.

She hadn't been inside the shed so late at night before. It was dark but it still smelt of sun-warmed wood, salt, and tar. There was a torch on the shelf by the door which she left there in case she needed it. Ginger spotted it immediately and snatched it up. The beam picked out the old wooden bench, the nets suspended from the ceiling, and the rusty anchor on the floor. A couple of fishing rods rested against the wall, and a plastic drum half filled with oil stood in the corner. The boat itself, tipped to one side, seemed to be resting, like an old man after a lifetime of hard work, at least that's what she always thought. She talked to it sometimes.

'Jesus, it stinks in here,' Ginger said.

The smell was one of the best things about the shed. Sofie put her hand on the boat's rough surface, fear was pricking her like tiny fishhooks. It had felt all right outside or at least not scary, but here they were forced close together, there was hardly room to step back. She could smell the boys' sweat, raw and unpleasant. Their eyes shone as if they were excited about something, they were breathing a little faster and watching her closely. She thought about lions again and how they looked when they slinked close to their prey, how their eyes gleamed with intent.

Jay lowered himself onto the bench with a grimace, patting the wood. 'Sit next to me.'

She sat down, leaving a little space between them. Her hands were clammy. He moved closer to her.

'Do you want to be my girlfriend?'

She stared at him; her heart was hammering. She couldn't take in the words.

'Girl. Friend.' He repeated slowly with a gap between the words, as if she was a child or else someone very old who couldn't hear properly. Her mind raced in circles. Would he want to hold her hand or put his arm around her? Kiss her on the mouth? How did you actually do that? Gabriella had tried it out on her old doll for practice, but it looked weird. What did you do with your tongue?

'Well?'

She nodded, it was easier than saying anything and she didn't know what to say.

'I need you to say it.'

Her face burned. She was being stupid. She should say the kind of thing Julia would say but she had no idea what that was.

'*Endaxi*,' she whispered. 'Okay.'

'Say it into my phone so I can play it back when I'm on my own, feeling lonely.'

Ginger made a noise from the shadows; it sounded like a pig grunting. She had forgotten he was here, and it felt wrong that he was listening.

Jay put his phone under her chin. Ginger was shining the torch straight at her.

'Go on,' Jay said.

'What shall I say?'

'Say "I want to be your girlfriend".' He seemed bored. He had told her this already.

'I want to be your girlfriend,' she whispered quickly.

'Louder.'

The impatience in his voice shook her, woke her up. He sounded angry. Did she really want to be his girlfriend? What did that mean anyway?

'Go on.'

She could just say it even though she didn't mean

it, then open the door and run up the path between the trees. The dark didn't matter, she knew the way by heart. She would go into her room, slip into bed and listen to Nico's breathing and the sound of rain. His collection of stones would be on the windowsill and everything would feel all right again.

'I want to be your girlfriend.' She made the words sound as loud as she could, though her voice shook.

'Good.' Jay smiled and touched her face with wet fingers. 'Now, take off your shirt.'

Chapter 8

London 2023

Julia

Rasul steps inside the house, he has come by appointment to plan his work, but he seems cautious as if I am to be feared and that's not surprising. This is my territory but he is very far from his. I have all the power and I'm ashamed of my unease.

I take him downstairs to the kitchen and make tea. We sit at the table while he shows me photos on his phone of the food he has cooked: fish dishes, vegetables, rice, bread, and salads; food from an unnamed country by the sea. I am not permitted to know where he comes from, or at least, not yet. He must have kept his phone very carefully, wrapped in plastic and strapped to his body, as he sat in a boat, jammed with others on a heaving sea. He has left everything he knew behind him. These pictures are his connection to home, even if home no longer exists.

He doesn't say much but the images show a hinterland of dedicated work.

'I'm impressed.'

'Thank you.' He looks tense, he is waiting.

'Shall we start with five lessons and see how we go?'

He stands and bows his head, his hand over his heart.

'I'll buy the ingredients, and you can keep what you cook. Anything you don't want goes to St Jude's. Does that seem fair?'

He nods again.

'When would you like to start?'

'In a couple of days?'

'And to cook?

'Bread.'

A good answer, the most basic of foods but hard to get right. James comes in unexpectedly as Rasul is telling me about the different types of bread he could make. He answers James's questions politely though he evades the ones about home.

'Did you see how he was looking at me, watching every move I made?' James says after Rasul has left. 'That's what they do; they work out how to use you and then they bide their time. You need to be careful, my love. I worry about your decisions sometimes.'

I don't argue and he moves in close. His hands slip under my skirt. My heart sinks. So this is why he came back; daytime sex, a new development that I'm not used to yet. Something would have started it off: a successful meeting or new building project, parents signing up or a secretary doing what he asked. The kick of power, the need to exert it. I wonder what those parents would think as he lifts my skirt and pushes into me. I let him. He doesn't take long. I'm not frightened, simply practical. I take the path of least resistance. Besides I couldn't fight back, he is bulky and very strong. If anything has changed it's me. I am no longer intoxicated by my husband; if it wasn't for Rasul I would have been safely in the café. That's where I usually am these days, where I am two days later.

The Garden Café is in a small street off Horseferry Road, small and set back from the pavement, partly obscured by large plane trees. The food is simple, and it's not usually crowded in the middle of the day. The waiters know me, they don't mind if I just order coffee. I can work in peace. James wouldn't come here, it's not grand enough. He has no idea where I am. He has begun to ask what I'm doing and who I'm with, but so far, he hasn't stooped to ask where I am. That would make him needy and give me power. James has to hold all the power.

Rasul is due to return to our house in half an hour. I tap out a recipe on my notepad and send it to his phone.

A message pings from Lottie. *I came back for my camera lens. There's a man outside who says he's here to cook. Should I let him in?*

Rasul is early. I'm glad Lottie asked. She could easily have let him in without a second thought, which would have mattered if he had been a stranger. Her generosity could get her into trouble one day.

Yes please, darling. That's my new trainee cook, Rasul. Can you make him tea? On my way.

Today's bill will be added to my account. As I slip from my sofa, the movement lifts the head of a woman sitting at a table near the door, also alone, also making notes. A woman in red, her dark hair twisted into a pleat. I glance away feeling disconcerted. I am seeing Laurel everywhere but when I glance back, I recognize those dark eyes.

I stop by her table on the way out and smile.

'Hi there.'

Laurel glances up. She nods politely and looks down again at her iPad.

She doesn't remember me. I should walk past her and out of the restaurant, but there is something about this woman that intrigues me; it might be the calm which surrounds her like a scent I want to breathe in.

'Forgive the interruption, we met the other night.'

She looks up again, scanning my face, smiling faintly. There is no flash of recognition. She must be used to this; our parents' meeting wouldn't be the only one she's attended recently. There will be other schools, teachers must seek her out all the time.

'Julia Grenville, wife of the headmaster.' I am aware as I say those words how medieval they sound. Wife of.

'Of course.' That pretty accent, Spanish or Italian. 'Do join me.' She indicates the seat next to her and moves her iPad to make space. I text Lottie as I sit down. *I'll be ten minutes late. Rasul can start cooking if he likes.*

'I discovered this café last week and I've come often since then.' She smiles. 'It's so peaceful, ideal for working.'

I must have missed her then or perhaps we come at different times.

She is dressed simply, a red cardigan, jeans and minimal make-up. Beauty is currency if you want it to be, mine bought me all the things I thought I wanted, but Laurel plays hers down. She might not want things anyway; she could be after something quite different.

'Is this a favourite place of yours too?' The brown eyes look interested.

'I come often, it's my escape.'

'Escape.' She echoes, nodding as if familiar with the concept. She doesn't say any more, she seems to be waiting. It's been a long time since anyone listened, the pause unlocks me.

'Well, things are little hectic right now.'

'You have a busy life?' She tilts her head, her eyes on mine.

'I cook for big school events, like the one you attended. And for a refugee centre.'

She nods and I find myself talking on, words spilling out, 'I organize my husband's diary, and I write most of his speeches. Then there's my daughter though she boards in the term time. The house too, of course, which has to be perfect, given my husband's job. It belongs to the school you see, and colleagues call round, then there's the pressure—'

For me to look perfect as well, though I won't tell her that, my heart rate is picking up already. I don't want her to think I'm crazy. I won't tell her that I come here to avoid my husband either, or that he's taken to coming back for sex during the day, though I've a feeling that wouldn't shock her. It might not sound bad; perhaps I'm to be envied. Maybe lots of women would like it if their husbands came back for sex at lunchtime.

Laurel doesn't seem to notice the sentence is hanging

in mid-air. 'It helps to work away from home some-times. No one to interrupt you, no jobs waiting to be done.'

'Exactly.'

A jug of coffee arrives with a second cup. The young waiter bows. Laurel pours out and passes mine over; sipping I feel restored, brave enough to ask her a question of my own.

'You mentioned your husband was a teacher too?'

'Ex-husband.'

'I'm sorry.'

She smiles, making light of it; she might have wanted out, perhaps she should be congratulated.

'It was a while ago now. I've made a fresh start.'

A fresh start. How cool and hopeful that sounds, like the mornings when I was young, those blue morn-ings on Paxos, when the air smelt of pine and all of life seemed spread out in front of me.

'I was a teacher once.' I rarely admit that these days, but as she leans a little towards me, her hand open on the table, she seems to be welcoming my confidences, even encouraging them. 'I loved it. To be honest, I miss it.'

Have I said that to anyone before? Even to myself? I usually maintain that I'm glad to be out of it, that the loss of my career was compensated for by my daughter, by marriage and cooking, but she is watching me with understanding, and I don't need to pretend.

She seems to be waiting for more, but the door of the restaurant slams and I glance round. No one else is here apart from us.

'I must go. I'll be late.'

Ridiculously late. Rasul might have given up and gone home.

'Take this.' She holds out one of her blue-edged cards.

'James has one—'

'This is for you.'

To refuse would be awkward. 'Thank you.'

'You might want to talk about finding a life that's right for you.'

I could tell her that I have too many lives already, that I am fine, but that would be glib, she already knows I'm not.

'I must hurry. Thank you for listening.'

I gather my bags and coat, worried now that I've given too much away.

'*Prego*.' She smiles up at me as if to excuse the Italian word that slipped out by mistake. There is a contract in that glance; she won't tell anyone what I've said. I feel relieved and, absurdly, I want to give her a hug.

I run all the way back home through the few quiet streets, pigeons flying from my feet. When I arrive, the hall is warm with the scent of simmering food, that deep perfume of slow cooking, the fragrance of wine and meat. Jazz thuds from the kitchen downstairs.

Lottie is grating a lemon and laughing. Rasul is by the stove, smiling, at ease. They glance up when I come in. Guilt flickers over Lottie's face. There is a little silence.

'You told me to let him in,' Lottie says. 'You've been ages.'

'Sorry, I met a friend.' Though that's not really who Laurel is, at least not yet, she was more like a listener. A rescuer perhaps. 'Hi there, Rasul. Something smells good.'

He bows.

'It's my turn to cook for my tutorial group tomorrow. Rasul's been showing me how to make this special Mediterranean dish. We used lamb from the freezer. I added James's wine.' Lottie sounds excited and defiant at the same time.

'Good for you.' James needn't know, there are so many bottles of wine in the cellar, stacked to the ceiling in their hundreds.

Rasul is meticulously dressed in chinos and a jacket. He must fold up his belongings each day, wash in some public facility, shave. Perhaps he has found a hostel. All the same, the effort he would need to expend to look tidy and clean must be continuous and exhausting.

103

'I started the bread,' he tells me, nodding to the bowl on the side of the stove where a pale heap of dough is already billowing. Salt, black olives, and needle-thin leaves of rosemary are laid out in tidy heaps. There is an unlabelled plastic bottle with green-gold oil inside. 'Oil from my country,' he says, noticing my glance. 'A gift.'

'How on earth did you manage to bring that with you?'

Rasul's face closes immediately. I have broken a rule and asked him a question about his past, his journey. I feel abashed. I don't need to find out how he secreted a bottle of oil on board a dinghy. It is important to him, that's all I need to know, and he is giving it to us.

Lottie nudges me out of the room and closes the door. Her blue eyes are bright though her face is pale with tiredness, there are dark smudges below her eyes. Her freckles stand out like little grains of sand. 'Why the cross-examination, Mum? You should be asking him to stay.'

'Stay?'

'Why not? He's living on the streets in Vauxhall.' Her colour is up, she's prepared to do battle. 'He can have my room. Anything's better than sleeping outside. It's cold. He's a refugee.'

'I know, darling, but there are so many refugees, we can't invite every one—'

'That's such a ridiculous argument. Doctors don't refuse to help one patient just because there are so many ill people. We are so fucking privileged, Mother, do you realize that?'

I'm taken aback, but also flooded with pride. When I was her age, I focused on my own battles. I didn't think about the world as she does. I hadn't thought of offering Rasul a room. I tread down the feeling that he seems watchful; if anything that should persuade me to be more welcoming. He feels uneasy, I need to earn his trust.

'You're right, Lottie, of course you're right. I'll have to check with James. There will be rules.'

'James won't find it easy to share our home.'

'It's not our home though, it belongs to the school. That's my point. We need permission, I'll let you know.' I study her face, the new pallor, the darkness under her eyes. 'Is everything all right at school?'

'Back off, Mum.' The blue of her eyes has darkened. 'Stop worrying about me.'

She walks into the kitchen; I can't hear what she is saying to Rasul. She comes out but she doesn't kiss me as she usually does, just a quick wave at the door and she's gone.

I was a tricky teenager, God knows, and distant from my mother, but I thought Lottie and I were different, much closer. We used to talk about everything, but now she's brushing off my questions. It's her age, as James said, but it's happened so fast and I've failed to keep pace.

Rasul divides the dough and gives me half as if he

knows the push and pull of kneading will soothe me. I drive the heel of my hand into the warm dough and flip it over, again and again. He folds in olives and then puts the dough into oiled tins, presses in rosemary and sprinkles the top with salt. I imagine his mother doing this when he was a child, giving him scraps of dough to shape. Later she would cut him a slice while the loaf was still warm; he might still carry the taste in his mouth. He looks absorbed as he weighs out the flour for rolls and begins to form more dough. I wonder if this is helping him too; it's impossible to know the thoughts behind that calm face, behind any face. I haven't any idea what Lottie is thinking these days. I wash my hands when I've finished and sit at my desk in the corner of the kitchen to answer emails.

There are many from parents about food, more these days, more every day. They want to know about vegetarian options, vegan, gluten-free and lactose-free diets. James thinks these food requirements extraordinary, a fad, but I understand completely. I was one of those whose day hung by the kind of food I ate, counting every calorie. I am still hostage to my weight, still, always, hungry.

When Rasul takes two loaves from the oven, shining with oil and crusted with salt, the pungent smell is familiar. This loaf could be one of those on that table in Paxos; it conjures up the warmth of the sun, the scent of thyme, the blue glitter of the sea.

Time ticks by peacefully. The six o'clock news announces itself on the radio. Rasul takes the rest of the bread from the oven: it has risen smoothly; the rolls are an even brown and perfectly shaped. He leaves, making me a gift of the loaves. I freeze one; later, James devours the other. I mention Lottie's suggestion that we provide Rasul with a room, and he looks thoughtful, his eyes shifting from side to side as he assesses the idea.

'I see no reason why not.' He replies after he has swallowed the last mouthful of bread. 'I'll check but personally I don't see a problem.'

I can't help thinking that several motives could be driving this decision: the favourable light in which it would cast him, the way I would become more available, simple greed perhaps. I should try to remember James is also being kind. I must tell myself this more often, my husband is a kind man.

It takes time to fall asleep but when I do, I dream of Paxos and Thalassa, but the dream becomes a nightmare. Red flowers lie on the steps of the terrace, the paths in the grounds are blocked by fallen pines. The beach is covered with rubbish. Goats wander in and out of the empty house, the contents wrecked by storms. No one answers my call. Some catastrophe has taken place. An old woman in black, wandering in the garden, shakes her head at me and refuses to talk.

When I wake at dawn, the calm English light filters around the curtain and the nightmare feathers away with an aftertaste of sorrow. My father never mentioned what happened the night I left the island; my mother shrugged and waved her hands in her dismissive way. The Greek family had left the day after I did, abandoning their home and their job mid-season. It had all been intensely irritating, something to do with the daughter who had made a nuisance of herself with some of the guests. She didn't mention her name, perhaps she'd forgotten it, as I had, which felt shameful somehow. What Mother said seemed unlikely, that little girl had been young and very shy, but she didn't elaborate. My parents decided to buy the house in Cornwall for holidays after that, though my father kept the Greek one as a pension plan, to be sold if they needed funds. It's been looked after by agents ever since.

Later I text Lottie to say James agreed Rasul can stay but my text seems to vanish without a trace, just like the dream of the wrecked house. There is no answer at all.

Chapter 9

Paxos 2003

Sofie

'Take off your shirt,' Jay repeated, his voice louder this time, sharper. 'You said you were my girlfriend.'

Dimitrios has known his girlfriend Roxana all his life. He bought her flowers, she made him cakes, they walked hand in hand everywhere but Jay was a stranger who lived in another country. He had pretended not to know her when she served the meals. She knew nothing about him, nothing at all. How could she be his girlfriend? Why had she thought it possible, even for one moment?

She glanced at the door, but it was shut. Ginger was standing with his back to it. Outside the branches of the pine trees sighed in the wind, rain was pattering on the roof. No one would hear if she called for help. She was trapped.

Jay's skin looked greasy in the torchlight; this close, his spots cast little shadows on his cheeks. There were white flakes at the edge of his hair. She hadn't noticed any of these things before. She looked away. Her legs were shaking, which made the edge of her skirt shake too.

'Buck up.' He was becoming irritated. 'Are you going to make this difficult?' He put on a disappointed face, but he wasn't really disappointed. His eyes were gleaming.

She shook her head. She couldn't take off her shirt. No one except her mother had ever seen her without clothes, apart from the boys this evening, when she came out of the sea, and then she'd been wearing her pants and had shielded her chest with her arms.

'I want a photo to remember you by when I'm in England.' The tone was wheedling but it sounded as if he was about to burst out laughing. Ginger chortled from the shadows. 'Just one photo.'

The shed didn't belong to her any more, it belonged to the boys. It had become like a cellar or a cave. A prison. Her mind was jumping in circles like an impala trying to escape from the lion. Her thoughts were dizzy, they made no sense.

'It's not as if there'll be anything much to see.' Ginger's voice was thick. 'But people like that. Get the skirt off her too.'

'Shut up, Ginge.' Jay didn't bother to look at Ginger;

he moved nearer to Sofie. 'Are you perhaps a little bit stupid?'

He sounded genuinely curious; perhaps she was stupid because she couldn't understand what Ginger had said. The teacher told her she was the best in the class in English, but it felt as if she'd never learnt it at all.

This close, the smell of sweat coming off Jay was making her sick, but underneath that, there was a faint scent of lavender. Athena had ironed Jay's shirt just yesterday, standing in the kitchen with tired feet and a headache, sprinkling lavender water onto the linen, scented water she'd made herself from the lavender that grew in the garden. She would be sleeping now, not dreaming of what was happening to her daughter. If Dimitrios and Christos knew, they would grab hold of both boys and throw them out of the hut, they would pound them where they lay, but they didn't know. No one had any idea. She had kept the secret so well.

Jay lifted his arm suddenly. Sofie cringed but he didn't hit her, he grabbed the front of her blouse. The fabric ripped and the buttons flew off. They spun on the floor for a few seconds, tiny circles of noise in the silence. The shirt gaped, she tried to hold the edges together, but they didn't meet any more.

'There. That wasn't so terrible, was it?'

Jay's voice sounded gentle again, as though she was a baby having to get used to something that was difficult but necessary. He said something else, but Sofie's heart was making such a noise in her ears that she couldn't make out the words. He slipped his hands inside the waistband of her skirt; his fingers were hot. She twisted away and something came up in her throat like vomit. Her mind was drowning in terror.

'For fuck's sake, stay still.' Ginger squatted to help Jay pull down her skirt, then Jay lifted her up, his hands gripping painfully, so Ginger could pull the skirt from her ankles.

'Good.' Jay sounded breathless. 'Now your pants.'

She stared at him, hearing but not believing.

'She's not going to do it, Ginge.' Jay sounded resigned and, for a second, for one brief second, she thought they would leave her alone. They would give up and go out, crashing the door behind them, shouting something rude, but she wouldn't mind. She would never say anything about tonight to anyone. She would lay the table very early in the morning so she wouldn't have to see them; she would ask Dimitrios to take the food to the table instead of her. She would never go to the beach again.

Ginger pushed forward and shone the torch straight at her face, scattering her thoughts.

'*Se parakalo*,' Sofie whispered. She would have said

please instead if she could have done, if she could have found the English word somewhere in the whirling chaos in her mind.

'Look at it, rabbit in the headlights.' Ginger grunted like a pig at the trough. 'It's not like those bitches at school.' His voice had a catch in it. He was excited, like a child about to rip open the wrapping around a birthday present.

'Do you realize we can do whatever the fuck we want?'

Chapter 10

London 2023

Julia

It doesn't take long to find Laurel's office: a ten minute walk along Millbank with the Thames on my left, a right turn down Vauxhall Bridge Road and then into the warren of Pimlico streets until I reach the tall white house with its black door and pillars either side. 'Laurel Rossi' is written on the label by the second bell in a pretty italic hand, but the instant the buzzer sounds, I want to escape. I've miscalculated. How can I share anything with a stranger? I should be cooking for the crypt or going through James's speech to the governors, answering emails that have accumulated in my inbox. The flowers in the sitting room need replacing, James gets annoyed if they look withered.

No one will notice if I turn around and walk away.

I can retrace my steps quickly, James need never know, but at that moment, the door in front of me springs ajar. Laurel's voice over the speaker tells me her office is on the first floor, second on the right. It's too late to escape.

Her door is open when I reach the landing and she is there, that lovely face smiling a welcome.

'Please come in.'

I step into warmth and colour. The walls are terracotta, lined with books and paintings. Candles glimmer on every surface. Water splashes quietly from a fountain in a bowl of stones. There is the sweet peppery scent of lavender. A little tree stands in a green and yellow striped pot in front of the window. Flute music plays in the background. All those things that are supposed to make you calm but, perversely, can make me more anxious, seem to be working here. I feel less tense already.

Laurel shuts the door behind me and indicates one of the two armchairs either side of the fireplace. Orange flames are flickering behind the glass door of a stove. She is wearing a knee-length leather skirt, a pretty shirt patterned with birds. Slim boots. That simple necklace. She looks professional though her beauty, if anything, is enhanced.

'You might be wondering about me.' Her tone is professional too. 'I approached your husband in an unconventional manner at the parents' meeting.

Therapists don't usually suggest treatment to potential clients, but my methods have evolved with experience. My qualifications, however, are very conventional.'

She opens the file on the table between us. Inside are certificates with wax seals and gold lettering: BSc(Honours) Psychology from the University of Rome, first class. She turns a page. A Master's with distinction in interpersonal therapy with stress management. She turns the page again. Distinction in a counselling diploma, awarded by Milan University.

'Impressive.' I hope I don't sound jealous. I have a first-class degree too, but my certificate is in a box in the loft, gathering dust.

'There are reviews, if you'd like to see them.'

I shake my head as if that's unnecessary, but in fact I've seen them already online, five-star attributes to her empathy and the way she's turned lives around.

'I record my sessions on a Dictaphone.' A small machine the size of a phone is lying on the table, a slim thing in shiny black with an edging of red. 'I use it with all my clients now; it means I can focus on what's happening in the sessions and listen later in case there's something I missed. Your words will be confidential, but we needn't use it if you'd prefer not to.'

'Oh no, that's fine.' I tread down worry about my words being recorded, all those reviews can't be wrong. She hands me the consent form for permission to record the session and I sign swiftly.

She presses play then settles back. 'Might there be questions you would like to ask me before we begin?'

There are, but hardly the kind that you can put to your new therapist. I'd ask what happened to her marriage, had she been expected to be perfect as well? Acquiesce to sex on demand? Had there come a point where the equation had ceased to balance, and what happened then? I want to know about her childhood, too. I imagine a privileged upbringing but there the similarities would end. Her mother would have had time to spare for her daughter, her father too; he'd have been a university lecturer perhaps. I picture a tall house in a wealthy suburb of Rome and imagine wide-ranging conversations over dinner. Meals with my parents had been silent. My father watched me while talking on his phone as my mother drank glass after glass of wine and I pushed my food round the plate, hiding what I could in my napkin and throwing it away afterwards.

'We don't need to dwell on the past,' Laurel says quietly, watching my face. 'That's not usually how this works but we could start with the things that brought you here today.'

'You might remember my husband said that I'm anxious enough for two.' I try to smile as if at a joke, but it hurt at the time. It still hurts.

She nods and the brown eyes darken, it wasn't a

118

joke to her either. 'Anxiety is hard to live with. What have you tried?'

'Medication and counselling. Exercise, yoga. Pilates. Everything I can think of.'

'What is the biggest cause of your anxiety?'

'The expectation.'

'Expectation?'

'To be perfect.' There, it slipped out by mistake, but it's too late to take it back.

'What does perfection look like to you?'

'Oh, you know, being a wonderful cook, and a great editor. A faultless organiser, housekeeper. Mother. Wife. Perfect looks of course, and perfect weight.'

'Is there a perfect weight?'

'As low as possible.' I laugh but she doesn't join in.

'Go on,' she says softly.

'I stopped eating normally at fourteen. It pleased my father.'

How quickly we have arrived here, at the very heart of it all.

'You don't need to talk about this unless you want to.'

'He liked me thin. Childlike girls are considered desirable, especially among older men. He wanted to gain leverage among his powerful cronies.'

'You had to please your father's colleagues?'

'We had a holiday home where he invited his friends,

119

nothing was forced. He wanted me to flirt with them, it meant they would owe him. Not blackmail exactly, nothing as vulgar. I would buy him an advantage that's all. If bargains were struck, I didn't know about them.'

'Did you sleep with them?'

'There was this man, Paul, who was very powerful in the media. He was in his forties, married, not that that made any difference. I began to sleep with him when I was fifteen.'

'What made you play along?'

'I craved my father's approval; ours was a loveless family, my mother was under his sway. She drank a lot, probably to cope with him. And I liked the admiration of his friends, the illusion of warmth. It was nice to be touched.'

Laurel doesn't look shocked although something flickers beneath the smooth surface of her face. Surprise? Pity? If so, it's gone in a flash.

'It's not unusual for patterns to repeat themselves,' she says quietly. 'Could this be what's happening now?'

'There's a price to pay for everything, if that's what you mean. My marriage allows me to give my daughter a stable upbringing, a good education.'

'How does your husband make you feel?'

'More anxious.'

'Because?'

'I have to look the part, constantly. I mustn't put a foot wrong for the sake of the school. Its reputation is all important.' I glance at her, she looks calm and trustworthy and I decide to trust her. 'It was threatened last year. I found that difficult to cope with.'

'Do you want to share what happened?'

'Oh, it's fine now.' It isn't though, it still makes me anxious. 'One of the art scholars falsely accused the art master of sexual abuse, it made us very vulnerable at the time.'

'I can imagine how worrying that must have been.'

'It was terrifying. Her father burst into the parents' meeting last year, threatening James.'

'So when I met you it was the anniversary of that occasion. No wonder you were anxious.'

She understands, I knew she would.

'You can't alter those kinds of things,' she continues. 'I expect it goes with the territory. But there is something you can do which might help.'

'Anything.'

'Eat more.'

'Sorry?'

'Not eating is a coping mechanism but it's self-sabotaging. Anxiety gets worse when you're hungry.'

'James expects me to be thin, I need to set an example.' And I'd be frightened to stop though I don't tell her that, I've been starving myself for years.

'It's your body, not his. It wasn't your father's. Don't punish it, make it stronger. Eat a little more every day, a piece of bread, a spoonful of rice, a potato.'

'I'm not sure if I can do that.'

'You have my permission. I'll want a report in two weeks. Let's call it your homework.'

A tiny bell from the Dictaphone sounds. The session has ended. I turn at the door to say goodbye, but she is bent over the table, making notes in a book. She catches my glance and smiles.

'Just noting the date and time for when I play back.'

She gets up and watches me down the stairs, an encouraging smile on her face.

I walk back along Millbank taking my time, watching the barges progress up and down the Thames. I pause opposite the Tate to touch Henry Moore's *Locking Piece*, bronze shapes that circle each other and look different depending on where you stand; things look different already, excitement jostles with fear.

When James comes in later, he is triumphant, the governors' meeting had gone well. To the victor, the spoils. Sex is in the hall against the mirror. The door is unlocked, anyone could walk in. James is a risk taker; to the world he appears calm and considered, the person who makes the rules, a safe pair of hands. No one could guess how close he likes to sail to danger.

Later still, while James is sleeping, I take Rasul's remaining loaf out of the freezer and put it in the oven. It was clever of Laurel to mention homework, she can probably tell I'm the type who always did my homework. When it's ready I pull off a hunk and eat slowly, savouring each mouthful. It's hot. The salty crust, the oily dough, and the warm hit of rosemary are like being held by a friend you haven't seen for a very long time; more than friendship, it feels sexual. Addictive. I eat half a loaf before I can stop myself.

Chapter 11

Paxos 2003

Sofie

'*Ochi*.' Sofie was crying. '*Se parakalo. Ochi.*'

She covered her groin with one hand, the other was over her chest. Sweat was trickling from her armpits down her sides. She was trembling. Ginger was right, she was like a rabbit, a dead one. When Papa shot rabbits, their bodies carried on trembling as if they were still alive.

Ginger grabbed her arm but her skirt, crumpled in his palm, prevented him from gripping tightly. He looked at it and shook it out.

'Jesus, do people really wear skirts like this? My kid sisters' are better. Gross.' And he threw it into the corner.

There was a banging noise which she thought was

her heart, but the door had unlatched, and it was thudding against the wall. She lunged for it, but Ginger moved quickly and stood in her way.

'*Voethia, Theous*. Help me, God.' Her voice was drowned out by the storm, no one would hear her.

'Help me, God!' Ginger mimicked her. He kicked the door shut and then grabbed her arm. 'Shut up.'

His face was close to hers; his breath stank of stale food and alcohol. She pushed him away, her hands sinking into the deep flesh of his chest. He stumbled back, and for a second she thought she might win, might dodge past him to the door, but Jay stepped forward and caught hold of her arms; for a skinny boy he was very strong. Now she had nothing to cover herself with. Ginger squatted in front of her and pulled down her pants with a quick, rough movement that tore them. He began taking photos. A noise started up from somewhere and got louder and louder before she realized she was making it herself.

Jay put an arm around her neck and pulled her head backwards. His arm across her throat made breathing difficult.

'Be quiet,' he told her softly. 'And stay quiet. You will never talk about this, do you get that? Your father will lose his job if you say a fucking word.'

Ginger shoved his hand between her legs, his fingers pushing and prodding. She twisted violently away, stumbled, and fell, hitting her head on the shank of the anchor. While she was still on the ground, stunned and breathless, something warm and wet fell on her shoulder and her neck. Rain? Raining inside? Then the stink of urine filled the shed. Ginger was peeing on her.

'You've got what was coming to you.' His voice was rich and warm; he was enjoying this. 'Slut.'

She tried to get up, but he pressed down on her shoulder, so she had to kneel at his feet.

'Open your mouth.'

She stared up at his flushed cheeks, his small eyes. She could see his double chin, his hairy belly. The way his blue shorts had slipped down. He wasn't wearing pants. Jay was behind him; he had his phone angled down.

'Open your fucking mouth.'

Chapter 12

London 2023

Julia

James watches whatever I put in my mouth. He raises an eyebrow when I help myself to potatoes, but I promised Laurel and I'm good at keeping promises.

The truth is, it's working. I thought eating would make me feel more anxious but it's the opposite. After a month I'm happier, more free of my worries. For the first time in decades, I'm enjoying food. Laurel is pleased. I tell her this is in large part due to Rasul. The scent of his cooking fills the house, as it must have done the narrow streets of the city where his parents had their restaurant, families sitting down, as we do, to plates of steaming food. He serves a mix of Syrian, Turkish, Greek, and Albanian food, we have *hummus* and *baba ghanoush*, homemade pita bread and vine leaves stuffed with meat. *Tabbouleh* and *falafel*. I have little to teach him, but I catch his eyes on me sometimes, as if he's trying to work out who I am, rather than the other way round.

Tonight, he left us bream baked in sauce with *harissa* and turmeric before he went out, as he usually does, giving us space. I close my eyes as I eat.

'Christ, Julia.' James's voice is amused. 'You look as though you are having an orgasm.'

I want to tell him that eating is far better than sex, but he wouldn't find that so amusing.

'You need to be careful, my love.' He pours himself a glass of wine.

'Careful?'

'After mid-thirties, extra calories go to the hips.' He glances at me over the rim of his glass.

Anxiety begins to burn with fierce little flames. I don't answer, at least not out loud. It's my body, I say silently, I am making it stronger. It's as though Laurel is in the room smiling at me and, gradually, the flames flicker and die out.

'I saw Lottie today,' James continues conversation-ally.

'How was she?'

'She was coming out of the art block on her own. She looked lost in thought.'

Maud said she went everywhere with Angel before Angel had to leave, but I don't tell James that, it wouldn't be worth it. He might lecture me about the danger of taking sides against the school or the importance of loyalty.

'Were any boys hassling her?'

'I told you boys don't hassle girls here.'

'We both know boys hassle girls everywhere.'

He doesn't reply but begins to talk about his day: a review of the music school extension with the architect, the year 12 curriculum planning lunch. The afternoon with the chairman of governors. I tune out his words, wondering how long it will be before he notices I skipped my hair appointment for the second time.

When I wake at five in the morning, the seeds of worry that he'd sown have flourished like a plant whose branches scrape against the inside of my skull. I slide quietly from bed, pull on my tracksuit and pad to the kitchen to send Lottie a text. *Tea. Garden café today?*

As I wait for the kettle to boil, I stare at the framed photograph of the Cornish house that my father bought after Paxos. I was happy there with my little daughter, surrounded by sea and sky and birds, the two of us together. I was between marriages. Lottie was enough, she was everything. There are no photos of Thalassa on the walls. James took them all down; there wasn't room for all my mementoes, he said, we had to get rid of the clutter.

I lace my trainers tightly. I need a run, a long one to clear my head. Outside the dark air is cold, autumn getting a foothold, the branches are dark against a darker sky. London is sleeping though not everyone, lights shine in the Houses of Parliament, policemen at the entrances shift on their feet. I turn left across the worn grass of Parliament Square, up Birdcage Walk and into St James's Park, into another world of trees, moorhens and pelicans floating on green-black water. I run through to Green Park and then to the underpass at Hyde Park corner, lined with sleeping bodies hidden under blankets. I leave several cards, informing them of the crypt, taking care to do it silently. Sleep is precious when the nights are long and cold.

The steely surface of the Serpentine in Hyde Park silvers as light seeps into the morning. Across the water, early swimmers pick their way to the edge, precise as herons. Geese sleep in ranks. I cut across the bridge, past the ribboning water of Diana's memorial and the bronze ibis. On the way back through the underpass, pink-faced crowds stream towards me, ignoring the huddled shapes at their feet as if they were invisible.

Back at home the house seems stuffy, the air dense and warm. James descends from his shower, two floors above, buttoning his shirt which strains against his stomach these days. He eats more than he used to and it's beginning to show.

'All well?' His hand on my shoulder feels heavy. I tread down the impulse to move away. His glance takes in the cup I left on the draining board, the glasses on the side, the socks he abandoned on the floor yesterday. 'Only it looks messier than it usually does in the morning. I wondered if you were feeling okay?'

'I'm fine.' I'm not going to feel guilty, not any more.

'You got up earlier than usual, so—'

'I couldn't sleep.'

'But you never sleep.'

Is that what he tells himself? That it's fine, since I get up early, to tidy the kitchen before breakfast? That I have nothing else to do while he is sleeping?

'I ran round the Serpentine. There were birds everywhere.'

'The therapist's instructions?' He grins.

'I always run in the morning.' I turn on the coffee machine.

'Breakfast isn't laid.'

'You could have fruit and cereal for a change, much healthier.'

'I need something more substantial. You know it helps with my ulcer.' He turns on the radio.

I don't bother to argue but fill the pan and set it to boil, slip in two eggs and set the timer. This is the man I chose and who chose me. He wasn't like this in the early days. He used to surprise me with theatre tickets or weekends away; he made jokes and left little presents around the house. He came home with flowers often. Those things seem to belong to a different era, another marriage.

'The timer's gone, Julia.'

I take the eggs out, put them in egg cups, and slide them both over, then put the toast in the toaster. Usually I do both simultaneously. James waits, tapping his neatly filed nails on the surface of the island, then unfolds the paper with a snap.

When the toast is done, I butter the slices, taking one for myself. It's been many years since I crunched into buttery toast. James's eyes meet mine. He isn't smiling now.

'I'm worried about you. Are you quite sure you're okay?'

I resist the impulse to tell him I feel better than I have for a very long time. After he has eaten, he slips on his jacket and inspects his speech which he left for me the night before. There is a short, deep silence. He looks up.

'This is unedited.'

'I'll bring you over an edited version.'

'I'm addressing the school in an hour.'

'I'll have it done by then.'

'Thank you.' He takes my chin in his fingers and kisses

me slowly, taking his time, his tongue pushing in. It feels like a punishment; I have to resist the urge to pull away.

I clean my teeth after that, then shower and towel my hair dry. In the mirror, without make-up, I look younger. I feel stronger, better. Laurel was right, food is helping. I pull on jeans. I've never gone to school without make-up or in jeans before; it feels as good as eating toast had done, as daring.

I speed read as I walk; his speech is plain but accurate. I usually add the warmth and depth, but this will do, it doesn't need to be perfect. I catch sight of James and Cosmo as I cross the large courtyard; they are deep in conversation, walking along the path by the far side, half hidden by trees. Their absorption is marked. Cosmo is laughing, he looks as unkempt as usual, but he's relaxed and clearly amused. James's head is inclined to his, his shoulders stooped, he seems subservient, even anxious. Neither notice me.

'You look well, Julia.' Libby smiles. 'Have you been away for the weekend?'

'Sadly not.' But I've had a piece of toast, I want to tell her; it was hot and steeped in salty butter. Someone has been listening to me for once; these things have made a difference, a bigger one than you might think. I don't say this of course, but simply smile as I put the speech in his tray, with a pencilled tick at the top to show I have read it through.

I watch a group of boys cross the courtyard through the mullioned window of the office. It takes a beat of time to see that the girl following them is Lottie, her head lowered as if in thought, her walk unrecognizably slow. While Libby chatters about the menu for the lower sixth music scholars' concert, I stare at my daughter until she is out of sight. Lottie would usually be in the middle of a group, chatting noisily and laughing, whereas now she is tagging behind. My stomach twists. I had been right to worry.

The traffic is slow across Vauxhall Bridge. I arrive late to the crypt, already filling up with refugees, more this week than before. I put my lasagne in the oven, where a large pot of macaroni cheese bubbles, browning in the heat.

'You've excelled yourself, Zoe.'

'Not me.' Zoe looks up briefly from the pot she is scrubbing. 'Your boy is turning out to be a bit of a lifesaver.' She nods to the corner of the hall where Rasul is talking to an emaciated old man we have been worried about.

'I saw you talking to that guy,' she tells Rasul when he brings plates to the hatch later. 'So lucky you can communicate in Arabic, at least I think that's what he speaks?' She seems to have got over her fear of boundaries.

Rasul's smile vanishes; he puts the plates down and walks away.

'Whoops.' Zoe looks guilty. 'Whatever happened in his past is serious.'

The past is always serious for refugees, she has only herself to blame.

I'm cleaning the stove when my phone buzzes a brief text.

My speech was unedited, what happened?

Fury curdles and I don't send an answer.

Two hours later, I'm in the Garden Café waiting for Lottie. It's busy today, the tables are full. Three women are in deep conversation, their heads close together. Two old men sit next to each other, sharing a paper, bickering amicably. An exhausted woman holds a grizzling baby on her lap, who quiets when she produces a bottle. I order tea and some muffins for Lottie then open my laptop. An hour passes before Lottie sits down in the opposite seat.

I shut my laptop and smile. 'How's things, darling?'

'What did you want to talk about, Mum?' Her skin is pale, the rings under her eyes are darker still, her shoulders droop.

'I just wanted to see you.' I hide concern under a cheery tone; not long ago she would have bounced in and given me her cheek to kiss. She would have expressed noisy despair at the amount of work she had to do and enthused about the photographs she was taking.

I order fresh tea and offer the muffins, but she shakes her head and stares at the people in the café. She seems miles away. The silence grows and I reach for something, anything, to say.

'I saw that photo of your feet in Maud's room, it's lovely.'

'That one?' Lottie's eyebrows draw together. 'I hate it.'

'Sweetheart, what's up?' I put my hand on her smooth one, the scattering of freckles make it look childishly young. The nails are bitten right down, which is new. My heart clenches with love and worry. 'Is it those boys?'

'What boys?'

'I was in Libby's office today; I saw you crossing the courtyard behind a bunch of them.'

'They're friends, Mum. I was probably just thinking about work. Jesus.'

'Would you let me or James know if you need help? He can seem remote, but he is in charge of the school, and your stepfather so—'

'I don't want favours from that man, and he wouldn't be interested anyway. I'll talk to my real father, or I would if he was here.'

She doesn't often mention Anthony, she must be feeling alone. She leaves soon after that.

I sit by myself, worry darkening the evening. We used to talk through her worries: concerns about work or disagreements with friends, but now I'm excluded, unable to help. I want to tell the girl at the next table with the baby on her lap to make the most of this time; the problems are simple, later she'll wonder why she worried.

I text Anthony to ask him to be in touch with Lottie, but he doesn't reply. She's on her own. The feeling of helplessness deepens. Her hurt hurts me but I can't do anything about it, like a wound I am powerless to heal.

Chapter 13

Paxos 2003

Sofie

The face in the mirror didn't look like hers. The right cheek was swollen and purple like an overripe plum about to burst. The eye that side was shut. There was a deep cut at her hairline. Her chin was crusted and so was her neck, her hair was stiff and matted. She wanted to vomit again, remembering.

A red and mauve bruise had spread under the skin of both breasts. She twisted round, another one darkened her lower back and buttocks, the skin was broken. If anyone saw her without clothes, they would tell her she should go to the hospital.

Bitch.

Slut.

The shower trickled water over her body, the stink of urine releasing in the heat. The pain was intense. She cried out, then stuffed her fingers in her mouth, no one must hear. It was lucky Nico wasn't in his bed, he must already be up at the house. Sofie endured the water for as long as she could, but afterwards, she felt just as dirty as before.

She wet the towel and pressed it against her face. In the mirror there was white between the split edges of skin on her forehead. Was that bone? She will say she tripped over in the dark. If she admits to being on the beach, there'd be trouble, but the trouble would be greater if they knew what had really happened. Mama might not be cross, but her eyes would fill with tears which would be worse. Papa would be silent with disgust. The cousins would be kinder, but she would be an embarrassment to them, a disgrace to the family.

The pain deep between her buttocks made it difficult to walk, and the skin between her legs felt torn. She put paper there and it came away soaked in blood.

Two weeks ago, Athena had told her never to go anywhere with a boy she didn't know. My lovely daughter, she had said, cupping Sofie's face in her palm which was roughened with washing clothes and scrubbing floors. 'My beautiful one. I don't need to tell you this, of course you won't.'

She hadn't given those words a single thought.

She closed her eyes but when she did, she was back in the shed.

She had thought she was going to die. She would die right there, with the rain on the roof and her knees on the concrete floor. After he had finished, Ginger pushed her face-down against the side of the boat and she had no strength left to fight. None. Jay took over.

She had woken on the ground outside the shed, with no memory of getting there; she must have crawled out of the shed to get away but collapsed beneath the trees. The ground was hot where the sun hit the earth between patches of shade. Every part of her was banging with pain, even turning her head was agony. She was naked apart from *Yia-yia's* chain round her neck. She couldn't see her pants, but her torn shirt and mud-stained skirt were next to her on the ground. She had struggled them on and stumbled back up the path.

Now she pushed herself out of the shower, holding to the wall. She wouldn't say anything, not one single thing. The boys wouldn't either, they would be too ashamed. She will bury what happened, like you bury dead things in the earth and stamp on the soil afterwards to make it firm. Once in the earth, dead things don't come up again.

She spent a long time combing her hair, so it covered half her face. She put on her school dress and cardigan and buttoned it up to the neck; at least the bruises on her body were covered.

She pulled on the cotton hat Athena so often tried to make her wear. She walked very slowly up the path to the kitchen, holding on to the trees as she passed them. Every step jarred.

She will tell them she fell over and perhaps they'll believe her.

Chapter 14

London 2023

Julia

Laurel tells me I look good. Each time we meet she says I look better than the time before, and I can see that for myself. My skin glows and my hair shines. The lines around my eyes have disappeared. For the first time I can remember I'm not hungry all the time. I'm less anxious about myself though the worry about Lottie seethes under everything.

Ironically James is anxious now, though not about Lottie. 'I'm really quite worried. To be frank, you've put on weight,' he says at breakfast, with his mouth full of scrambled egg. 'I mention it because I care about you; it won't do your health any good if you get fat.'

'Would it change how you feel about me?' I am curious rather than concerned.

'The PTA meeting is coming up soon.' He avoids my question, but his stare is intense. 'Your hairdresser might be able to fit you in today.'

'I've decided to grow my hair. It was long when we met, you liked it then.'

'That was seven years ago. You're almost forty now. It's different.'

My face feels hot. I pick up my jacket. I don't want him to see that right now. I'm wondering why I am here, in his kitchen. 'I have an appointment. Your papers are on the side.'

His face relaxes. An appointment, he will be thinking, a haircut or a manicure. Maybe a body wax.

'It will be good to have you back to your lovely self.' He drops a kiss on my head and turns back at the door, smiling the old charming smile, the one that used to make my heart turn over. 'We'll go for a holiday together soon, just us. You've earned it, sweetheart. I know you'll want to look your best.'

Rain is pocking the surface of the Thames as I hurry along Millbank to Pimlico. Laurel is waiting at the top of the stairs when I arrive.

'You look fabulous.' She smiles her wide smile, and we hug.

'James thinks I'm getting fatter.'

The fire crackles quietly, we sit either side. Watery light shines through the window onto the leaves of her potted tree and the room smells warmly of lavender.

'He hates fat women, though he's put on weight himself. He thinks I should take care.'

'You, fat?' She sounds incredulous. 'And you are supposed to do whatever he says?' She passes me a glass of cinnamon tea.

'I represent the school, looking good is my side of the bargain.'

'What's his?'

'A home. Financial stability.' I glance down at my hands; the thick gold wedding band gleams. The diamond on my engagement ring is ridiculously large; tilted, it catches the light, sending tiny rainbows over the wall. 'But recently that's not enough, other things feel more important.'

'What kind of things?' She sips her tea, glancing at the rainbows.

'My career. I'd like to go back to teaching. I used to love it. I'd return in a heartbeat.' I'm surprised at the fervour behind the words even as I say them. 'It would be tricky though.'

'Because you are working for him?'

'That and the cooking and everything else. He wants me to look perfect, but it's hard to find time for all the maintenance he thinks I need: the hair and the nails, the waxing, the make-up, the clothes. He's complained about my hair already.'

'Or you could let it all go.' The room is quiet after her words; only the sound of the flames hissing in the grate as her words sink in. 'Why should he control your appearance?'

'James controls everything, even sex. Especially sex.'

'Sex,' she repeats. The word in her mouth is like the faintest sizzle of oil in a pan.

'He dictates how much and when.' I've talked about sex before but not like this, not so honestly. 'He comes home at lunchtime sometimes, he likes it in the hall, he takes risks. I know there are women whose husbands don't desire them. Maybe I should be grateful.'

She listens, entirely unshocked.

'He's rougher than he used to be, quicker. He likes me to acquiesce. He prefers it if I wear skirts and stockings, more accessible. He likes unusual positions. It often hurts.'

'It's your body,' she says evenly. 'You can always say no.'

When the session ends, I feel lighter and happier than I can remember. I pull my coat from the hook by the door and glance back. She is bending over her notebook again, writing with concentration. 'Just referencing the date.' She gets up to see me out.

I jog home in the rain, passing Enzo Plazzotta's bronze dancer leaping high over Millbank, my heart is soaring too. My mascara will run and my hair will be flattened, but I don't care. It doesn't matter.

You can let it all go.

It's your body.

You can always say no.

Back home, I log on to a careers website for returning teachers and cancel my hair appointment again.

Chapter 15

Paxos 2003

Sofie

'I tripped over a big stone,' Sofie whispered.

Athena cupped her chin, tilting her face towards the light from the open window. All the smells of summer were coming into the kitchen: thyme, sage, lemon, lavender, tomato. The spray of water from the hose hissed from the vegetable patch and the cicadas had started. The normal sounds of a summer's day although nothing was normal any more.

'Which big stone?' Athena's eyes narrowed as she scanned Sofie's face. She looked as though she was trying not to cry. Athena never cried. 'We have spent years removing all the stones from the garden, there aren't any.'

'It was on the beach,' Sofie said quickly. 'It was hot, I couldn't sleep.'

'The beach? What's this?' Babas entered the kitchen with a bag full of fish. He put the bag in the sink and then sat down at the table, staring at Sofie.

'We understand.' Athena put a hand on her husband's shoulder. 'It was stuffy last night. There was probably a breeze off the water so you went to get cool. No harm done.'

'No harm?' Papa growled. 'Look at her.'

Sofie turned her face away. There was more harm than her parents could possibly guess, but she could never, ever tell them.

Dimitrios came whistling through the door to collect the shopping list and stopped.

'*Skata!*' he exclaimed before he saw Babas who didn't allow swearing in the house. 'What happened to your face, Sofie?'

She couldn't reply, not straight away. She must hold back tears; she must think of anything else but what happened.

'She tripped over a stone in the dark,' Athena told him, but her eyes were troubled.

'What are you not saying, *pedimou*?' Babas's tone had softened, which made it worse. 'Something bad has happened to you.'

Sofie looked at her feet to make sure she didn't cry. The skin on the top of her left foot was bruised but she had no idea how that happened. Did one of the boys stamp on it? She glanced at her father then away again. Dimitrios's face was creased in concern, he probably didn't believe her either.

Your father will lose his job if you say a fucking word.

'And a cardigan in this heat?' Athena asked. 'Are you poorly?' She put her hand on Sofie's forehead. The roughness of her palms was usually comforting. Today it hurt.

'You are hot, *pedimou.*'

That couldn't be right. She felt cold. Icy cold.

'Has it started?' Athena whispered. She would forgive her daughter anything if she thought it was her period; she'd been hoping it would begin this summer. Maybe it had, perhaps those pushing fingers had torn something deep inside.

'Go and lie down. There are pads in the pink box in your cupboard. We'll manage. It might have been the fall that brought it on.' Her eyes were kind but there were dark rings beneath them; she looked very pale. How could Sofie tell Mama anything, when she looked so ill? Babas was shaking his head. He knew there was more to the story. He would ask her again; he would make her tell him the truth.

She went back to her room, step by step, and found a pad. She needed to put one on anyway, her knickers were soaked with blood, so she changed them too. She lay on her side in bed watching the curtains become transparent as the light grew stronger. The distant bleating from the goats in the farm next door sounded unreal, the roar of Dimitrios's motor bike starting up was from a world she didn't belong to any more. She was sliding into a darker one where the sounds were louder:

Bitch

Slut

The thud of her face being hit.

The smash of her body against the side of the boat.

'*What if she tells?*'

'*She won't. Do it, bro.*'

Blackness closing in.

She lay in bed for an hour, but sleep didn't come. She pushed herself to sitting and got up very slowly. It was more difficult to walk than before. She felt dirty but she didn't need another shower, she was going into the sea.

It hurt to breathe as if something had cracked in her chest. Outside the sun had baked the soil that the rain had loosened last night. Her bare feet landed on crusts of mud, pine cones, and sharp stones but those sharp little cuts were far off, nothing to do with her. She left the path and crawled over the hill which separated their property from next door. No, it wasn't theirs, it belonged to Peter. Why did she keep forgetting that?

The path downwards was so steep she lost her

footing and half slithered onto the pebbles of next door's beach. The pain so intense that the world went black. She came to, lying awkwardly on the beach and had to pull herself up. No one would find her here, not until it was too late. The owners weren't at home though the workmen were somewhere on the cliffs above, building an extension near the edge. She could hear them whistling; men who knew Dimitrios and Christos, friendly guys who waved to her when they drove past.

She crawled to the edge of the sea and lay down. The water stung, that didn't matter, but it was too shallow. She couldn't walk out further, or the workmen would spot her. She would have to wait till they went home. No one must see her slipping under the water, they might drag her out too soon. Her body would be washed very clean. She would look normal, like any other girl of thirteen. She'll escape Mama's sorrow and Babas's questions. They will think it was an accident, that she was trying to swim but wasn't thinking properly because she was muddled after the fall. They would be sad of course, but they wouldn't be angry. If they knew what had really happened, they would be angry for the rest of their lives.

Chapter 16

London 2023

Julia

James and I are on either side of the fire, we are on our own. Rasul is out, Cosmo left a couple of hours ago. He and James were drinking in the sitting room, their conversation punctuated by loud bursts of laughter. Cosmo refused supper and disappeared, but the smell of tobacco lingers in the room. Bach is playing, a sonata this time, but I want to turn off the music, throw back the curtains, open the windows and listen to the birds. I told Laurel about our evenings once, the ceaseless music, the claustrophobia. Most people would think I should be grateful, but she understood.

'I've been thinking about re-training.' I watch James for his reaction. 'I want to study something new.'

'Of course.' He is reading Thomas Hardy's early poems and doesn't look up. 'What's it to be?'

'Arabic, I think. Maybe Mandarin.'

He turns a page. He's getting a double chin, I hadn't noticed that before.

'Good for you,' he says abstractedly. 'I don't know much about Arabic food. It'll be interesting to be enlightened.'

'I mean the language not the food.'

'Why would you want to do that?' He looks up, smiling, his finger keeping his place in the book.

'I've always wanted to learn Arabic, and it would look good on my CV—'

'What's your CV got to do with anything?' The smile fades. He sits up straighter, the book slides to the floor.

'It's time I went back to work.'

'You work already.'

'What I do isn't a career.' I avoid his eyes. 'I've applied for an MA at King's.'

'Part-time?'

'If that can be negotiated.'

'Is it about money? You think it will get you a job?' His tone softens a little. 'You know you can have whatever you want.'

'It's nothing to do with money.'

'I rely on you.' His eyebrows draw together.

'It shouldn't be hard to find an editor to work on your speeches.'

'What about the catering? It works so well.'

For you, I reply silently, it works so well for you.

'And you love it.'

'I didn't study languages at university to be a PA or a cook.'

'The plans we make when we are young often have to change.' It sounds like a sixth-form lecture.

'Yours didn't.'

His face hardens.

'But you're right, I enjoy doing school events, I'll continue those at weekends.' My heart is hammering but I speak calmly. 'Rasul can carry on cooking for us if he wants to, and I can ask him to help at school functions during the week.'

'Has someone persuaded you to do this?'

'Of course not.' Why tell him about Laurel? What we talk about belongs to us, Laurel and me. In any case, she doesn't persuade, she listens and encourages, but he wouldn't understand that.

'When is all this supposed to happen?'

'As soon as possible.'

He doesn't speak for the rest of the evening, but when we're in bed, he nudges himself into my side. His skin feels cold, rough.

'Not now, James. I'm tired.' I rarely turn him down

and he doesn't take any notice. His hands find my breasts, he moves on top of me and I can feel his belly, softness which used to be muscle.

'I said no.' I turn away, but he grabs my arms, pulling them above my head and then stops, and stares.

'Christ. Armpit hair. What the fuck is going on with you?'

I twist sideways and get out of bed and leave the room, my legs are trembling. I go into Lottie's room and contemplate locking the door, but I also feel like punching the air.

The next day I ask for an extra appointment with Laurel, and she fits me in. The euphoria has faded by the time I'm sitting in her office.

'I was excited but scared at the same time. I've always said yes to men: yes to my father's friends and yes to my husband, it felt safer. Last night I said no but he took no notice. I got away but it was frightening, he's stronger than me.'

Laurel looks thoughtful. 'It might be an idea to let him do without you for once, allow him to come to his senses. He'll appreciate you more. Can you escape to your holiday house?'

'Cornwall? He'd come straight after me.'

'I meant Paxos.'

I'd forgotten I told her about Paxos, but I must

have done. It floods back in a heartbeat: the blue light and the heat, that white bite of beach. The garden and the trees and those long lazy days by the pool. The Greek family who looked after us so well and then disappeared.

'You still have the property? I forget what it's called.'

'Thalassa which is Greek for the sea. It's been boarded up for years. An agency looks after it for us.'

'Have you been back?'

'Not once. James hates the heat; he refuses to go. He much prefers Cornwall.'

But her words have opened a door through which I glimpse the glittering sea and those brilliant flowers. I would be alone. Blissfully, completely alone. It would be easy enough to arrange; the agency could remove the boards and clean the house, put sheets on a bed. It will be half-term, but Lottie will be on a GCSE history trip to the battle-fields of France and not even at home. She won't need me at all.

'You know, that just might work.'

On the way home I phone Lefcothea, my mother's agent in Gaios. She sounds worried.

'It's not in a fit state, Mrs Grenville.'

'I don't need luxury.' It's James who likes luxurious things; he refurbished the Cornish house after our marriage, organizing expensive fittings, the most costly fabrics, the latest appliances.

At home I cook three quiches for the staff party I'll miss when I'm away, and phone Lottie in her lunch hour to let her know.

'Good for you, Mum, you deserve a break.' She sounds happy for me, a glimmer of my lovely girl again. My eyes fill with ridiculous tears that I'm glad she's not here to see. I hadn't realized I needed her approval quite so much.

'Thanks, darling. I'll miss you.'

'But why now?' She sounds curious.

'I thought I should check on the house, it's been a while.'

She doesn't answer, she probably knows that's not all.

'I'm going to see your granny later today. Any messages?'

'Tell her I'll come by soon.'

I agree, though it's unlikely she'll visit her grandmother soon. I can't remember the last time she did.

'Has Dad been in touch?'

'I saw him last week on his way to a music festival in Madrid. We had a picnic by the Serpentine. Do you ever think you guys might—'

'No, darling. The memories are good, and of course we made you, but it was over a long time ago.'

Anthony helped me escape but he belonged to a time that's long gone. I need to escape again, but this time I'm going back.

Mother is in her usual chair by the window when I arrive. A nurse is giving her the daily medication in a little cup which she obediently swallows. Her glance flickers over me, uninterested.

'We have good and bad days. This isn't a good one,' the nurse whispers. 'I won't be far.'

I take my mother's hand, a cold claw crusted with jewels. She stares at me blankly, as if meeting a stranger.

'Lottie sends her love.'

Her face brightens, and she looks searchingly into mine as if she looked hard enough, she would discover her granddaughter instead of me.

'I've come to say goodbye. I'm going to Paxos soon.'

She flinches and turns her face away.

'I'll take photos so you can see how it's doing.'

She shakes her head and pulls her hand from mine, her rings scratching my fingers. Her head remains turned towards the window. I wonder if she is seeing the dry landscape of Paxos, the olives groves and lemon trees instead of the withered leaves on the lawn and the empty beds outside. Perhaps the Greek family is hovering somewhere in her mind, along with the mystery of their departure which she never really shared.

Chapter 17

Paxos 2003

Sofie

'Sofie! Where are you, *pedhaki mou*?'

Dimitrios's voice echoed from the wooded cliff between the coves. He sounded upset. Sofie crouched down on the pebbles and closed her eyes. Shame beat hot like the sun on her back. Everything was spoilt. She had made up her mind what to do and she didn't want to see anyone. Go away, Dimitrios, she prayed silently. Please just go away.

'Sofie! Wait!'

His voice was louder. He was closer. She couldn't wait after all. The men on the cliffs might see her but that needn't matter if she was quick. She started walking into the water. Papa always said drowning was quick. He said it didn't hurt.

'Sofie!'

She had to hurry but it was hard to move, every step hurt. She pushed against the sea as fast as she could, knees, thighs, waist, chest. Just another couple of steps. Dimitrios's hands lifted her just as she went under. He carried her out of the sea as carefully as a baby, up the beach to where the rocks had tumbled from the cliffs in big blocks. He set her down on a smooth stone. One of his eyes was puffed up like hers, both cheeks were bruised.

'What were you going to do?' he asked, but then he shook his head, he knew exactly what she had been going to do. 'Thank Christ I got here in time. Nothing is ever as bad as that. Do you hear me? Nothing.'

He sounded angry and, unexpectedly, she began to cry.

'No, Sofie, no.' He put his arm around her. She saw there was blood running into his red trainer from a deep cut on one knee and bruises on his face. Something must have happened to him since she had seen him earlier, but she was scared to ask him what that was. It was probably her fault too. His arm round her shoulders was painful and comforting at the same time.

'I'm sorry, little one. I'm upset, that's all.' It sounded as though he was going to cry too. He lowered his voice, speaking gently. 'Roxana phoned and told me what happened.'

'Roxana?' She stared at him through her tears. 'How does she know?'

'Those boys, the ones that hurt you, came to her bar in Gaios this morning.' He spoke hesitantly as if he didn't want to tell her, but knew he had to. 'They were showing images on their phones, and she saw them.'

Sofie didn't know what he meant at first and then she did. She didn't think it was possible to feel worse than she already did, but something heavy seemed to fall down inside her chest as if she was coming apart. She'd forgotten the photographs.

She wished she'd had time to walk into the sea and let it close over her head. She would never have had to think about the boys again, or the photos they took. Everyone would know she was dirty, stupid and dirty. A wasp landed on her arm and then another. She watched them crawling over her skin, sipping at the graze which had begun to weep fluid. She couldn't feel them at all.

'After that, Christos came with me on the motorbike. Those boys had taken Peter's car. It was parked across the pavement by the bar, so we knew exactly where they were.'

Everyone knew Peter's car. The number plate had two Ps, one for Peter and one for Paxos, as if he owned the island. It was the kind of car that took up all the space on the road, other cars had to crush into the hedge to make way.

'We found them inside.'

Sofie can see Jay and Ginger as clearly as if she was standing next to them. Ginger would be holding his phone and laughing his pig laugh. Jay would be standing further back, smiling and watching everything, as he had in the shed. There would have been a crowd of other boys clustering around; their faces would be avid. The thought of what was on the screen made the vomit rise in her throat.

'I took the dark-haired one outside, and Christos took the fat one. We punched them in the face, the chest, the gut. They fell over, squealing like pigs, and we carried on punching. I think we would have killed them if Roxana hadn't sent her boss out to stop us.'

Lots of people would have watched the fight. They would have thought it was an ordinary punch-up between boys who were drunk even at this early hour. Then a whisper might have gone round that some stupid girl had asked for it and that photographs had been taken.

'Christos told them we were going to call the police and they would go to prison. The boys said if we did that, they would put the photos on the Internet and that everyone in the world would see them.'

Sofie's eyes stung so badly she wanted to close them, but she had to watch Dimitrios's mouth to work out what he was saying, because she couldn't hear properly. The noise in her head, a low kind of humming, was blocking everything out.

'Don't go to the police.' The tears had started again. '*Se parakalo*, Dimitrios. Don't tell anyone.'

'We made a bargain with those pigs. They promised to delete the pictures if we didn't go to the police.'

'So it's all right? Mama and Babas won't find out?'

Dimitrios's face turned away from her and he gazed at the sea. His expression was angry and sad at the same time. He didn't answer her questions and for a moment she thought it would be as simple as that. She actually thought that no one else would ever have to know what had happened.

Chapter 18

London 2023

Julia

'Why go now?'

It's the question Lottie asked but James is angry rather than interested. 'Isn't that why you have an agent in Paxos?'

He is by the door, jacket in hand, it's time he left for assembly. I chose this moment on purpose so we wouldn't have long to talk about it.

'It's been twenty years since anyone has checked on the house. I should have gone before.'

'Like I said, you have an agent. This is a busy time. I need you here,' he raps out.

'Busy? It's half-term.'

'We have the trustees planning committee coming up.' His face is flushed. 'I was relying on you to edit

171

my speech. There's Simon's leaving party to organize. It's what you do, Julia. It's your job.'

'Libby will edit your speeches, and I've already cooked for the party.'

I have answers to his objections, but I have to be careful not to sound triumphant, that would make him angrier still.

'It's not the same.' He shrugs on his jacket then stares down at me, brows drawn. 'And what about Lottie?'

He wouldn't ask about her usually, but luckily, I'm prepared.

'She's off to France for the battlefields trip with the school, remember?'

'I don't understand why you can't wait for me to have a break. I'd like to do some fishing; we haven't been to Cornwall for a while.'

'We can go to Cornwall when I get back.'

Beyond the bluster, none of the protests hold up. I'm not sure why he is making so many.

'I'll only be away for two weeks; you'll hardly notice I've gone. Libby knows exactly what to do, and Rasul will cook. Everything will continue normally, just as if I was here.'

Apart from sex. I don't mention the fact that he won't have sex, but I've been evading that already. He'll work out why when I've gone: that's Laurel's theory and I agree.

His glance travels over me, his eyes are narrow, assessing. He wants the last word.

'You aren't looking good, Julia, but then you haven't for a while. I warned you to take care.' He shakes his head. 'It's a great pity you've let yourself go like this.'

Chapter 19

Paxos 2003

Sofie

Sofie's face throbbed with every step, as if blood had leaked from her heart and was collecting under the skin. If Dimitrios hadn't been holding her, she would have fallen. They stumbled up between the trees together, stopping to rest every few steps.

'It's lucky none of the guests are around today,' Dimitrios said, panting a little. 'Julia's gone and Paul drove everyone else to Lakka for lunch; apart from Peter who left to collect those thugs from Gaios by taxi because they took his car, apparently without his permission. They haven't returned yet.'

Sofie imagines Peter hauling the boys up from the ground. He wouldn't be gentle. He'd be furious with them for taking his car and for getting into a fight.

He would shout at them like he did when Jay spilt the wine. They wouldn't dare show him those pictures, they'd be far too ashamed.

Everyone was in the kitchen. Mama, Babas, even Christos which felt wrong. Christos should have been cleaning the pool by now, or working on the yacht, adjusting the rigging, checking the engine and the sails, but he was here, because of her. He had bruises on his face as well. His mouth was set in a tight line and he was frowning. Sofie had seen him serious before but never angry, not like this.

The kitchen was different too. There should have been bread on the rack and the scent of tomatoes and aubergines bubbling on the hob, but the stove hadn't been lit. For once the kitchen didn't smell of anything. There should be music coming from the radio, Bouzouki music, Mama's favourite, but the only sound was the buzzing of flies at the window.

Athena was standing with her back to the sink. Her face was tight, as if she were holding on as hard as she could to every scrap of her strength. Her hair had fallen down which made Sofie feel unsafe. Mama's hair was always neatly pinned. What other things might come apart, things she hadn't thought of?

Babas was in front of the stove. He was always the same, quiet and serious. When you looked at him from a field away, you could see the dark of his eyebrows before you could make out any other features; now they were drawn like a thick bar across his face.

The only thing on the table was Christos's phone; even from where she was standing, Sofie could see the screen was lit up with her face; her face and her body and the sea behind that. She understood why Ginger had called her a rabbit because that's what she looked like on the phone, a frightened rabbit who'd been caught in the headlights. Christos must have showed Mama and Babas the other pictures as well. They knew then, they all knew exactly what had happened. No wonder they looked angry. Everything they'd believed in had been a lie. It was like coming out of the cinema in Gaios, when real life returned with a rush. You felt stupid you'd been caught up in something unreal, like a child who believed in fairy stories. She'd done that to her parents, she'd made them feel stupid for believing in a fairy story. They'd thought if they worked hard and followed the rules there would be a happy ending, a reward for being good. It was clear now that was a myth; being good didn't even keep you safe, bad things happened however good you were.

Athena was the first to move. She pulled out a kitchen chair, placed a cushion on the seat, and helped Sofie sit down.

'So now, *pedhaki mou*, tell us what really happened.'

Sofie's tears were pointless, they seemed to have nothing to do with her. The world had exploded like a bomb; tears made no difference when everything had been blown apart. She wiped them away with her sleeve although they kept coming.

Athena gave her a glass of orange juice. Most mornings Sofie turned the inside of halved oranges against the ridges on the little glass cone until her wrist ached. She had put the jug full of juice on the breakfast table so many times, poured it out for the guests and watched as they sipped a little. She'd had to throw away what they hadn't drunk, while her mouth parched with longing. Now she had some to herself, but when she tried to sip the juice, it stung the inside of her cheeks.

'It's important you tell us exactly what happened.' Dimitrios's voice was kind. He was a kind man; they were all kind, but no one could make a difference to what had happened.

'I know you couldn't tell us before. We understand.' Athena sat down next to her. 'But tell us now, we need to know.'

Sofie looked round at the familiar faces. They wouldn't like her once they heard her story, but they probably knew most of it already; there was nothing more to lose.

'They came to the beach.'

'Last night?' Athena asked.

Sofie nodded then shook her head, then nodded again.

'Tell us the whole story from the beginning,' Athena said. 'It doesn't matter how long it takes.'

Dimitrios sat in the chair next to her. Now she had Athena one side and Dimitrios the other, it felt safe.

'They came in the mornings as well as last night.'

Babas was staring at her. She turned her head so she couldn't see him, not even out of the corner of her eye.

'How do you know they came in the mornings?' Athena asked.

'Because I was there.'

The silence was full of questions, but she forced herself to continue, what could it matter now?

'I've been taking Nico to the beach every morning, he likes splashing in the sea. One day the boys came.'

'You take Nico to the beach?' Babas's voice was incredulous.

'Uncle,' Dimitrios said, just one word, but it stopped Babas.

'I watch him.' Sofie didn't look up. 'I watched him all the time.' Had she? What about when Jay held her so she could swim? But she couldn't think of that, she should have realized that was the beginning of everything wrong.

Christos looked up and stared around the kitchen and under the table as if searching for his shoes, then hurried out. No one took any notice, they were all looking at Sofie.

'You can't swim,' Babas said quietly.

Dimitrios put a hand on her wrist, it was meant to comfort her. He couldn't know it was painful. Jay had twisted her wrists tightly and the skin was broken, it stung with the warmth of his touch.

'He doesn't go far. I can reach him if I need to. He loves jumping over the waves.' Nico had deserved that time of being happy, they were all too busy for him, but she knew that wouldn't seem important now.

'So, those boys,' Athena said. 'What did they do?'

'They taught me to swim. I was going to show Christos after they went home. It was going to be a surprise.'

'What are their names?'

'Jay and Ginger.'

'That skinny one with spots and the fat pig,' said Dimitrios. 'Not the one who is always on his phone.'

'You thought they were your friends,' Athena said. 'So you trusted them, we understand that. No one is cross.' But it sounded as though she was going to cry, which was worse. 'Now tell us what happened yesterday evening.'

So, in a whisper, Sofie told them everything she could remember. She tried to pretend that Babas wasn't there, that she was just talking to her mother. She tried to be as truthful as she could. When she had finished, no one said anything for a while.

Dimitrios looked at Babas though Sofie didn't dare.

'She would have had no choice,' Dimitrios told him. 'None at all.'

'They hit me when I tried to escape,' Sofie whispered. The shock of that blow came back, and she put her hand to her cheek.

'There are no pictures of that,' Dimitrios said grimly.

'Did they do anything else that wasn't in the pictures?' Athena asked slowly, as though someone was dragging the words out of her mouth.

Dimitrios moved closer, leaning his shoulder gently against Sofie's. All her life she would remember the warmth of that.

'She is asking if they raped you.'

She was glad he'd said that word. It was simple to understand. It should be simple to answer but she couldn't. Ginger had put his fingers inside her, she could still feel them. Did that count? And then there was that thing she couldn't remember, after they turned her over and pushed her against the boat, that pain. That tearing pain. Then blackness.

She shook her head though the truth was more complicated, she didn't know, not really.

'Don't talk any more.' Athena knelt and put her arms around her. Sofie leaned her head against her mother's shoulder and closed her eyes, although that made them sting even more. She wanted to stay there for ever, but after a while Athena got up and began to move around the kitchen, opening cupboards and taking things out that belonged to them: the flowery apron and the lace cloths with embroidery that *Yia-yia* had made. She picked up the jug with the painted olives and the little saucepan with the curving handle that just fitted your hand.

Sofie began to feel frightened, a different kind of fear from before.

'I don't want anything to change.' She tried to speak loudly but her voice cracked. 'I want everything to go back to how it usually is.'

'Things have changed, little Sofie,' Dimitrios said. 'Of course they have. We can't go back.'

They heard footsteps running across the drive outside and then Christos was standing at the door. He was panting and he looked different, he wasn't angry any more he was terrified.

'What?' Athena's voice had a new, raw note of fear, as if she had already guessed what Christos was going to say next.

'I can't find Nico anywhere.'

Chapter 20

Paxos 2023

Julia

The autumn sea is a deeper colour than the sea I remember, navy rather than turquoise, but as the hovercraft approaches Paxos the colour lightens. I am standing on the deck. The crew would prefer all the passengers to be inside but out here the wind tugs my hair, the sun is warm after the cool English October. The clear blue sky looks endless.

Gaios with its harbour of boats and yellow and white and pink buildings looks as it always used to, but as we near the harbour, more masts come into view, the yachts are larger than before. On the quayside a slim woman with cropped grey hair is waiting, her dress stamped in aquamarine leaf shapes. Lefcothea, the agent. Her eyes sparkle.

'You look just like your mother,' she says. 'The same smile and those blue eyes. I would have known you anywhere.'

I can't remember how my mother used to look when we were here, but I can't picture her smiling. Her eyes are dull now, shrunken in their folds of skin.

'We've prepared the house as well as we can,' Lefcothea tells me as I settle in the passenger seat of her new Audi, business must be doing well. 'We removed the boards over the windows yesterday, except for the guest cabins of course, and the building where the Greek family lived.' A glance at me. 'We didn't think you would want to stay there.'

'That family worked so hard for us, it's a shame they left so suddenly.' I return her glance, but her eyes are back on the road.

'I'm afraid I know nothing about it. It was twenty years ago; a lot of things have happened since then.'

We drive up the steep hill from the harbour in silence. Bougainvillea tumbles red and mauve over the walls of the houses we pass; a tree of blue flowers stands against a yellow wall. Pots of herbs line the roadside gardens.

'The flowers at Thalassa have long gone.' Lefcothea navigates her car past a bus. 'But the olives and the bay trees are still there, and the citrus trees too, though some have died. The vegetable garden has disappeared; once your family left there didn't seem

184

any point in keeping it up. Your father told us to look after the house. He said the garden would look after itself.'

As we leave the town, the road becomes narrow and twisty in places. We have taken an inland route and are climbing and turning. A steep wooded valley opens to the left. This part of the island is unfamiliar but then we lived in a little kingdom of our own, ignorant of the island landscape and the people who lived here.

'There have been many changes in Paxos recently, so much progress. Look around you.' Lefcothea's tone is bright. We are passing diggers as she speaks, cement mixers and half-built houses by the road. Things have moved on since we were last here, and she doesn't want to talk about the past.

'Tourism has replaced olives: we don't sell the oil any more.' She sounds happy, though it seems like a backward step to me, but then I've never had to get up early and pick olives as the women did back then. Perhaps the islanders are glad of tourists and their second homes, but as we pass stacks of breeze blocks and coils of blue piping dumped in olive groves, it's as if something precious has been stolen and a shoddy gift left in its place.

Then we are there, at the gates that I closed behind me twenty years ago, the evening I made my escape. The wood has faded to pale silver which looks better than the dark brown paint I remember. Lefcothea gets out to unlock them, then back in. The drive twists ahead like a long grey snake, the borders are empty; there had been oleander bushes with pink and white flowers on either side, but they must have long since died.

'Is there anyone there at all? Another caretaker?'

'No one has lived on the premises since your father left, but we're in and out all the time.' She flashes me a reassuring smile. 'We inspect regularly, log the necessary repairs, get workmen in then bill the estate, just as he told us to.'

Lefcothea parks her car on the drive, once a smooth sweep of paving that shone in the sun. Now the slabs are dull and chipped, tall weeds have pushed themselves through the mortar. The house looks much as I remember, a sprawling old building settled into the landscape. I get out of the car and gaze up at the high tower in the centre. I'd thought the first sight of those terracotta walls would conjure unhappiness, that my father's power might still linger here, and all the old tensions come flooding back: his coldness and control, the sense of being trapped. Surprisingly, I feel none of those things or perhaps I don't feel them yet. It's as if I'm being greeted by a friend from the past, someone who endured the storms as I did and survived. I rest my hand on the wall that circles the drive, feeling the sun's warmth in the stone.

Lefcothea ducks under the straggling branches of an old olive tree avoiding a battered iron table and chair. Close up the paint on the walls is patchy and the blue of the shutters has faded. She unlocks a door at the side of the house and ushers me into a small kitchen which is cool and very clean. The furniture is simple: a deal table, a stove, and a fridge. Scrubbed wooden sideboards. This is where our food was cooked. I never saw it prepared, never thought to thank the beautiful woman who did the cooking for us: those fragrant fish stews, the courgette fritters, and pies bulging with cheese and spinach, all of which I ignored. Six chairs are arranged neatly around the table. I doubt it has changed much since she put everything in order before she left, stacking dishes in the cupboard, wiping the table, casting her eyes around the room to commit it to memory. What thoughts had been going through her head as she walked out of the door for the very last time? Did she know she would never be back?

'I've switched on the fridge, but we didn't light the stove.' Lefcothea's brisk voice cuts across my thoughts. 'We put in an electric hob instead, we thought it would be easier for you. Our cleaning girls have left you some food.' She opens the fridge, there is a packet of ham and one of cheese, bread, olives, a bottle of wine. 'It'll start you off, it's a long way to the shops. I'll send a car in the morning.'

We walk outside and across the weedy drive;

shards of the old terracotta pots have collected in the corners of the steps we descend. There were flowers on each step back then, yellow and blue and pink though I don't know what kind. I never stopped to look properly. There is no water in the pool either, instead a deep layer of leaves and twigs cover the bottom, along with broken glass and plastic bags.

'Winter storms bring all sorts of rubbish.' Lefcothea sighs dramatically. 'I'm sorry there wasn't time to clean or fill it, but I'll contact our usual man who'll do that for us.'

'Please don't worry.' The last thing I want is a chatty workman and his noisy machinery. 'I haven't come to lounge by the pool.' Though that's what I used to do, for hours at a time, sleeping off the drugged nights with Paul. 'I'll swim in the sea, I'd much rather.'

'Your father would have preferred us to have it all in order. I'll send someone.' She glances up at the house with pursed lips. 'The place needs a lick of paint too.'

Her phone shrills, she answers, then looks up, grimacing. 'One of our guests has backed his hired car into a gate. I must go. Enjoy your stay. Here are the keys.' She puts the jingling bunch, warm from her hand, into mine. 'Call me if you need anything. I'll send you photos after we've repainted.'

She drives out, the engine fading as it travels away up the drive.

The silence that floods back is as thick and golden as the light. It's as though a door has closed on a babble of voices calling my name. The hubbub of meetings, of plans and lists and cars and planes has disappeared. Even my mobile is silent.

I open the French doors to the sitting room on the garden side of the house with the third try of the key. My footsteps echo as I walk through empty rooms. Dried leaves lift and eddy around my feet as though someone has come into the house and is walking beside me. I turn my head sharply, but there is no one there, of course. The wide reception rooms are silent, dust sheets are folded on the table. The white linen sofas are as I remember, the cushions plumped, one or two indented as though my mother had got up and walked out earlier this very day.

I climb the winding stairs that lead to the top of the old mill that is the core of the house; my parents' old room opens to the side; the wide bed is still here and the wall of glass that slid back at a touch. My father stood on the balcony and looked over the grounds, watching everything, especially me. Even now I can feel that harsh green stare. I shiver though the room is warm with sun.

My room is up a further turn of stairs, the highest in the tower. My father would have preferred the topmost room, but my mother couldn't walk up the spiral staircase; odd that she was the most fragile but has lasted the longer of the two, though her mind has failed. Hubris, as Anthony might have said.

My room is still lovely, the view still breathtaking; timeless, as though the landscape we occupied has reverted in spirit to the past, back to the years before we came. The ocean glitters between the pine covered cliffs. Paul made love to me under those trees, there were wild cyclamens growing in their shade. I was Lottie's age, fifteen years old, accomplice and victim, but hardly innocent. My father watched as the pine needles fell from my hair to the tablecloth, his eyes glinting like the sea.

I dump my case on the pale floorboards which are dusty but still silky smooth, pull my costume out, wrap my towelling gown around me then run down the stairs and out into the garden, away from the ghosts. The emerald lawns that sparkled under rainbow arcs of water have vanished, replaced by a low-lying tangle of tough-looking weeds. Huge plants have sprouted by the side of the path that leads down the garden, some as tall as my head, distant relatives of the vegetables that grew here in ordered rows. All that effort gone to waste. The young man I used to glimpse tending the garden would be heartbroken to see what's happened, but at least nature has flourished, reclaiming what we stole.

The concrete jetty that leads to the beach from the garden is cracked in places, slimy with algae. I slip twice, catching my feet on ropes of seaweed but the sea is as crystal clear as it used to be. The pebbles hurt my feet when I take my shoes off. Did we wear shoes or were my feet hardened back then? I shed the gown and hobble over the stones and into the water, throwing myself forward as soon as it's deep enough. The sea is warm from months of heat. My rings flash as my hands pull through the shining water; what if I were to slip them off, free my hands of those tokens of ownership, watch them fall glinting to the seabed? I imagine James's face if I were to return without them. I would pay dearly for that gesture.

I swim far out and then float, face to the sun, rocked by the sea, empty of everything, as though for a few precious seconds my mind has been washed clean. Then a wave catches me out, saltwater fills my mouth and I turn over and swim back, looking at the familiar cliffs. There is a change though, there are no birds flying against those white crags, and none in the air. They used to float above the sea and by the cliffs. Fish ribbon away from me, though there are fewer of them now. They used to be darting this way and that in shoals.

The rocks on the side of the beach are as warm

and smooth to lie on as I remember. The sun turns the inside of my eyelids red. The sound of the sea fills me, and I sleep, waking chilled as the shadow of the cliff creeps over the beach and a light wind feathers the water. The woods above me have grown shadowy in the evening light and quite suddenly I have the sensation of being watched.

Chapter 21

Paxos 2003

Sofie

Nico was missing.

Babas's face became very still. Sofie had never seen him frightened before: tired, angry, worried but never afraid. It made her frightened too. She hadn't seen him running either, but he ran out of the kitchen ahead of Dimitrios, jowls shaking as he thudded past the window. Athena told Sofie to stay put, but how could she sit quietly and wait if Nico was missing? She followed them down the garden, each step slamming through her head like a hammer. All the cicadas were screaming.

Christos had remembered about Nico, but she hadn't. She knew what must have happened though, and it was her fault. They went to the beach every day, so he had become very used to it, it was their routine. When he woke this morning and saw she wasn't there, he must have thought she was on the beach already. He would have hurried to join her; running down while she was crawling back, they had missed each other. There were so many twisty little paths and so many trees.

The water would have been choppy after the storm. He might have waited for a little while, but he loved waves, he would have been lured in. He would have stepped in carefully at first. No, he would have run in, talking to himself, jumping over the waves, one jump after another until he jumped too far, and the water came up to his chest. He would have been in much deeper than ever before. One of the waves need only to have been a little bigger than the rest and he'd have lost his balance. He wouldn't have known how to right himself, especially if his feet couldn't reach the bottom. If someone had walked onto the beach at that point, they would have seen a disturbance in the water like the thrashing of a fish, but it would have stopped after a little while.

She met Dimitrios and Athena on the path near the wood. Dimitrios's face was running with sweat. They had been to the beach, but Nico wasn't there. Dimitrios said Nico couldn't have gone into the sea, because his flip-flops weren't on the beach. Sofie didn't tell him that Nico always ran to the beach barefoot, there wasn't any point, it was too late. Christos was looking in the woods and Babas, among the olive trees, but she knew there was no point in that either.

'Let's go back.' Athena was gasping for breath. 'Nico could be in the kitchen. He might have come back while we've been away.'

The sun was blazing. Athena's hand holding Sofie's was slippery with sweat as they hurried back through the gardens. Everything was quiet. The guests would be on the beach in Lakka by now, and Jay and Ginger might now be sleeping in the back of Peter's car on their way home. They would be splayed out, heads back, mouths open, snoring. Their phones would be on the seat beside them. What if they had been too tired to put their seat belts on and a lorry ran into the back of the car, having skidded on a twisty road? Accidents like that have happened before. The phones would be smashed into tiny fragments, the shards scattered over the floor, the images lost forever. Peter would be in the front seat wearing his seat belt, he might survive, but the boys would be killed, decapitated instantly, she decided, both of them. The story of what had happened to her would vanish for ever.

Athena let go of her hand as they passed the cabins; she wanted to check in case Nico had gone inside to play though he wasn't allowed. She searched under each bed, in every wardrobe, inside the bathrooms and behind the shower curtains. Sofie didn't follow her into the boys' room, but she could see Ginger's blue shorts had been flung into the corner. She turned aside quickly and retched into the flower bed; by the time Athena came out, she had finished and wiped her face on the edge of her skirt. They climbed the stone steps to the drive. The flowers in the pots were drooping, the leaves hung down like flat sheets of paper. They hadn't been watered that morning and were dying already. Going back into the empty kitchen was like entering a kitchen that belonged to another family. Sofie began to shiver although she was sweating.

'Stay here, my little one.' Athena kissed the top of her head and laid her rough palm on Sofie's cheek for a moment, then she filled a plastic bottle full of water and left again. Sofie didn't tell her Nico wouldn't need water, it was clear he had drowned in the sea, and it was all her fault.

The only sound was the tap dripping. Athena had asked Dimitrios to fix it weeks ago, one of those jobs he put off because he was so busy in the garden. By now on any normal day, he would have brought in boxes of lettuce and onions and tomatoes, courgettes with those big yellow flowers that Athena fried in batter. Piles of little potatoes, dusty with earth, bunches of thyme and sage and a dozen sharp-scented lemons.

A drop of water bulged at the lip of the tap, fell, bulged and fell again.

Sofie's abdomen and pelvis ached with a throbbing pain; she hunched over but it didn't help.

Ten minutes later Athena came back and so did Dimitrios, then Christos, and Babas last of all, he looked exhausted. They hadn't found Nico. Of course they hadn't, her brown-eyed little brother had drowned. It didn't seem possible that she wouldn't see his smile again or hear the humming noise he made when he was happy. His breathing at night timed with her heart beat. Athena looked pale; she was panting for breath. Dimitrios phoned the police though Babas shook his head: they would find him, he said, they always did. Surely Babas knew by now there was no such thing as always. Things changed with no warning, new dangers could spring out when you were least expecting it, destroying everything you had taken for granted.

They sat in the kitchen, waiting for the police. The pain in Sofie's pelvis got worse, perhaps she really was going to get her period. Gabriella had told her having her periods would mean she was ready for a boyfriend. She wanted to laugh but if she started laughing it would turn into screaming. The room was silent, so when the police car came down the drive with its siren blaring, it filled the kitchen with the noise of a wild animal rushing towards them.

Chapter 22

Paxos 2023

Julia

The silence at Thalassa feels ancient. I move with care, loath to break it. The small noises of insects and bees in the lavender skate on its surface. Time becomes liquid, flowing from day to day, pooling at noon when nothing moves. Details shine: the glitter on the skin of a lizard, the pink tongue of the cat who comes to the door to lap milk from a saucer, the silver green of olive leaves, glimmering in the heat. I text Laurel to thank her for advising this trip. I tell her I am resting and healing. She texts back that I must stay longer, that I should stay as long as I can. I reply that I'd better stick with arrangements. I miss Lottie and I promised James I'd be back in two weeks. She doesn't reply and nor does James when I text to ask how he is. I message Lottie who is in France, hoping she's happy; she texts back a kiss but no words.

Today the sound of sweeping filters through the silence. The swimming pool is being prepared by the man the agency contacted, but despite my fears, he disrupts nothing. He moves slowly as if respecting the peace. I'm not sure of his age, he wears a cap pulled low and I can't see his face. He is accompanied by a dark-haired boy of fifteen or thereabouts. Their movements are similar, perhaps it's his son. They climb down into the pool by the marble steps and sweep up the leaves and the rubbish, the boy taking basketfuls away. They scrub the base with buckets of water; the boy sits often, drinking from his water bottle; the older man works on stolidly, unbothered by heat. When the bottom of the pool is clean, he connects the hosepipe to the tap by the back door. He seems to know his way about. I offer tea, but he nods his head, that Greek refusal. *Ochi*. No; though his face turns to follow my movements, watchful.

I leave them to it and pace the estate, following the overgrown paths between the shut-up cabins that used to accommodate our summer visitors. Paul is the one I remember most clearly, the only one. He had been given an extra cabin at the edge of the wood, necessary for him to work in peace away from his family or so my father pretended to believe. I try several keys on the bunch, before I find the one that works. The lock is rusty, it takes two hands to turn it.

The room is smaller than I remember, the bed is still where it used to be, opposite the window. It's dark because of the boards covering the window but then it always used to be dark. The shutters were closed. I stand at the door and remember:

'Sit down.'

I comply. I even smile.

'Take off your dress.'

The first time, I am fifteen. He is in his forties, but I am cool with this. I think I can handle it though my hands are shaking. I want to do it. I'm the bribe that puts Paul in my father's power and makes him vulnerable though he doesn't know that yet. I like the power that I think this gives me. I don't mind being naked, my body is thin, my skin is tanned. I know I look good.

He sits on the bed and touches me. He doesn't undress. I hide the sensations he unlocks, the fact that they confuse me, the fact that I don't want him to stop. I say nothing, which provokes him. His mouth twitches and tightens. He wants reassurance and becomes craven.

At supper later, I see the woman he brought along watching him bend his head towards me; she watches me too. I smile at her, little beast that I am, liking the knowledge I am the more desired.

It occurs to me now she might have been sorry for me. I had no idea back then that I was a victim, losing, not winning. That I was being used, rather than the other way round. It continued until that last summer, when I saw the Greek girl watching me. I began to watch her back, though she didn't know that. We had been friends before but now I ignored her. I was jealous of her innocence. That's partly what drove me away; I wanted what she had, though it was far too late for me. I saw her once on the balcony of my parents' room as I walked with my family to board the yacht on what became my last day. She was collecting sheets, content in her world. Unsullied. Meanwhile Paul was pressing close behind me, touching me as we walked. I'd had enough, enough of being a plaything, of doing what my father wanted. I left that evening. Anthony was the escape route, but it was pregnancy that changed me; it took my daughter to make me grow up.

The sun is high. I go swimming but I feel watched again as if the ghost of that little girl and her brother are studying me from the cliff tops. Hurrying back to the house afterwards, I come across an old shed I haven't seen before. The trees that formed a tight belt behind the beach are broken with age, a roof is revealed. The door is part rotted and gives with a deep groaning whine when I push it open. Inside the dark air is rank with mould.

An old boat is tipped on its side, the planks splintered with age. Nets hang in tatters from the rafters and a rusted anchor lies on the floor. Cobwebs have blanketed a wine bottle on the chair. It's hot and very quiet. There is a rustle in the shadows at the back. Rats. I back out.

The next day I don't want to go to the sea again, through those silent woods or along the jetty by the shed. I swim in the icy pool instead, then shower and comb my hair in the mirror in the sitting room. Backlit by the windows, my face looks younger, smoother. I have freckles. I haven't had freckles for years. As I lean to look closer, a shadow crosses behind me in the glass, moving too swiftly to make out. I step onto the terrace that extends around the house, calling out, but no one replies.

I phone Lefcothea. 'Is the pool man still here?'

'He left yesterday; is there a problem?'

'I have the feeling that someone may be about. Have there been reports of an intruder? Drinking in the shed?'

'What shed?'

'The one in the trees at the back of the beach.' If I tell her about the feeling of being watched or the shadow across the mirror, she will think I'm going mad; maybe I am.

'I shouldn't worry.' She laughs breezily. 'It will only be kids from Loggos or walkers that hike along the coast. Tourists pay little attention to privacy, but they mean no harm. I'm sure you're fine.'

I phone James but there is no reply. Later, much later, he texts that he's sorry but he's too busy to chat. I text Lottie to tell her I miss her; she sends back a heart emoji and a smiley face. Still no words but I feel cheered.

I've hardly used the car Lefcothea sent, but today I drive into Loggos. The old woman in the shop on the corner looks familiar but her stare is disconcerting. I remember her in cheerful middle age, greeting customers with a friendly grin, but chilled by the hostility in her hooded glance, I don't chat. I buy white grapes, cheese, bread, and figs – picnic food to eat on the little table outside the kitchen – and hurry home.

Every day the sky is flawless, the air grows a little cooler but it's still as warm as an English summer day. The sensation of being watched persists but I make my peace with it, perhaps there are always ghosts in a place that's been empty a while.

I drive to parts of Paxos I never visited before; ancient Ypapanti church with two towers drowsing in its hidden valley; Mongonissi beach; the hills behind Gaios with the remains of old dwellings, and a trip to the far side of the island, to Tripitos Arch, that famous bridge of white limestone arching over the sea. My father used to take our guests, but I stayed behind with Paul, and he turned a blind eye.

I can't find the start of the footpath that leads to the arch, so leaving the car in a layby near the church in the ancient village of Ozias, I cross the road to the village café. Two old men quarrel over glasses of cloudy ouzo under a wide-roofed veranda. They stop talking at my approach. Both have identical hooked noses and longish grey hair that's untidy in the same way. They wave me to a seat and the taller one brings iced coffee.

I ask about the birds and, looking guilty, they tell me they've all been shot. The sky was once black with quail and collared doves migrating to the cooler countries of Europe from Africa. They were machine gunned out of the sky, a pastime for the boys. They shrug, what can you do? That's how it was back then. They introduce themselves as brothers, Jakob, the taller, older one and Valentin, joint owners of the café. They want to know where I'm staying and, when I tell them, Thalassa, they mistake me for a tourist, rather than homeowner. I don't correct them, because that's true, I am a tourist as well.

'We thought it was boarded up.' Jakob shakes his head, his lips tighten. 'We hoped it would be sold by now. Good riddance.'

'Good riddance?'

'To those English bastards who own the place. They haven't dared show their faces for years.'

'Why not?'

'The way they treated the caretakers. They must be ashamed.'

'Why ashamed?'

Surely they have this wrong; the caretakers left without warning. My parents hadn't been ashamed, why should they have been?

Valentin picks up the glass of ouzo, tosses back the contents then glances at his brother. 'Bad things happened to the caretaker's daughter, because of the owners,' he mutters. 'Jakob thinks it was our fault it was missed. It's why we ended up here.'

'I don't understand.'

Jakob scowls at his brother, rolling his eyes impatiently. 'You haven't explained anything properly, as usual.' He looks at me. 'We were there, you see, back then we were the police. We'd been called to the house, because the caretaker's little boy had gone missing during the night.'

Chapter 23

Paxos 2003

Sofie

'Woah. Have you been in a fight?' The taller of the two policemen stared at Sofie. His eyes narrowed.

She stared back. Were they friendly? They looked the same; both had bumpy noses and dark stubble. The taller one had older eyes, that's all. Would they listen?

Their faces were wet with sweat. They had come back for water having been all over the grounds, in the woods and down to the beach. They hadn't found Nico. Of course they hadn't, he'd drowned, but they didn't know that, they didn't know anything. They didn't know she was stupid and dirty, but if she told them what the boys had done last night, they would look disgusted. They shared a jugful of iced water and it was only when the taller one put down his glass that he noticed her. He stepped closer. He had a thick truncheon and a gun; his uniform crackled as he moved.

'What happened to you?' he asked. His voice was fierce.

Athena put her hand on Sofie's shoulder and faced the policeman. 'I'll tell you.' Despite her worry about Nico, she sounded determined. 'I'll tell you exactly what happened.'

Sofie tensed. Athena was going to tell them everything. She wanted to get up and go to her bedroom, climb into bed and pull the covers over her head, but she couldn't move because Athena's hand was pressing down on her shoulder.

'It was an accident.' Babas pushed himself quickly between the policeman and Athena. He looked angry. 'She had a fall on the slope coming up from the beach, the seaweed is slippery there. You probably saw that for yourselves. She hit a rock.' His voice was low and hard. 'Do not let this distract you from finding our son.'

The tall policeman stepped around Babas and spoke to Sofie again. 'How old are you?'

'She is thirteen,' Babas growled. 'Thirteen years old.'

'You look younger.' The policeman didn't even look at Babas, he looked at her. 'Who hurt you?'

Babas was staring at her. He looked furious and anxious at the same time. If she spoke out, she would shame them all, and worse than that, the search for Nico might be delayed.

'No one,' she whispered.

The policeman looked harder at her. He seemed about to say something, but the other, shorter policeman pushed himself away from the wall.

'We need to co-opt help from Corfu, Jakob. Time is passing, every single minute counts when it's a kid.'

He banged his fist on the table. Sofie felt that bang through her bones, as if she was being hit again, a helpless prisoner in the shed.

The shed. She hadn't thought of that. She sat up straighter though even that hurt. The shed was hidden in the trees. No one would have seen it. No one would know if a little boy was locked inside, because he had followed his sister in and got trapped. If he had been calling for help, no one would hear.

'The shed,' she whispered.

Chapter 24

Paxos 2023

Julia

'We were there to find the caretaker's boy who'd gone missing, but Jakob noticed that their daughter was badly bruised. We believed the old man when he'd said she had fallen over and hurt herself. Why wouldn't we? He was her father.'

Valentin stomps into the dark interior of the shop behind the terrace, returning with a half-full bottle of ouzo. He waves it at me in invitation, but I shake my head. He pours another glass for himself and pushes the bottle across the table to his older brother.

'Pretended to believe him,' Jakob says, looking above my head towards the church. Regret is stamped on his heavy features. 'More's the pity.'

'So he wasn't telling the truth? She hadn't fallen?'

Jakob's head moves up and down. '*Ochi.*'

'How do you know?'

'A cousin of hers returned to the island. He had been there when we were called to find the boy, and he came back years later, looking for us.'

'Why?'

'He thought we should know,' Jakob mutters.

'Know what?'

'That the things that were done to that girl changed her life. He thought we should have stepped in.'

'For Christ's sake, Jakob.' Valentin shakes his head. 'Let it go.'

'Who did things to her?' I persist.

'A couple of boys, guests in the party.'

'What do you mean?' I stare at Jakob; it had been a trivial incident surely, the little girl was complicit, in fact she'd led them on. I recall the scorn in my mother's voice, the way she had flicked her hand. It wasn't the boys' fault; the girl had made a nuisance of herself. Those had been her very words. I remember because it had surprised me at the time.

'Let me explain properly.' Jakob plants his elbows on the table. He speaks more loudly; his face is flushed. This is a memory that haunts him and he needs to make me understand. 'The estate where you are staying is owned by these English cunts who used to bring friends out for a holiday. Two of their guests hurt her.'

212

'She was badly bruised; she told us she'd tripped and fallen,' the younger brother says. 'I believed her.'

'I didn't, which makes it worse,' Jakob says, lowering his voice. 'I knew something bad had happened, you only had to look at her.'

Their mouths turn down in the same way.

'What did the cousin say?' I look from one to another, but their faces are closed. 'The one who came back?'

The pause stretches. Jakob tosses back his glassful of ouzo. They don't answer. Why tell a tourist something you're ashamed of? They look at each other. Valentin seems unsure but Jakob clears his throat. He may sense my concern is genuine, or he might be plagued with guilt. It could simply be the ouzo, but he starts to talk quickly.

'The cousin said two "nice" English boys of fifteen and sixteen had taken the child into a shed on the beach at night, and ripped the clothes off her. They took photographs. They forced her into degrading sex acts. An innocent thirteen-year-old girl for fuck's sake. She was probably raped but she didn't know because she lost consciousness. She never saw a doctor, which may have been down to the father.'

'The child's father? Why wouldn't he want her to see a doctor?'

'His daughter had been dishonoured; you don't shout about that if you're a Greek orthodox patriarch.'

I'm glad I'm wearing sunglasses. My eyes fill with tears. Those boys should have been charged with assault and statutory rape and sent to a detention centre for serious crimes. My father would have got to the truth very quickly, why didn't he help? But I know the answer as soon as the question shapes itself. He wouldn't have wanted any ugliness to attach to himself or his family; it might have threatened his investment portfolio. Who would do business with a man whose guests had raped a child? He would have made very sure the truth never came out.

How much did my mother know?

The shadowy terrace has become cold. I think of Lottie; how I would feel if this had happened to her. The horror and fury that would transform everything, the justice I would pursue, whatever it took.

'We let ourselves believe the girl's father; we were distracted at the time,' the younger brother says, but he doesn't meet my eyes. 'Everyone was. We'd been looking for their little boy for hours, and kids don't last long in the heat. A death would have been the worse shame.'

He looks down at his drink; this must be how he thinks of it, so he can live with himself.

'In fact, it was the little girl herself who gave us the lead in the end.'

Chapter 25

Paxos 2003

Sofie

The younger policeman opened the kitchen door to go out, light and heat flooded in. It must be noon or later. He hadn't heard what she said, it would be too late if she didn't make them listen. Sofie made herself stand up though she had to lean on the table. They all looked at her, her face burned and stung, but she had to speak out for Nico's sake.

'He might be in the shed.' She spoke loudly this time, as loudly as she could.

'What shed?' The taller of the two policemen looked puzzled.

'There's a shed in the trees at the back of the beach that's used for storage, but it's kept locked,' Christos told them.

'So the little boy couldn't have got in then,' the younger policeman said.

They all stared at her as if she was stupid. They couldn't see the thoughts that were darkening her mind like those storm clouds across the sky yesterday. They didn't know she had unlocked the shed, that Jay had taken the key and must have locked it again after they had finished with her. They had no idea that during her ordeal, Nico could have heard noises coming from the shed. He might have thought they were playing a game and have sneaked inside. When he saw what was happening, he would have hidden in the boat, too terrified to move. Perhaps he had gone to sleep in the end, then found himself trapped.

Or that was all wrong, and he had really drowned. He wouldn't be found for days, bodies take a long time to wash up, even if they're small. Papa had had his share of finding drowned bodies; he told Christos that you have to look at their feet sometimes to find out who they were. Feet stayed the same though the water changed everything else. She'd know Nico's feet anywhere; all his toes were the same length. He had a little mole under the bone on his right ankle.

Dimitrios got up so suddenly his chair fell over. He left it lying there while he ran out of the door, followed closely by Christos. The taller policeman walked out quickly and the shorter one followed; beyond the window she could see them beginning to

216

run. Athena and Babas followed but more slowly, their heads bowed. Sofie knew they didn't believe Nico would be in the hut, but they were checking it out all the same.

She bowed her head as if she was in church and clasped her hands.

'Please. *Se parakalo, Theous*. Please, God.' She began to whisper prayers that she had known when she was small. '*Panayeea mou. Voethia*.' Virgin Mary. Help me.'

Fragments only, all she could remember but what good would they do? Nobody was listening. Nobody heard her last night, certainly not God.

A minute passed. Three, Five. Ten.

How long would it take them to walk to the beach, force open the door, look inside and come back?

Fifteen. Twenty.

When they saw he wasn't in the shed, they might climb up the headland to the next beach if they hadn't looked there already, but they wouldn't find him there either. Athena might start crying.

Twenty-five. Thirty.

If you keep him safe, God, I'll look after him for the rest of my life.

Her head was still bowed, and she was still whispering promises, so she didn't see Dimitrios at the window; it wasn't until the door was flung wide open that she looked up, startled, and saw he was carrying Nico and that her brother was very still. His head

217

had fallen back, and his arms hung down. He was bleeding from a cut on his head. The blood had trickled down the side of his nose, so it looked as though he'd been crying tears of blood. Dimitrios was actually crying, which she had never seen before. Christos was walking behind, he had Nico's flip-flops in his hand.

The world, the whole spinning world with its sunshine and sea and flowers, stopped turning. Nothing would ever be as bad as this again.

She stood up and took Nico's hand and that was when she got a shock. His hand was warm. And then, very slowly, his fingers closed around hers.

The world began to turn again.

Athena came running into the kitchen at that moment. She must have gone in a different direction to the others, so she didn't yet know Nico was all right. Grief had altered her face, she looked much older.

'He's alive, Mama. He's alive.' Sofie wanted to shout but it came out as a whisper.

It was enough. Athena didn't smile but her face changed, it lost that desperate look. She took Nico from Dimitrios and held him tight against her heart. The police arrived a few moments later. Their faces were wet, and the necks of their shirts were dark with sweat.

'Where was he?' Babas had followed Athena into the kitchen. Sofie never really thought of him as old before but now she saw he was an old man. His shoulders were hunched, and he walked very slowly as if something had broken inside.

'He was in the shed, like Sofie said,' Dimitrios told him. 'The policemen broke the door down. He had climbed into the boat and fallen asleep.'

He must have heard everything. Everything. Sofie closed her eyes.

The policemen were looking at Nico asleep in Athena's arms. There were so many questions they could have asked, like how did he get into the shed if it was locked, or if it wasn't, how come it got locked up again afterwards? If they had asked those questions, she would have told them what had happened despite what Babas said, but they didn't ask anything. They were actually smiling.

'He seems okay,' the younger one said.

The older one nodded.

How was it possible that anyone can think they know a person is okay just by looking at them? The older one had been worried by her appearance it was true, but now he had forgotten about her. Athena was looking at Nico, absorbed by him; if you think your child has drowned and then he is found alive, your mind would be so full of thankfulness there wouldn't be room for anything else. The policemen nodded and then simply left. Christos went outside with them to close the gates of the drive behind their car.

The light outside had softened, a whole day had passed, and the evening was approaching. Someone should start cooking but no one was doing anything. Babas was looking at her, his lips clamped tight. It was difficult to know what he was thinking. Did he hate her? She wouldn't blame him if he did: she hated herself. She wanted to go to her room and had just pushed herself to standing when there was a loud knock at the door. She jolted and everything began to hurt again.

Dimitrios opened the door. Peter stood there, his hands on his hips, his face impassive.

'Take Nico,' Babas told Dimitrios quickly. 'Christos, go with them.' His voice was as hard as a rock.

Athena glanced at her husband then handed the sleeping boy to Dimitrios who walked past Peter, his hand over the child's head as if to protect him. Christos followed. Sofie wanted to go with them, but Peter had stepped into the kitchen and was blocking the doorway. She was trapped. She sat down, it was difficult to stand for very long. Athena sat down beside her and took her hand.

'Your boys hurt two of my guests,' Peter said calmly.

Sofie realized she had been wrong, he hadn't been angry with the boys at all, he was taking their side. He looked very calm, as if stating a fact.

Babas's head was lowered as he waited to see if

Peter had anything else to say. He looked like a bull about to charge.

'They called me from Gaios today. When I arrived, I had to organize urgent medical help,' Peter continued, as if reading from notes that he has kept carefully, knowing they would be useful. 'Both had their scalps stitched. One needed a skull X-ray.'

His words passed through Sofie fast, sharp arrows of pure gladness, leaving her body trembling.

Babas moved close to Peter, ragged patches of red glowed on his cheeks. 'Your guests visited an abomination on my daughter,' he said, spitting the words into Peter's face.

'What do you mean?' Peter's voice was very cold.

'Look at her.'

Sofie lowered her face, but Babas walked behind her chair, took her head in both hands and turned it towards him. There was a flicker in Peter's cold green eyes, extinguished instantly.

'There are other injuries too,' Babas said.

'She made herself available to our guests. I cannot help that.'

Athena let go of Sofie's hand and stood up, for once she seemed larger and stronger than Babas.

'Those boys were lying in wait for her. They coerced her. They forced themselves on her in disgusting ways.'

'She asked for it.'

This must be how Peter became successful, by

refusing to acknowledge the truth if that truth wasn't helpful. He must have damaged many people over the years on his way to getting rich.

'They are just young boys,' he continued, shrugging.

'One is sixteen,' Athena spoke very clearly. 'I know that because I made his birthday cake myself. My daughter is a child of thirteen. What they did was a crime. Both boys should face charges and be punished.'

'She made herself available,' Peter repeated. He sounded regretful. He was good at this. 'She has been pestering those boys all holiday.'

'Of course she hasn't.' Athena was very calm; she was good at this too. You would have to know her very well to detect the tremble in her voice. 'This is a matter for the police and the courts. You only have to look at the bruises on her face.'

'You will never be able to prove she didn't make those bruises herself, to blackmail us.' Peter's voice had risen very slightly. 'Make no mistake. I have the best lawyers in the world at my disposal. Whatever she claims, we will prove her wrong. One of the boys has recorded her voice clearly asking to be his girl-friend. There are pictures of her standing in front of them naked and other, more intimate images. We will release these if you pursue the case but destroy them if you agree not to.' He pauses, his eyes narrow. 'Do you want her to be more shamed than she already is? Shamed in front of the whole world?'

Babas moved towards him, but Peter stepped aside; he was surprisingly agile for an old man. At that moment, as if by a signal that had been arranged beforehand, Paul came into the room. Paul, with his thuggish looks and bulging muscles. The two men stood side by side. Babas was outnumbered. He looked swiftly at the mantelpiece for his gun, the one he used to shoot rabbits. It was lucky, Athena said later, that she had taken it down and hidden it after Christos told her what happened. If she hadn't, Babas would have had to go to prison for murder.

'You can't win,' Peter said quietly. 'I won't let you. There is no way in the world that I will permit my guests, myself and my family to be dragged into the mire along with your daughter.'

'You are wrong. We will win.' Mama touched Sofie very lightly on the head, a sign or a promise. 'Even if we can't now, we will one day. Wait and see.'

Sofie didn't care about winning. She wanted those men out of the room. She wanted there to be tomato sauce bubbling on the stove, the scent of bread and the sound of music, for Athena to be singing as she washed the lettuce, shifting from foot to foot in a dance. She wanted Dimitrios to catch her by the waist and twirl her around and for her to gasp and sit down at the table, out of breath and laughing.

Peter walked out of the door without another word. Paul glanced at them all in turn and then he looked at Sofie. Something gleamed in his eyes, interest, excitement even. Athena saw that glance. She walked towards Paul and this time her voice was raised. When she spoke she broke Babas's rule about swearing in the house, although Sofie had never heard her swear before.

'Get the fuck out of my kitchen.'

Paul bowed his head and walked out.

Athena turned to Sofie; she bent and kissed her very gently on the cheek that wasn't bruised and then she made a cup of tea which she put in front of Sofie and cut sandwiches which she wrapped up. She filled all the water bottles they had, took their rucksack from the top of the cupboard and put the water bottles and sandwiches inside, along with the apron and the embroidered cloths, the jug and the pot with the handle, that she had gathered earlier. She looked round at the table and the chairs and the stove and the fridge as if she was saying goodbye. Then she took Sofie's hand, and they walked out of the kitchen. Sofie didn't know it then, but she was walking away from that life forever.

Chapter 26

Paxos 2023

Julia

'What became of the children?' My hands feel cold but then I am clenching the cup of iced coffee very tightly. 'Were they okay?'

'You are never okay after something like that. The little boy survived if that's what you mean. Nico. Odd that I remember his name but not the girl's. That's vanished. I have no idea what happened to her, the cousin didn't say. I had the impression things didn't work out so well.' Jakob took another swig of ouzo, this time he didn't bother to drink it from the glass.

'Her face still haunts me. After the cousin told me what had happened, that was the end for us. We didn't want to stay on as police. The regrets were too sharp.

225

We should have insisted she went to the hospital right away. They could have done swabs. We could have got those boys.'

Valentin looks at him. 'For Christ's sake, Jakob, let it rest.'

'It might have been trickier than you think,' I tell Jakob, feeling an urge to comfort him though God knows why. He was right, they hadn't done their job. 'Money would have been brought to bear.' If that family had sought justice, my father would have thrown hundreds, no, thousands of pounds at the problem. He would have made it disappear completely.

'You think we could have been bribed?' Jakob stares at me, his voice is louder now, angry.

'Of course not,' I reply swiftly, though that's exactly what I think. My father was ruthless. He would have found out the name of the boss of the local police force, and the boss of his boss, all the way up to the chief of police. He would have made it his business to know members of parliament if necessary, and possibly the prime minister. That little girl would not have stood a chance. I understand now why her parents left; it was to protect their daughter from further harm.

'Thank you for the coffee.' I get up. 'And for sharing the story.'

As I walk across the road, I sense the two old men staring after me, wondering exactly who they had been talking to. They might find out: it wouldn't take much.

I was as bad as they were. I'd failed that child too. We all did in our different ways, but if I'd been kinder, it might never have happened. I had been friendly to her when I was younger; if only I'd been friendly again, if I'd painted her toenails once more, or thanked her for her bracelet instead of losing it, she might not have turned to them. She might have told me about the swimming lessons. I could have warned her to take care. I have no memory of the boys' faces but what persists is an impression of arrogance, fuelled by entitlement. They wanted someone for their sickening games and that child had been the perfect victim. No wonder the woman in the shop seemed hostile. I should have questioned my parents further, pushed for answers. What the hell had I been thinking about? I know the answer of course, I'd been thinking about myself.

I forgot to ask for directions to Tripitos Arch after all, but it isn't hard to find; the stony path leads me across four fields, past olive groves, a shelter for goats, and a line of cypress trees. From a distance, the white stone arch is blindingly bright and curves high above the turquoise sea. The strip of green that roofs it looks as narrow as a knife. I creep nearer, step by sliding step, down the crumbling cliff path. No one would know if I lost my footing or witness my fall through the hot air, the smash against rocks. I force myself to go on and, when I reach it, the bridge is wider than I thought, the distance had been deceptive. I stand in the middle feeling neither triumph nor fear; poised high above the water and surrounded by space, I'm not even sure where I am.

That night the regrets crowd in. I don't want to be on my own. There would be comfort in confiding in James, but he doesn't pick up when I phone, nor does Laurel. I text both then Rasul, to thank him for holding the fort. I message Lottie again. I wish she had been here with me, swimming in the sea, lying in the sun, and exploring the woods. She would have loved the colours here, she could have photographed the sunrise and the woods at dawn, she would have captured the shifting blues of the sea. She might have confided in me.

The waterfront restaurants in Loggos are quiet. They will soon close for winter. As I eat a bowl of seafood, I catch sight of the man who filled the pool, sitting at a table outside the café opposite. He is wearing the same hat and is side by side with a woman with thick grey hair and a pretty pixie face. They sit close, shoulders touching, murmuring to each other from time to time. This is the way they must sit at home; the way James and I have never sat. Is that my fault? Perhaps we should have, we still could.

They look content. I should try harder. I'll organize that weekend in Cornwall, I could try fishing to keep him company. We'll sit together like the couple I'm watching; we'll discuss what happened in Paxos and work out how to find the family. We'll think of a way to make amends.

Sleep is deep but on the terrace early next morning there are tiny stones, as if someone had come up from the beach in the night. They might have been carried on an animal's paws, the little cat perhaps, but all the same I am disconcerted; it's as if the house is telling me it's time to go home, and I understand. I've discovered the past and now I should leave.

My flight is in two days but there is a space on a plane later this morning. It turns out to be easy to transfer my ticket, there are plenty of spaces at this time of year. I text Lottie and phone James, leaving a message to let him know the time my plane arrives. I tell him I'm looking forward to seeing him then I pack and close the house. I don't look back as I drive away, leaving the house to its ghosts again.

Chapter 27

Corfu 2003

Sofie

Sofie looked at ghosts every day, framed in tarnished silver on the windowsill in Grandfather's flat. A younger Sofie stared back at her, carrying baby Nico.

Was she smiling? The image had been bleached by light, so it was difficult to see. Sofie peered closer, looking for the shape of her mouth or the glimmer of teeth.

Open your fucking mouth.

She had to look away from the picture, but her gaze was drawn back all the same. She wanted to shout a warning to that faded child, tell her not to trust anyone, not to talk to boys when she was on her own, never to believe anything promised by a stranger or even a friend.

The ghosts in the picture belonged to a life that was gone. She couldn't remember how it felt. She couldn't recall the colour of the flowers Mama planted or how the garden smelt in the morning. She couldn't bring to mind the sound of the wind in the olive trees or the noise of Papa's fishing boat as it chugged back into the cove at the end of the day. But she could still feel those fingers inside her and the searing pain between her buttocks; she still heard those voices and the bang of the door as it slammed, trapping her inside the shed, with them.

Grandfather's flat in Corfu Town was small and dark, high up in an old building that was stained with weather and graffiti. A new block of flats had been grafted on the side, old and new, stuck together. When they arrived, she had looked up at it from the outside, trying to guess which one might be his, but her neck hurt. Everything hurt. They walked up the stairs as the lifts didn't work. Babas led the way with a suitcase, Dimitrios, Roxana and Christos carried the other bags, and Athena gripped Nico's hand to stop him trying to wriggle through the banisters. The door of the flat had been left open. It was dark inside and smelt musty. They walked down a narrow corridor which only fitted one person at a time. Grandfather stood up slowly from his old cane chair in the kitchen, but he was still looking at the floor because his back and neck were bent right over. He sat down again, leant back and smiled at Sofie. She was glad he didn't ask her any questions, not what her favourite hobby was or where she was going to school, or even, with a chuckle, if she had a boyfriend. Those were the kinds of questions that people used to ask and which had nothing to do with her at all, especially now. She had no school and no hobbies. She wouldn't talk to a boy again, ever. Grandfather didn't say anything, he just lifted a hand in a kind of salute. His eyes were small and sunken, but they were kind. She lifted her hand too, without saying anything either. Her mouth wouldn't make a smile, but it didn't seem to matter. Nico didn't say anything either. He hadn't spoken since the day they found him in the shed, curled in a ball in the bottom of the boat.

Mama put some things to eat on the table, but Sofie wasn't hungry. She followed Roxana further down the corridor to a small room. Roxana had helped Grandfather put two mattresses on the floor for her and Nico. Sofie was glad that she would be with Nico, and that the window was high up so no one could see in.

She washed her hands in the bathroom which had patches of mould on the wall. She was washing her hands so often there were little cracks in between her fingers and the skin was sore. Then she lay down. There was darkness inside her head, a big lump of it, rough-edged like the tar they put on the roads which hardened like rock. She couldn't think properly, there wasn't enough space in her mind. She stayed in her room for a few days, sleeping and waking, losing track of time. Once she felt on her bed for Aries before she remembered that they had left him with Kolena. Athena had said that a town was no place for a little island cat. Nico came in at night and went to bed; he liked the door left open. Sometimes Sofie got up when he was asleep and sat in the corridor outside the kitchen door, just so she could hear Mama's voice.

Some nights she wet her bed, but no one said anything. Athena took the sheet away to wash and then hung it from the balcony that opened off her and Papa's room. Sofie thought that meant everyone would be able to tell that she had wet her bed, but there were lots of sheets hanging between balconies, draping down into the narrow streets, perhaps it didn't matter.

There were doors on the side of their building that opened into space. Sofie didn't like looking at them, what if someone opened one by mistake and stepped into air?

Sometimes she put her hands on her body to see if she could still feel things because it didn't seem to be her body any more. She was getting thinner: every time she put anything in her mouth it made her want to vomit. Mama took away her unfinished food, her lips pressed tight together but she didn't say anything.

Washing smells and the scent of polish begin to creep into the flat, replacing the damp and mould smells. Athena was working as hard as usual, cooking and cleaning, looking after the family and Grandfather; she looked thinner too. She sat more than she used to, often putting a hand to her head as if she had a headache. She screwed up her eyes when she looked at things as if it was difficult to see. Babas disappeared for hours each day looking for work, but there were no olive trees in the city and no fishing boats in the harbour; when she heard him climbing the stairs slowly each evening, she knew he hadn't been successful. She didn't ask him any questions; he might blame her for everything that had happened, and she already blamed herself.

Nico started at the new school. He held himself more stiffly than he used to, and he didn't hum any more. She heard Grandfather say he had the look of someone who was just about surviving, and he should know because he had been in the war.

Sofie would have to go to school soon; she knew because she heard Babas tell Mama in the kitchen one night when she was sitting on the floor outside. He said she needed a routine, something else to think about. It was time she moved forward. She should put everything behind her, but she couldn't do that, it would make it worse; when she looked in the mirror in Grandfather's hallway, the corridor behind her already bulged with frightening shadows.

Christos was back at university in Athens, but Dimitrios and Roxana were living nearby. They had found jobs in a café that belonged to some friends of Roxana's, and they were living together in a flat above it. All their plans about buying land and building a house had gone, but they didn't complain. Roxana had an argument with Babas about the clothes Sofie should wear to school. Sofie was surprised that Roxana won. She bought Sofie a hoodie and tracksuit bottoms. It would mean she would look like everyone else at school, but she didn't feel glad, she didn't feel anything. She didn't want to go to a new school. She would have liked to go back to her own school, though Gabriella would have another friend by now. She might have seen those images; her older brother went to the bar where Jay and Ginger had shown the photos around. If Gabriella had seen them, she wouldn't want to be her friend again. In any case, Babas said they wouldn't ever return.

'There's one thing that's certain, we can never go back,' she heard him tell Mama. 'We just have to keep going forward.'

That night she imagined herself walking along a path that went on and on, with the earth stretching either side as far as she could see. She knew she mustn't go back because the earth might start to shake and tremble and the things she had buried would rise up, like monsters coming back to life.

The bruise on her face had faded and she had stopped bleeding by the time the week for school came around. The cut on her forehead had knitted together in a thin red line. Roxana trimmed her hair in a fringe so no one would notice, and Athena took her to school that first day. Sofie walked behind her and Nico, through crowded streets and across roads. It was the first time she'd been out since they'd arrived in Corfu, and everything seemed very noisy. The school building was much bigger than she'd thought it was possible for a school to be. It was painted bright white, and it shone in the sun. There were no trees outside like her old school, just marks on the ground for football. A group of boys were kicking a ball around. She wanted to go back home when she saw them, but Athena took her inside to her classroom. The teacher's forehead was creased into worry lines already, so Sofie didn't ask her anything. When she looked round to say goodbye to Athena, she had already gone.

Sofie sat at the wall side of the third row of desks. When the lessons started, she heard the words that the teacher said, and they seemed simple enough, but they flowed past her somehow. It reminded her of standing in the sea, waves passed by, you felt them, but you couldn't grasp hold of them. The teacher had to come over and point to the sheet on the desk before she could begin and, even then, there wasn't enough space in her head to think properly. When the bell went halfway through the morning she followed everyone to the playground and stood with her back pressed against the wall, wondering how the girls could play in the middle of the playground where the boys barged into them. How did they keep from screaming? There was screaming anyway, everyone screamed, and after a while she had to go inside. The teacher was in the classroom, so she went to the toilets where she washed her hands three times. She sat at her desk when it was lesson time, but her head was so full of the screaming it was hard to hear what the teacher said.

When Athena asked her how she had got on at school, she didn't answer.

That night Babas came into the bedroom and sat on the bed. Nico was asleep. It was dark but she could see Babas by the light that shone into the room from the street through the high-up window. He was thinking and it was a little while before he spoke.

'Remember when you were with me the time the boat was caught in the storm last year?'

She nodded.

'What did we do?'

She wasn't sure what the right answer was, so she

didn't say anything, and, after a pause, Babas began taking again.

'We carried on,' Babas said, 'I steered the boat and I kept my mind on all the things that were happening to us: the waves that were high and the wind which was strong and the way the current was tugging us. I thought about all those things and at the same time I kept going steadily on. In the end I saw the lights of Loggos. We made it into harbour, and you got out with the rope and pulled the boat in. Do you remember?'

Sofie nodded; she hadn't heard Babas say so much at one time before, at least, not to her. After a while he nodded and patted her leg through the bed covers and went out.

The next day she walked along the street with Nico. Athena didn't come with them this time because she had a headache again. It was raining. Sofie held Nico's hand and thought about what Babas had said. She tried to think about the pavement and how hard it felt under her sandals. She thought about the noise of the cars and how cold the rain felt on her face. In lessons she thought about the numbers in the sums and about the words she was writing, even the feel of the pencil as it made each little stroke on the paper. At break it was noisier than before. Today the bigger boys came out at the same time as the girls. They watched the girls and whispered to each other, grinning. She felt the monsters stir deep underground, so she went back to the girls' toilets and washed her hands. The soap stung the cracks between her fingers. The paper towels scraped her skin, so it bled, and afterwards her hands were even redder than before. She sat on the toilet seat and locked the door and stayed there until the bell went and she went back to the classroom. She stayed in the toilets at break time from then on. No one seemed to notice.

Babas was right. She should keep her mind on all the things that were happening to her: how the pavement felt, the noise that the cars made, the rain on her face, the grittiness of the pencil on the paper and the roughness of the towels. That way, it was possible to keep going from one moment to the next. The moments added up to a morning and then an afternoon and then a day, and when it was evening, she could lie down on her bed. She thought she might be able go on like this, day after day, week after week but everything changed when Athena dropped the tray.

Athena had come into the bedroom one night as she usually did, with glasses of water to give to Sofie and Nico but when she put the tray down, it missed the table and clattered to the ground, shattering one of the glasses. Water soaked into the rug.

'How silly,' Athena said. 'Silly me. Stay in bed now, or you'll cut your feet.'

As she walked out of the door to collect the dustpan and brush, one of her shoulders hit the door frame. That was all, but it made Sofie worried. After school the next day she watched her mother as she got the supper. Athena looked thinner and older. She moved more slowly than usual. Was that her fault too? Had her mother been so concerned about her that she had got older and weaker somehow? That night the new worry about Athena slid into bed like a snake, writhing together with all the other worries that surrounded her.

A few nights later, when Nico was already asleep, there was a loud noise, like the noise Dimitrios made when he came back with the shopping and dropped the bags on the floor all at once. But it was a Sunday, the shops weren't open on Sundays. Sofie got out of bed and tiptoed along the corridor, but neither Mama nor Babas noticed her standing at the doorway. Babas was kneeling on the floor next to Mama; it was as though an animal had hold of her and was shaking her from side to side. Her eyes rolled back and Sofie could see there was wet between her legs. Babas was holding her hand, saying her name loudly.

And then it was over. Athena lay very still, she wasn't breathing. Sofie was too frightened to move but then Athena took an enormous breath and pushed herself up so she was sitting upright. Babas gave her a glass of water. She drank a little, spilling some. She looked up, catching sight of Sofie by the door.

'It was just a little fall. Go back to bed.' Athena waved her away though her voice sounded strange. She frowned at Babas. 'No need to make any fuss.'

Sofie went back to bed. She lay completely still watching the light under the door. She could hear Babas talking to her mother and her mother replying. Her voice had begun to sound the same as it always did. Babas sounded angry but he often sounded angry now.

'It was just a little fall,' Sofie whispered to Nico who was still sleeping. 'No need to make any fuss.' She had lost so many things: the house and the garden, school and Gabriella. The beach and the sea and the olive trees. Aries and the little owl. She couldn't afford to lose anything else.

They were in Corfu Town, a place where ordinary families were getting on with their lives and nothing particularly unusual happened. They were the same as everyone else, getting on with their lives as best as they could. Bad luck wouldn't find them again, and pick them out of all these people. They were safe, they had to be.

Chapter 28

Corfu and London 2023

Julia

Corfu Town is ridiculously colourful, the kind of place tourists think of as the real Greece because in the parts of the town they visit, the houses are painted pretty colours, the windows have blue shutters, and cobbled roads twist past old churches and cafés. There are arches over the streets and there are bright flowers in the gardens behind wrought iron gates.

I have a couple of hours before my flight, so I make my way through the crowded streets where the shops are full of ornaments, clothes, jewellery, and plastic icons. I buy a blue pendant for Lottie to match her eyes, and a leather bracelet for James; he won't wear it, but he'll know I made the effort. Further and higher in the town is the part where most people live.

There are fewer painted houses and several high blocks of flats, some of them dilapidated looking. I saw nothing of this when I last breezed through aged nineteen, hand in hand with Anthony, but then I didn't look.

I order coffee in a tiny café half hidden by a fall of ivy. A black clad old woman sits near the inner door; she has tired eyes and a face as finely wrinkled as a piece of tissue paper. Her grey hair is in a bun high on her head and her hands are busy with knitting. The slim waiter in a white shirt and black trousers pauses by the door to touch her on the shoulder and exchange a few words. I stare at them as I sip my coffee and a thought flares from the smouldering regrets in my mind. What if the waiter was once the little boy who lived at Thalassa and the old woman, his mother? They might live above this very restaurant, the daughter with them. There are hundreds of families that work in restaurants, mothers and sons together, thousands of them, it's almost impossible these two could be part of the family that helped us. Nevertheless,when the young man returns to ask me if I want anything more, I stare at his face for remnants of that long-ago child. I don't know what I'm searching for, I wouldn't know him anyway. I never looked at that boy properly, he was just a child, playing at the edge of things, a little boy I ignored completely.

The young man waits for my answer, his eyes evading mine as I continue to stare at him. After a moment he asks me if I want the menu. I shake my head, thank him and pay, glancing around the café to see if there is anything familiar, but I never got close enough to the Greek family to be invited in as their guest. I have no idea what things would have been precious to them. They looked after us, made our beds, cleaned our showers and gave us food, vanishing unthanked; if this young man and his mother were part of that family, I'd be the last person they would want to greet.

A taxi gets me to the airport just in time. Later, the plane lifts smoothly over the town. The tiled roofs and blue sea make a colourful scene below, like a postcard. From here there is no rubbish in the streets, no stains on the pavements, no broken cars, no families working hard to make ends meet.

The young couple next to me on the plane hold hands, legs hooked over each other. I'll come back with James. We'll return to Paxos and find out where the family went. We can ask the woman in the shop in Loggos or the people who live next door. Someone must know where they are.

James is waiting the other side of the arrival doors at Heathrow; his face is lowered. He is talking on his phone, smiling in a way I haven't seen for a while.

There must be good news to share, but when he looks up and catches sight of me, the smile fades. He looks wary.

I hug him, he feels different. Softer, a little fatter. He pats my back and takes my suitcase. I wait for him to say I'm looking well or that he's missed me, but he seems so serious, a wave of fear hits me.

'Is Lottie okay?'

'Fine, as far as I know. Let's get some coffee.'

Coffee? Here? I follow him through the crowds, too relieved to protest that I'd rather go home and have coffee in our own kitchen. He chooses a table in the corner of the café.

'I thought this might be better if we were sitting down.'

He indicates a table and goes to the counter. I slide into the seat against the wall. I think I understand, if he's planning an apology, he'd want a neutral space.

Just beyond the entrance, people are walking fast, focused on their destination. Everyone is hurrying. I want to hurry too. I want to go home and start our new life, a new and better life, both of us trying harder. I'll tell him what happened to the child in Paxos and listen to his suggestions; he's good at making plans. I glance at the tall, familiar back view as he pays at the till. The girl taking his money smiles at him, another woman glances at him as she collects her tea. An attractive man, they might be thinking,

246

I wonder if he's taken. They might watch to see where he goes and register me. It's not as easy as you think, I could tell them, but I'd stop there. I wouldn't tell them about anything else, why would I? It's about to change for the better.

He returns and sits down with two espressos.

'I have something to say, and I need you to listen.' A quick guarded look at my face. 'Things have changed.'

It's as though he has read my thoughts. He glances down, as if uncertain how to continue. Apologies don't come easily to James, he might be finding it hard to admit that he's been reflecting on our lives and now he's ready to support my career as I've supported his. I want to put my hand on his, but he has crossed his arms.

'I've changed too. I've missed you. I'm glad—'

'Please don't make this more difficult.' He looks rapidly around the café then back at me. 'There's no easy way to say this.' But despite these words his eyes are bright, his voice sounds excited. 'Since you've been away, I met someone.'

'What do you mean?' A stupid question. In retrospect it will be completely obvious what he means, but sitting in that bustling restaurant with a warm cup of coffee in front of me and within touching distance of my husband, I know where I am. I feel secure. Life is back on track, and things are about to improve, or so I think. I'm still smiling. I assume he must be referring to a new member of staff or a PA, someone he hired to take over my role.

'We've become close,' he continues.

'Close?'

I think, ridiculously, of him sharing his office with this new employee, that their desks are close together.

His voice becomes patient, a little slower, as if he's talking to a child. 'As in fallen in love.'

I am still smiling because what he says doesn't make sense. 'Is this a joke?'

'You deserted me. What the fuck did you think would happen?' He is speaking very calmly, as if we were having a normal conversation which makes what he says that much worse, the swearing more of a jolt.

'I explained at the time,' I tell him, also calmly though I want to speak loudly, shout even, which is why James must have chosen this place. You can't easily make a scene in a coffee shop. 'I went to see what needed doing at the house, it was an opportunity—'

'Don't say it. I know. An opportunity to find yourself.' He laughs, unbelievably, he laughs. 'Well, while you were searching, someone else found me.'

'I've been away for just two weeks. How is that possible?'

'She only just missed you. You'd literally just left in the taxi when she rang the bell to return a book or leave one of hers for you. I never found out which, it didn't matter, it still doesn't. We got talking and things moved very quickly. You'll find this hard to believe but we've hardly been apart since then. We have so much in common, you see.' His voice trembles with emotion.

'What do you mean?'

Did he mean sexually? I feel hollow, convinced that nothing he is saying is the truth and yet it so clearly is.

'It was as if we had already met in another life.' An incredulous little chuckle he doesn't bother to suppress; the kind people give when they can't quite believe their good fortune. 'We could be soul mates.'

'What on earth do you mean?' I repeat, though that's stupid too. I don't want to know.

He leans forward and the words begin to pour out of him, as if he's been saving them up, which he probably has.

'She listens to Bach sonatas and reads Thomas Hardy. She adores Cornwall and fishing.' He throws up his hands as if newly astonished. 'I mean, what are the odds? She was even wearing my favourite scent.'

I feel cold in the way you do at the start of fever. My hands are icy though my cheeks burn. His words continue to come at me. I want to turn my head away, and let them fly by unheard.

'She diagnosed my ulcer. We're seeing the doctor next week. How about that?' He sounds proud and indignant at the same time, as if he's forgotten I've been trying to persuade him to get help for months. 'Don't look so worried, you've enough money. I won't contest Lottie.'

Has he lost his mind? Lottie was never his.

'It's good timing as it happens.' He sweeps on. 'She's interested in your old job, she loves cooking.' In a minute he'll thank me for conveniently leaving the coast clear.

'Which job?'

'The one you despise. Cooking for events.'

'But cooking for events is exactly what I said I'd carry on doing.'

'It's a bit late to pick and choose, she's already made plans.' He looks at me with what might pass as sympathy. 'I thought this would come as a bit of a shock but then, you shocked me when you left.'

'I went for a fortnight; you've been away for far longer before now. What about the teachers' conference in Switzerland or those weeks in the States last year?'

'This was different, you said you didn't mind, but I asked you not to leave, remember?' He has all his answers ready; he must have thought them through. 'You've brought this on yourself, Julia.'

'You haven't told me her name.' My heart is beating very hard, because although I think I know what he's going to say, it will still come as a shock.

'Oh, sorry.' He sounds anything but sorry, triumph tinges his voice. 'Didn't I say? It's Laurel, of course. Your therapist, Laurel Rossi.'

Chapter 29

Corfu 2003

Sofie

'It's time to go and see the doctor.'

Athena had put on her best dress, the one with the tiny white birds flying on a silky black background. Her hair was in a tidy roll, tucked into the back of her neck. She looked beautiful but tired. Sofie thought the appointment would be about her headaches and the fall, the shaking and the funny way she had spoken afterwards, but when Mama touched Sofie's cheek, Sofie realized that the doctor's appointment was for herself, and that Athena was going to talk about the things that had happened in the shed.

'The doctor is the same one who looks after Grandfather.' Athena sounded calmer than she had for a long time. It was as though with the cooler months the view had cleared, and she could see clean back to the day they left Paxos. 'She's very nice. We must make the most of this chance. Babas has taken Nico to the sea.'

Babas wouldn't want anyone to know what had happened to his daughter, not even a doctor; Athena must be worried to be doing this behind his back. But Sofie was just home from school and bone tired. She didn't want to go.

'Do we have to, Mama?'

'The doctor is very nice,' Athena repeated, wrapping up a piece of cake for Sofie to eat when they got there.

'What can she do?' Sofie knew that sounded stupid, but she really didn't know.

'She'll help you get rid of the memories.'

She had no memories, that was the point. She had buried them deep; monsters shouldn't be disturbed, but at the thought of the doctor's questions, she felt them stir.

'And *pedimou*,' Athena spoke slowly, 'I want her to look at you, properly.'

Look at her? Which part of her? But she knew and she backed against the wall, shaking her head. It was too late for that. Things must have healed up, at least those kinds of things. But it didn't make any difference. Athena was pulling their coats from the cupboard and rooting for the shoes which were always in a

252

muddle no matter how careful they tried to be. As the front door of the flat closed behind them, Sofie felt pure panic. Normally she wouldn't take her mother's hand but today she agreed to.

They stopped at a road crossing and Sofie felt something soft around her ankles and looked down to see a little black cat. Aries? The cat lifted its head, and she could see it wasn't Aries. Of course it wasn't, he was miles away across the sea, with Kolena. The light changed, her hand was pulled, and she stumbled over the kerb and across the road. When she looked back, the cat had vanished between the legs of all the people. Would he be safe in the crowds? Do cats know about cars? She wanted to go back and pick him up, but they were late, she had to keep walking, almost running. They hurried down streets and turned corners, until they were both gasping for breath and Sofie's arm was hurting from the way Athena was pulling her along.

They stopped in front of a glass door in the side of a building, and it slid open. There was a queue of people up ahead and a desk with a woman behind it, tapping on a computer and talking to the man at the top of the queue. There were a lot of grey plastic chairs and people sitting on them: an old man with a yellow face who had fallen asleep with his mouth open; a bored-looking boy with a bloodstained bandage round his hand; and a woman with a smiley face, talking to the baby on her lap. None of them seemed at all frightened, perhaps it would be all right. Sofie looked up at Athena, she wanted to catch her eye and smile, but at that moment, her mother's hand pulled itself roughly from hers and she fell. At first, Athena seemed to be tumbling in slow motion, but when her head hit the floor with a crack, everything happened fast. Her body began to writhe and jerk as it had before. Her eyes rolled back. She made that noise, a harsh kind of moaning, and a large wet patch appeared on the floor between her legs. Her beautiful, dignified mother. Sofie stood still, torn between terror and shame. She watched as Athena's handbag came open and her brown purse fell out, spilling coins which rolled away between the legs of the patients who were staring silently. The cake bounced from its wrapping and broke up on the floor. When she saw Athena's lips go blue, Sofie forgot the people and fell to her knees by her side, calling her name as Babas had done. A moment later, a doctor was there, a bulky young man with a red beard and a red face. He turned Athena onto her side with his huge hands. He was gentle though his eyebrows slanted downwards in two rusty lines.

'Is Mama going to die?'

She didn't realize she had spoken aloud until she heard the words. The doctor didn't answer, he was listening to Athena's chest, his stethoscope pressing hard against the white birds. Sofie's hand was taken by a woman wearing a plastic apron who pulled her to her feet, whispering that no, her mother wasn't going to die. The whisper buzzed in her ear, but it felt comforting.

'Is your father here?'

Sofie shook her head. 'It's my fault.'

She didn't realize she said this out loud either, until the nurse replied. 'Of course it's not. Look, she's getting better already.'

Athena was trying to sit up but men in uniform had arrived with a stretcher and they lifted her onto it.

'Sofie,' Athena said in that strange voice. She was looking around and sounded desperate. 'Sofie!'

Sofie wrenched away from the nurse and took her mother's hand, but Athena was carried out of the doctor's surgery on the stretcher and their fingers were pulled apart. The nurse put her arm around Sofie, and together they watched as the ambulance doors were opened, the stretcher slotted inside, and the doors closed. The ambulance drove away, the siren screaming.

Sofie didn't cry, it was too bad for that, it felt as though her worst nightmare had come true.

The nurse took her back inside and Sofie stood next to her as she tapped on the computer in her room and asked questions. Sofie told her that her father couldn't come because he was looking after her brother, but her cousin Dimitrios could, Dimitrios Mundis. The nurse looked up his name and said he was a patient of the practice as well, and she would call him. She brought a glass of water and told her to sit in the waiting room as she had to see other patients. Sofie didn't want a drink, she wanted to wash her hands, but she couldn't in case Dimitrios came to find her. Sofie's thoughts churned in her head like the sea: if only Athena had gone to see the doctor after her first fall, she might be better now; instead she was in hospital. People die in hospitals, like *Yia-yia* when they took her away and she didn't come back.

The waiting room had changed, people seemed more ill. A man came in who couldn't breathe properly; he was making wheezing noises and the doctor came out again and took him away. The baby was crying now, a strange, high-pitched cry and his face was blotchy. His mother wasn't smiling any more, she was pacing up and down, jiggling the child but it didn't make any difference.

After a long time, the nurse came running out and said she was sorry and was sure that her cousin would be coming soon. Sofie could see she had forgotten all about her until now. She looked at the ground rather than the door so her hopes wouldn't be dashed every time it opened, but when feet in red trainers stopped by the chair, she knew she was safe. Dimitrios led her outside to the car, cold rain was pouring down, but

Roxana got out of the passenger seat and hugged her tightly.

'Athena's all right,' Roxana said into her hair. 'She's at the hospital, they need to do tests but she's doing fine.'

Sofie felt dizzy with relief, but the other worries that had been hiding inside that one escaped and began to fly around in her head, buzzing like wasps.

'Babas? Nico?'

'Babas is with Athena.' She brushed Sofie's hair away from her face. 'Nico's at our home with your grandfather. You're going to stay with us too.' She smiled. 'We'll all be cosy together.'

'What if Mama comes home later and we're not there?'

Roxana looked at Dimitrios, a swift, unhappy glance.

'She needs to stay in the hospital for now,' Dimitrios said calmly, but she knew that voice, it was the careful one he put on for guests, when he told them things he thought they wanted to hear. It wasn't real. 'You can see her tomorrow.'

Roxana took her hand. 'Let's get you home.'

They got into the car and drove through puddles which sprayed dirty water against the window. She wasn't going home. At home the rain would be falling through the leaves of the olive trees. By now the olives would be lying on the ground and because no

257

one had been there to pick them up, they would be going rotten. The kitchen would be dark and empty, or another family might be living there which would be almost worse; someone else might be lying in her bed, listening to the wind in the pine trees and the waves crashing on the beach and the little owl crying in the dark.

Chapter 30

London 2023

Julia

I leave James sitting in the Costa coffee shop in Terminal 5 at Heathrow, and walk outside, pulling my suitcase after me, rattling and bumping over the pavement. It has started to drizzle. I'd forgotten about rain. Paxos had been hot and dry but now my face is soaked as if I was crying, though I don't feel like crying. I feel numb.

I hail a taxi and ask him to take me to Paddington before I've had a chance to change my mind. I can't go to our Westminster house though I long to go home. Laurel might be there. I am going to Cornwall. I am tired of travelling, but at least I have somewhere to go, and as clearly as if she had been sitting beside me, I hear Lottie's voice, 'We are so fucking privileged, Mother. Do you even know that?'

Was that why Laurel had taken everything she could? She might have envied me the houses, the sexy-looking husband with his important job, my job, my clothes, and the large diamond ring. So much good fortune in one person's life must have seemed unfair. She might have desired those things at first and then plotted to steal them.

I'd trusted her completely. I'd believed she was on my side. I had revelled in that warmth like some needy child. How crazy, how stupid, how blind I'd been. The traffic is thick and the taxi crawls through the streets. I turn my phone off. I don't want James to contact me and what if Laurel should try?

When did it start? She'd been on my side when we first talked in the café, but a new thought hits me like a slap. It was possible, likely, that she had stalked me there. It would have been easy: my movements weren't complicated. She could have had the idea at the parents' evening and followed me after that. I'd seen her or thought I had, in the courtyard of the school, hidden among a group of teachers. Once I'd been enticed, she hadn't had to work very hard, the facts she needed poured from me in an unstoppable flow. I told her everything: the way my husband wanted me to look and behave, his favourite music, the books he read, and the scent he preferred. The sex he expected. She'd stored it all on that Dictaphone of hers, writing down times and dates in her little book, the better to retrieve what she needed. She would have replayed the important bits; she might have learnt them by heart. James would have been easy to seduce, but she had seduced me first.

I must have paid the taxi when we reached Paddington, bought a ticket, walked to the platform and climbed aboard, but I find myself in the train with no recall of getting there. The train, the last one to Penzance, is quiet which is lucky. I sit next to a window and put my coat on the seat next to me. I want to hear my thoughts.

I had followed her instructions to the letter when she told me to discard my diet, abandon my grooming, and stop having sex. I went to Paxos because she told me to. She'd only had a fortnight, but she got to work immediately; two weeks is a long time if you look like Laurel does and know precisely what to do. She would have listened to James and praised him while pouring his favourite drink. She would be groomed, sleek in the ways she'd advised me not to be, ready for the kind of sex she knew he wanted. I imagine her whispering his own fantasies into his ear. I pictured her slim body under his, on the table or the floor, against the mirror.

My eyes in the train window are dark. I look different, older. Defeated. I hardly know where I am. Time has stopped. It's impossible to believe I was in Paxos today, those sunlit weeks have disappeared as though they'd never been. What she has done as a therapist must be illegal, but she'd know I'd never sue. The publicity would be unbearable, especially for Lottie and what would be the point? She's beaten me already. Taunton and Exeter pass in a blur of rain. Totnes, Bodmin, Truro; more passengers get out than in. Eventually the train stops in Penzance. It's cold now and very dark, pouring with rain. I get a taxi after a wait in a queue with others hunched in their anoraks. I'm wet through, my jacket was meant for Greece not Cornwall in a downpour.

'The house is through Zennor,' I tell the taxi driver, a small man with grey stubble and a snake tattoo curling around his right ear. 'The furthest one on the left.'

'Holiday, is it?'

I don't reply and he studies me in the driving mirror, curiosity in his eyes. What is he seeing? A nameless woman with rain-soaked hair and unhappiness stamped on her face; he might have transported a few of us over the years, escapees from wrecked marriages looking for peace. I pay him off at the gate, and he drives away with a backward glance.

The house is long and low, an extended one-storey building that gropes its way across the garden in the dark. The key safe code is unchanged; when I enter and snap on the lights, the long white corridor springs at me, bright and exhausting. I peel off my jacket and avoid the mirrored wall facing the door. The luxurious kitchen at the end of the hall is as immaculate as always. A large American fridge-freezer hums in the corner, a huge stove with multiple hobs lines the opposite wall. James had it installed so it would be easy for me to cater for the groups of friends he likes to bring down here. Lit glass cupboards display the expensive glassware that we'd had for our wedding. There are several bottles of Scottish malt in the rack. I pour a generous measure into a tumbler. The cupboards are full but I'm not hungry. Ortiz tuna, black truffles, caviar, tins of foie gras. De Cecco pasta and jars of Genovese pesto. Harrods fruit cake. James had stocked up well; he was the last one here with Cosmo, a boys' weekend.

The whisky takes effect quickly. I lean against the doorway of our room staring at the bed with its white velvet cover and leather trim, the soft fur rug on the floor. All James's choices. Could he have brought her here already? They would look good together on the bed or even the rug, James's long physique and Laurel's slim body. I imagine the noises they would make. She would massage his back afterwards because she knew he liked that. She would bring him a glass of whisky with two clinking ice cubes, and he'd be thrilled by her insight, because she knew, somehow, that was exactly how he liked it.

I turn on my phone and it rings immediately. Lottie.

'Are you home yet? Was it lovely?'

Tears rise for the first time; she sounds so pleased to hear me. 'I'm back but not really at home.'

'Are you okay? Only you sound a bit weird.'

I don't mean to tell her, but it comes out or most of it. I don't mention Laurel by name or that she had been my therapist, I'm ashamed of how gullible I'd been. I always tell her not to believe what strangers say, yet I'd poured my heart out to someone I didn't know at all. I told her that James was having a fling, and it would probably be over soon.

'I knew he was a total shit, but I didn't expect that. Do you want me to come down?'

'You can't leave school,' I make myself say, though there's nothing I'd have liked more. 'I just need a few days to get my head together and make plans. How are you, sweetheart?'

'I've got tons of art coursework. Rasul's been great, he cooked me a brilliant meal a couple of nights ago. We chatted for ages. James was out, there was no sign of anyone else.'

'Can you let Rasul know where I am? Perhaps he could send on my post, I may be here for a while.'

I have no idea where I would stay when I return. The Westminster house is for the headmaster; his jilted wife would get short shrift. James will want to move Laurel in, though not quite yet. A headmaster with a live-in mistress wouldn't be the right image for the school. He'll do it by the book, a divorce and new marriage, if only to please the governors.

I pour myself more whisky to stop the thoughts and it works; it takes minutes to fall asleep on Lottie's bed.

The security lights switch on, waking me in the dead of night. My heart thumps as I stand at the front door, catching the bronze flare of a fox's tail disappearing into the trees. The lights switch off again, but I stare into the dark until my heart slows. The sea is crashing against the cliffs but there are no other sounds. Laurel, the Laurel I had trusted, might have told me there was no need for fear. I am disturbed by old memories that's all, the peopled past: my father, his cronies, Paul. Anthony, the little Greek girl most of all. Laurel would have listened carefully and maybe offered tea. Grief hovers as I stand in the cold darkness. She had belonged to me first; she was mine before she was James's. She came into my life like a guardian angel, and I'd loved her. But that's stupid. Wrong-headed. She wasn't mine: she hadn't loved me back. I was a means to an end, that's all. My Laurel didn't exist, she had never existed. I shut the door and lock it again. She had only held out a helping hand in order to reach the man standing behind me. She had invented her credentials for all I know, forged the documents she showed me, posted her own reviews. My head thuds. I find an old box of paracetamol in the kitchen cupboard behind a jar of truffles and swallow two with another glass of whisky. I curl up and drop back into sleep. If there are any more foxes prowling around the house, I am not disturbed again.

Chapter 31

Corfu 2003

Sofie

Sofie woke in the night, fear crackling in her head like a fire.

It was dark and hot. The door was shut. Her heart was hammering.

She wanted to scream but had to keep quiet in case she woke the boys, and they started all over again. She held her breath until she heard the noise of singing then the quieter noises of breathing. She wasn't in the shed. Her body slowly relaxed. Nico was in the bed next to her, the boys weren't here, Nico was. The singing came from a café in the street outside the flat. She was in Roxana and Dimitrios's flat in Corfu Town and Mama was in hospital. She tiptoed to the door. Roxana was in her bedroom with

Dimitrios, she could hear their voices and see the light under the bedroom door. She sat down outside their room, leaning her head against the door just as she had done outside Mama and Babas's room in Grandfather's flat. She only wanted to hear their voices, but the words were as clear as if she had been inside the room with them.

'. . . caused by stress.' Dimitrios's voice was quiet.

'Stress can't cause a disease like that, surely.' Roxana sounded upset, there were tears in her voice.

'Of course it can. It lowers your resistance. Things take hold.'

There was the sound of Roxana's footsteps as she moved about the room, a drawer was opened and shut again. She blew her nose.

'We'll know more in a few days.' Dimitrios sounded as if he was trying to be cheerful, but it was obvious there was nothing to be cheerful about.

Sofie got up quietly and went into the bathroom. She washed her hands several times with Roxana's pink soap, which stung more than ever. Then she went back into her room and got into bed.

It was all her fault. She had caused her mother's illness. If she hadn't made friends with the boys, if she'd managed to fight them off and run away, she wouldn't have been attacked. Athena wouldn't have been stressed; the illness wouldn't have taken hold. They would be at home now. Mother would be cooking at the stove, and, in the day time, they would be cleaning the house, room by room, washing the curtains and pegging them on the line, watching them billow like sails in the wind.

The door of her bedroom was pushed open, and she closed her eyes quickly. It was Dimitrios, she could smell his warm tobacco smell. She heard him sighing as he stood there then he walked back to his room. She would have to pretend she didn't know what they said, but that wouldn't be hard, she was pretending all the time anyway.

When she got up the next morning, Roxana was already bustling about her little kitchen, apron on, her dark hair held back with a flowery headband. Dimitrios was making coffee from a big machine the owner had given them from the café when he got a new one. Babas and Grandfather must still be asleep. Roxana gave her a kiss, she seemed cheerful, it was as if Sofie had imagined the conversation she'd heard in the night. The kitchen had a blue ceiling and yellow walls. There were green and red plates shaped like flowers displayed on the shelves, along with books and plants and photographs of both Roxana's and Dimitrios's families. One was of her, under the olive tree by the back door. The girl that she used to be was reading. She looked happy, but then she had no idea what was coming. Sofie looked away quickly, but there were so many things in the kitchen, and so many colours, that they jumbled up in her head, and she had to close her eyes.

Roxana pulled out a chair for her; there was only room for two to squeeze round the table which was the size of a tray.

'It's so nice for me to have another girl here.' Roxana handed Sofie a cup of coffee. Sofie didn't tell her she wasn't allowed to have coffee, Babas might not mind today.

'What time are we seeing Mama?'

'It turns out that we have to wait a while, she's still poorly.'

'What's wrong with her?'

'She has a swelling in her head.' Dimitrios sat next to Sofie, he spoke slowly as if he was taking great care with every word.

'What kind of swelling?'

'It's called a brain tumour.' He said, 'It's quite big. The doctors have to take it away.'

Nico came into the room. He stood close to Sofie. Roxana tried to lift him and put him in a chair, but he shook his head and put his thumb in his mouth. He never used to suck his thumb.

'How will they take it away?'

Dimitrios glanced at Roxana again, and she nodded.

'They will send her to sleep for a little while and then

they'll make a small opening in her head.' He traced a circle the size of an olive, maybe two olives, on the tablecloth. Sofie wished she hadn't asked; the thought of a hole being made in Mama's head made her feel sick.

'I want to see her.'

'We can't go today, *pedhaki mou*.'

The flowery plates swam against the yellow walls. 'You said we could.'

'I was wrong.' Dimitrios put his hand on Sofie's. 'She's been taken to a hospital in Athens for the operation; she'll come back after that. We'll see her in two weeks' time.'

For the next two weeks Sofie tried not to think. She tried to be good. She took Nico to school every day and brought him back. She painted a picture so she could show Athena when she returned from her operation. She painted the sun and the cliffs but most of her effort went into the blue of the sea; her mother used to look at the sea with a smile, as if the colour was a present just for her.

Dimitrios rang the ward several times and after two weeks and three days he was told Athena had come back. Sofie didn't sleep that night. The next day Babas said she and Nico had to go to school first, so Dimitrios collected them afterwards and took them to the hospital in the evening.

* * *

271

The hospital was the biggest building Sofie had ever seen. She whispered to Nico that it was like two big Lego bricks stuck together, and he smiled for the first time she could remember. It took a while to find Athena's ward; they went to two wrong ones first by mistake.

Babas was by the bed when they got there. He looked different, smaller, and his face was twisted up as if he was trying not to cry. If it hadn't been for him sitting there, Sofie wouldn't have known that it was Athena lying in the bed. She had a bandage that covered her head and half her face. The eye you could see was swollen shut and she had a bruise that reached to her mouth.

Sofie didn't want to look at her, but she had to. Athena's arms were on the outside of the sheet, and the tube that was going into one of them was attached to a plastic bag full of fluid hooked to a stand next to her bed. Her hands were thin, her fingers looked like a little collection of white sticks. Nico began crying and Roxana put her arm around him; the sound of his crying woke Athena. She opened the eye that was visible and said something, but it wasn't her usual voice, and the words didn't make sense. She turned her palm upwards and Sofie put her hand into her mother's hand; it was cold and smooth and felt as though it belonged to someone else. Nico didn't want to go any nearer, so Roxana talked to him very softly. Mama was smiling but a tear trickled down her cheek. They were only there for about ten minutes then the nurse came and said they had to go. Sofie asked if she might stay, she said her mother wanted her to; she knew that she was the rope that would pull her mother safely into shore and that she mustn't let go of her hand. The nurse said she could come back the next day and maybe stay for longer. When they got back in the car, she realized she was still holding the picture of the beach that she had painted for Athena.

'Give it to her tomorrow,' Roxana told her.

But there wasn't a tomorrow for Athena. She died in the night.

A week later, Babas died too. The doctor said he'd had a heart attack. He died at night as well.

Roxana found him. He wasn't in the kitchen first thing as usual. Babas had always been the first to get up: after years of fishing at dawn it was hard for him to change. Roxana had waited for him to appear; when he didn't, she had taken in his morning tea. Sofie was in the bathroom washing her hands when she heard the cup drop.

Even though she saw Babas's face, which was completely still, even though his eyes were empty, she couldn't believe it. She put her hand on Babas's but it was very cold and she took hers away quickly. She knew he was dead then. She wondered if he had known in the last minutes of his life that he was dying, and whether he had been able to keep himself going steadily on towards the end, just as he had done in the storm.

The bodies of Mama and Babas were put into caskets first of all, side by side, in the church, their feet pointing towards the east. The tops of the coffins were left off in case anyone wanted to see them, but Sofie didn't. What if Athena's bloodstained bandage was still in place, what if it wasn't?

On the day of the funeral none of their old neighbours and friends showed up. Sofie didn't know if they knew, besides it was too far away. Kolena might have wanted to come but she wouldn't have had the money for the boat. It was just Christos and Dimitrios and Roxana, Nico and her and the priest. Mama and Babas were buried in the cemetery outside town. It was a windy day, and the wind made a crying noise as it blew through the trees around the gravestones, but Sofie knew it wasn't the wind; it was the sound of her mother calling to her, adrift in the storm because Sofie hadn't been there to pull her into the shore.

Chapter 32

Cornwall 2023

Julia

The wind howls around the house and down the chimneys, waking me in the early dawn. Through the windows, white shreds of fog cling about the higher ground. The heather is black in the rain, bare trees crouch low over the humped granite.

The house is dark, the rooms shadowy. I try one light after another but none of them work. The power lines must be down. I feel completely alone. Father chose the house for its isolation at the end of the track; he disliked prying eyes though he brought his acolytes here. I never came then but I brought Lottie later. I haven't been here on my own before. This is the kind of house that works best with family about; on a dark morning in November with no lights it feels threatening.

There are spare anoraks hanging in the lobby and a pair of Lottie's boots. I need to be outside in the raw morning to clear my head. Rain blisters my cheeks. The grey sky and heaving sea echo my mood. The double betrayal fills my mind, I changed my life for James. I stood by his side for years, played host to his friends, worked and cooked for him, dressed in the clothes he chose, had sex I didn't want. No more. Gulls scream. Waves crash against the cliffs; their icy spray reaches me. There is salt on my lips. They used to rub salt into the wounds of victims, but I don't have to be a victim. I'm done with that. Anguish and disbelief are giving way to elation. The wind tugs my hair, and the truth comes at me fiercely. James's affair has cut me loose.

Rain soaks through the old anorak but I don't care. My mind fills with the sounds and colours of the storm. There's no room for pretence. The truth is, I'm glad. I don't love him any more. I'm not sure I ever did. I tried. I was going to try again but now I don't have to. Hundreds of feet below the cliff, the sea swirls and seethes. Birds swoop above me. I have been in a cage, but the door has swung open. Laurel betrayed me but she's given me my freedom. Did she know what she was doing?

I walk on for miles, my thoughts whirling, trying to make sense of what happened, of Laurel. The future has been torn open, revealing a great space in front of me, the choices are dizzying. The storm buffets me almost to the ground. The light changes. It could be dangerous to be by myself on these cliffs as the day wears on. I turn for home, clambering over boulders and stiff bushes of heather until the house comes into view again. From a distance it crouches like an animal in its lair, the surrounding trees look like predators prowling along the boundaries.

Back inside, the lights still don't work. I discard my sodden anorak and kick off the boots, light candles and make a fire in the sitting room from the vast pile of logs stacked in the hearth. My thoughts crackle and flare with the flames. I will leave my marriage. James's infatuation may not last, but I won't wait to see. He has squandered my trust. There will be a battle, he'll want this house; he feels he owns it already. When friends visit, he walks about showing off the view and the way the garden fits the landscape, the blue hydrangeas planted by my mother but I have power of attorney over her estate. I'll need to sell to provide for Lottie. She'll have to change schools.

I feed the fire with more logs and sit close, the heat fuelling my thoughts. James took my career and my identity, but I can get both back. I feel stronger already. Laurel stole my husband, but I don't want him any more, and it's hard to believe that she does. Did she need money so badly she was prepared to take him on, despite knowing his faults?

Was it about companionship? Sex? The flames leap high as the questions burn unanswered. The dry wood snaps so loudly that I don't hear the footsteps. By the time I sense there is someone in the room, and hear breathing behind me, it's too late for escape.

Chapter 33

Corfu 2003

Sofie

Mama was dead.

Babas was dead.

The words played again and again like drumsticks on the skin of Sofie's mind, but they didn't make sense. Everything had happened so quickly, though even that wasn't true.

'The tumour had been there for a while,' Roxana said. They were in the kitchen after the funeral. Roxana had made her hot chocolate and was sitting at the table with her, her warm hand over hers. Nico was next to her. She spoke softly. 'You remember Athena had those headaches?'

Sofie nodded.

'And the fits?'

She nodded again.

'That was the tumour growing; the doctor said it might have been there for a long time.'

'But she went to see the doctor for her headaches. Babas took her, they could have done something then.'

'The doctor organized tests but she didn't go for them,' Dimitrios said. He was leaning against the door looking serious. He had the sort of face that was meant for smiling, but it had been a long time since she had seen him smile.

Mama didn't look after herself because of what happened to me, Sofie thought. She was worried about me, so she didn't think about her own health, she never did and now she's gone for ever. It was impossible to imagine that. How would she and Nico manage without her tomorrow or the day after that, or for the rest of their lives?

'Babas didn't take his tablets for blood pressure either,' Dimitrios said. 'That might be why he had a heart attack. People make their own choices.' He looked at her and tried to smile. 'It's no one's fault.'

That was wrong, it was her fault. Babas had died of a broken heart after Athena died, which wouldn't have happened if she hadn't talked to those boys in the first place and caused all the stress. Dimitrios said stress lowered your resistance and that was why the cancer took hold. What she had done had destroyed their old life like some ravenous beast and then, still hungry, it had taken Athena and Babas too. The black tar-like lump inside her head grew darker and larger than ever, until there was almost no space left.

Grandfather went back to his own flat; he preferred it that way, Roxana said. He was used to it. Sofie saw him on Sundays. She lay down in her old room or sat in the kitchen with him. She liked the quietness and the fact that she didn't have to say anything. Sometimes she slept all day when she was there: she was always tired. It was noisy at night in Roxana and Dimitrios's flat because of the restaurant below; they had to keep the windows closed and then it was too hot. Every morning before it was light, the rush of bottles being tipped into a truck woke her with a clatter.

Some nights Nico would slip into bed beside her in the night and she didn't mind. She liked the warmth from his body, the feel of him pressing up against her back. She never sent him away. He still didn't say anything, but she felt closer to him than to anyone else and she knew he felt the same.

Roxana told Sofie she needn't go back to school until she felt better, but Sofie knew she would never feel better, so she said she would go. Roxana hugged her and told her she was brave, but she wasn't brave. School was just a line like the lengths of string Dimitrios had tied between sticks as a guide for planting seeds in a straight row. She knew where she was if she kept to the line.

There were more things to bury now, like the way Mama had sounded in the hospital when she tried to speak and the different feel of her hand. Babas's twisted face as he sat by her side. The coffins in the church.

She worked all the time she was awake, so she didn't have to think. She had heard Babas say to Athena that no good came of looking back so she tried not to; instead she read and wrote and went to the language club on Wednesdays after school. She helped Roxana and Dimitrios in the café on Saturdays and visited Grandfather on Sundays and she didn't think about anything. Life continued in the same way until one Wednesday in early December.

School closed early on Wednesdays. Nico was collected by Dimitrios; they were taking a football to the beach with some other boys. The teachers were worried about his silence and Dimitrios thought a team game might help. Sofie went home. She didn't want to go to the beach or look at the sea.

She had to wait in the café, but she didn't mind, there was homework to do. She sat just inside the entrance and pulled out her books. A few boys were drinking at a table further in, two girls sat chatting together at a table beyond that. The noise melted into the background. She began to read a story in English for the language club the next day. She could hear plates clashing in the kitchen and the sounds were comforting somehow.

A loud male laugh and a sharp scream jerked her head up. She hadn't meant to look but it was as though she was a puppet, and someone was pulling the strings. The scream had come from one of the girls. Two boys from the group on the table next to them had got up and were standing either side of her. One of them was bending low over the girl and had put his hands on her shoulders. His face was close to hers. The other boys were laughing. The girl's friend was sitting very still in her chair as if frightened that if she made a fuss, the boys would come to her too.

Sofie stood up so quickly that her chair fell over backwards and hit the floor. The noise alerted Roxana who came out from the kitchen; she saw the boys and strode over to help the girl. Sofie didn't wait to see what happened. She left her books on the table and ran upstairs to the flat. The door had been left open because Nico and Dimitrios had just returned and were inside, taking off their coats. She yelled at them both for not having shut the door, anyone might have come in, she shouted. That night she didn't want supper, she pushed her plate away. Later, Nico was making a noise under his breath as he walked his Lego man over the sheet. She got out of bed, snatched it up, opened the window and threw it out. Nico began to cry but she ignored him. She washed her hands and didn't stop even though they were bleeding. She refused go to school the next day and the next and she didn't eat anything. Roxana tried to talk to her, but it was difficult to hear anything, the monsters were roaring.

The day after that Roxana had a day off, it was the weekend. She said they were going for a bus ride out of town to visit the mother of her friend, who lived in a village. Sofie looked up, it was the word *mother*.

'She has had six children and she's very kind,' Roxana said. 'She has a garden and a cat. You need space of your own, *pedimou*, time away from all of us for a few hours.'

Sofie didn't believe the woman had a cat, it was probably something Roxana was saying to make her go. She didn't care about space or time either, there was too much time already. The problem wasn't Roxana or Dimitrios or Nico, but she hadn't the energy to explain. She was too tired to explain anything. She didn't care. She already knew the woman wouldn't be able to help. How could she? She couldn't wind the clock back, stop Sofie going to the beach with the cake or make her mother go to the doctor earlier or tell her father to take his pills, but she didn't have the energy to say any of that, so she nodded.

She wanted Nico to come to the woman's house too, but he had football practice. He hadn't said anything about the Lego man but then he wasn't saying anything anyway. Roxana said she needn't feel bad about it, but she didn't feel bad, just empty. Roxana told her that someone at school, a counsellor, had been talking to Nico since they arrived. Sofie thought that was pointless, it didn't seem to make any difference, if anything he was quieter, but Roxana said that he was getting better bit by bit.

There was no one else waiting by the bus stop next morning, and when it came there was only one woman with her bag of shopping at the back, which was a relief. When they were sitting down, Roxana offered her an apple, but Sofie shook her head. Roxana opened a book and began reading. She was the one who needed time, not her. Roxana hardly had any for herself, like Mama, and Sofie felt a stab of worry, what if something happened to her too?

The bus was driving along the sea front, so she closed her eyes. It was warm, the seats were comfortable, and the driver drove very carefully, even the noise the engine made was soothing. Without meaning to, Sofie went to sleep, waking when the bus turned a sharp corner. Outside the windows were olive trees, rows and rows of them, stretching back either side from the road as far as you could see. Sofie stared. It was like being given a glass of cool water when you were thirsty. She hadn't realized she was so thirsty for olive trees.

285

The bus lurched into a village with stone houses and orange roof tiles and front gardens. It came to a halt by the side of the road. Roxana got out of the bus, smiling goodbye to the driver. How did you do that, Sofie wondered, smile and say something friendly to a stranger? People managed that all the time, they must be stronger than she was or much cleverer.

They walked down a lane with houses strung out either side and cypress trees sticking up over white walls. They stopped outside a small house; there was a wall around it too and a bell with a twisty rope which Roxana asked her to pull.

The clanging noise echoed down the street. She must have pulled too hard, other people might come out to see what was happening. She shrank back against Roxana but then the gate was opened, and a tiny woman stood there, with grey hair piled on her head and strands which had come loose around her face. She had an apron with roses on it, like Athena's, though the roses on Athena's apron had been red and these were blue. She was smaller than Sofie, so despite her wrinkled face, she seemed a bit like a child herself.

She held out her hand to Sofie first. It was warm, and the skin was rough, so Sofie knew she had looked after a family, cooked their food and scrubbed the floors. She didn't smile back but she felt her mouth relax just a little.

'Hello Sofie,' the woman said, still holding her hand. 'My name is Eleni.'

Her voice wasn't trying to be anything special; it wasn't being careful or quiet and it wasn't as if she was talking to a child. Eleni turned to Roxana and said how lovely it was to see her again. Roxana chatted for a bit, then she touched Sofie lightly on her shoulder. 'I'll be back later,' and then she disappeared.

Eleni was waiting but Sofie wanted to turn around and run after Roxana. She was very frightened, everything that was familiar had vanished.

Chapter 34

Cornwall 2023

Julia

There is a dark shadow inside the door. My mouth dries. I had been stupid to not have locked the front door behind me in this lonely place. I'm alone with an intruder and there are miles and miles of empty moorland around the house. Nobody will hear if I call for help.

'Who are you?' I grab the poker, my heart beating so hard I feel sick. 'What the fuck are you doing?'

The shadow moves, and I bring my arm back ready to lash out with as much force as I can. A figure steps forward into the firelight.

Rasul.

'What the fuck?' I want to hit him, scream at him

for terrifying me. I drop the poker and make myself stand very still, but I can't control the trembling. Had James been right about Rasul all along? About the watchfulness, the sense that he was waiting for something, that he was just biding his time?

'I'm sorry.' He is trembling too. 'I rang the bell, but no one came.'

'There's been a power cut, the bell's not working.' A new fear catches me. 'Is it Lottie?'

'No. She's fine. This is not to do with her. Absolutely not.'

My heart slows a little. 'Why didn't you tell me you were coming?'

'I tried many times, but your phone was turned off yesterday, and today you didn't pick up.'

'How did you know where I was?'

'You asked Lottie to give me the address for the post. I walked from the station. I thought it was nearer.'

He looks exhausted, his shoulders are bent, his clothes are dripping on the floor.

'Sit down.'

He half tumbles into his seat, and his rucksack drops by his feet.

'Have you had anything to eat?'

He shakes his head. 'I didn't see any shops.'

I leave him sitting by the fire while I make strong coffee. I spread crackers with the caviar and take the plate to him with three thick slices of fruit cake. The food seems to melt into him. He drains the coffee then sits up.

'Lottie's fine, truly. She called round when you were away; your husband was out, and we talked for a long time. I think she's been missing you; she shared a lot of stuff. She rang me yesterday, and said she was pleased you'd left your husband.'

'What were her words exactly?'

'She said "finally".'

I smile, I can't help it, that was pure Lottie. She must feel she can trust Rasul, and I begin to relax though I'm still wary.

'Why are you here?'

'I wanted to see if you were all right; you've been so kind to me.'

The tables are turned, is that what he means? That I am the refugee, the one who has lost the trappings of my life? But I've been escaping a marriage not a war, running from one house to another, it's not the same. Rasul's dark eyes are watching me, as if waiting. There's something else he's keeping back.

'Thank you but tell me why you've really come.'

He doesn't reply but picks up his rucksack and, delving inside, draws out a small machine, a familiar object that looks like a phone; it's black and shiny with a thin band of red around the edge. He puts it on the coffee table between us.

I feel sick, more deeply betrayed if that was possible. I can hardly get the words out. 'It looks exactly like the Dictaphone my therapist used. Has she been sharing my sessions with James?'

Rasul shakes his head. 'It's not that at all. It's something worse.'

Chapter 35

Corfu 2003

Sofie

Eleni led the way into her house. Sofie followed, there was nothing else she could do. The house was quiet. There was the smell of freshly made bread and Sofie felt her shoulders relax. A house which smelt like this must be all right. Eleni took her into a room that was pink or maybe orange, the walls glowed as if a light had been switched on. There were paintings everywhere, beautiful paintings of flowers and cats and birds. The shelves were covered with photographs of weddings, children, and babies. There were stripey mats on the floor and shells on the mantelpiece, a little table with a vase of yellow flowers among tubes of paint and brushes. An easel with paper on it. The windows were open, and she could hear wind chimes.

There was a cat on a chair. Roxana had been right after all, a little tabby cat asleep in a shaft of sun.

Eleni made her a cup of tea and put it on the table. She lifted the cat off the chair and when Sofie sat down, she put him on her lap. He began purring; he sounded just like Aries used to.

After a while Sofie began to cry, and Eleni gave her a hanky made of linen and smelling of lavender, it had a blue border and a little 'e' on it. When the crying had stopped, Eleni put Bouzouki music on the record player. It was like Grandfather's record player, with a turntable and a sharp little needle. Sofie sipped her tea. The music seemed to fill all the spaces inside her. When the record had come to an end, Eleni smiled and got up.

'Shall we let Theron into the garden?'

Sofie carried the little cat as she followed Eleni through her kitchen to the back door. She passed strings of garlic hanging up and basil in pots on the windowsill, an embroidered cloth on the table and a yellow cake under a stiff netting cover. There were slippers by the back door, they were dark inside and the backs were trodden down. They were so like Athena's Sofie wanted to pick them up too. The back door was stiff, and she helped Eleni tug it open. The garden was full of birds, more than in the city and more than there had been in Paxos. They were in the trees and on the wall and pecking the grass.

There were birdfeeders hanging everywhere. When Sofie put Theron on the ground he crouched low, and she felt her heart clutch with fear.

'Don't worry,' Eleni said. 'He has a bell around his neck. They know when he's nearby. Come and look at the garden.'

They walked along the paths. There were bare beds either side, with nothing to see but brown crumbly soil even though she looked closely.

'There are plenty of plants deep down,' Eleni told her. 'They will come up when it's warm enough. There will be hyacinths, cyclamen, and irises. It will be time to do more planting soon; you can help me next time, if you'd like to. My bones are getting old.'

When she got back home, Sofie took out her books and began doing some sums. Roxana took her back to Eleni's house the next week while Nico stayed with Dimitrios who was going to let him help out in the restaurant kitchen. Sofie could tell Nico was pleased; he began to hum very quietly.

Eleni made tea again, and they listened to folk songs. When they went into the garden, Eleni gave her a wooden basket filled with round bulbs that looked like onions. She handed a trowel to Sofie. 'You can make little holes in the earth if you like.'

Sofie looked at her hands. She didn't want to get them dirty because she would have to wash them, and Eleni might not have enough soap to get them clean. She could feel the sweat collecting at the back of her neck.

'On second thoughts, it might be more helpful if you just threw the bulbs on the grass for me.' Eleni said. 'I'll dig them in wherever they fall. That way it looks natural when they grow into flowers.'

So Sofie threw handfuls of bulbs on the lawn, and Eleni made little holes where they landed and dropped the bulbs in and then covered them over. Afterwards, Sofie only had to wash her hands twice. That night she sat in the kitchen with Dimitrios, looking at books about olive trees that he'd borrowed from the library. He was planning to buy a couple to put in pots for outside the restaurant. They chose the same kind that had grown in Paxos.

Sofie went back to school and to Eleni's every week after that. Roxana didn't ask her for details about the visits, which was lucky because she wouldn't have been able to tell her. Nothing much seemed to happen each time but when she was there, it felt like everything was happening.

In January there was a rainy spell, and they couldn't go into the garden.

'Well now,' Eleni said. They were in the sitting room, and she had lit a fire which was crackling. Theron was on Sofie's lap. 'I think I'm going to do some painting today.' She was wearing her flowery apron and there was a smaller one for Sofie. She had put some paper on the easel; it was rough to touch, like Eleni's skin. Like Athena's had been.

'You could look at the paintings on the wall if you like, and see if any of them give you an idea.'

Sofie walked around the room and stopped in front of a picture of the sea, the sea on a stormy day. The kind of day when they would worry if Babas took the boat out. There was a small red dot on the sea which was probably a boat. The sky in the picture was black and thick with clouds. Sofie's throat tightened.

'Some things don't fit into words or even pictures,' Eleni said. She had tied her long grey hair back with a bright red scarf. 'Sometimes colours are enough.' She scattered some tubes of paint on a plate and put it on the table between them, with two little saucers and a pot of water.

Sofie chose the tube of black paint and squeezed a thick black worm of it onto her saucer, dipping her brush into it and then painting a line on the page, then a bigger, thicker sweep. Eleni was right, there were no words that fitted what she was trying to express but something was happening. The sweep of black over the paper was like night closing in, the kind of dark in a shed at night, dark that could stay in your mind, week after week. She painted more layers until the black was thick and it was as though she was taking some of the darkness out of her head and putting it down on the paper instead. When it was time to go, Eleni covered her picture up very carefully with a towel.

The sun felt warmer as the weeks passed. It might have been the bowl of yellow daisies that Eleni placed on the table, or the colour of the sunshine itself which made Sofie paint thin lines of yellow in between the slabs of black; when she saw them on the paper it reminded her of lightning piercing the darkness.

At the end of that day, Eleni put a slice of warm ginger cake in a saucer and made a cup of mint tea, and they sat on the step outside the back door in the garden with the sun on their faces.

'Look,' Eleni said, pointing to where shoots had begun to appear, small green daggers under the trees. 'Our bulbs.'

As the year turned into spring, Sofie was back at school, she needed new shoes which Roxana said was a sign that she was growing. Each week more flowers appeared in Eleni's garden, the ground turning blue and yellow and red. Eleni bought her a pair of gloves so she could help put the tomatoes into the ground. Sofie knelt to tie the stems to the sticks with the twine that Eleni had given her, but when she got up there were dark marks on the knees of her trousers. Clouds rolled into her mind, black clouds. She was dirty, careless. Stupid.

Eleni leant over and brushed the mud from the trousers. 'It's not really your fault if you get dirty, *pedimou*.' And she smiled.

Her words arrowed into Sofie's mind like the thin lines of lightning she'd painted.

They flashed over and over again the next day as she walked to school with Nico.

'It's not really your fault if you get dirty.'

'It's not really your fault.'

'It's not your fault.'

The hard black stuff in her head began to shrink and soften; it didn't disappear but now there was room for something else. Something that was pushing through the darkness like the shoots in the soil, something she could look after like Eleni looked after her plants and feed so that it would grow strong. It wasn't pretty like the flowers; it didn't smell nice like them or taste good like tomatoes. It was simpler than that.

It was anger.

Chapter 36

Cornwall 2023

Julia

'How did you get hold of it?' The Dictaphone held my most private thoughts, what the hell has Laurel been up to?

'It was on James's desk,' Rasul said. 'She's been using his study for work. I saw it when I was cleaning. When I heard Laurel asking James about Cosmo, I grabbed it quickly. I wanted to record every word.'

'How did you know what he'd say?'

'I didn't know but I guessed. I'd heard James warning Cosmo to be careful earlier that evening, I knew it would be on his mind.'

'Careful?'

'Not to get caught. It was said as a joke, but Lottie told me what happened to her friend at Cosmo's hands and that he'd avoided being caught. It wasn't a joke to me and it put me on my guard.'

Lottie had told him about Angel then, just the sort of thing my impetuous daughter would do. I imagined her blue eyes flashing with fury as her words spilt out. I hoped Angel wouldn't mind.

'I know all about abuse,' Rasul continues quietly. 'Refugees make easy targets. I've seen what it does.' His face is dark. 'It wasn't hard to put the Dictaphone behind the bottles on a tray of drinks, then hide it on the mantelpiece when I put more logs on the fire.'

'Didn't they see what you were doing?'

'They barely looked up.'

'What if Laurel goes back to the desk and sees it's not there?'

'She's gone to London about her divorce. She told James she'd be back in three days. I'll replace it before then.'

Laurel is moving closer to James, inch by clever inch. She's planned carefully, her reward won't be long in coming now.

Rasul picks up the machine and presses play.

'*Whisky?*'

James's voice is solicitous, tender. It makes my skin crawl.

'*Thank you, honey.*' That familiar warmth. Laurel could be speaking to me, my throat constricts.

Glasses clink together.

'Go on then, I'm curious. I honestly can't imagine why you give him so much time.' She sounds amused.

'Why shouldn't I? He's a mate.' I can almost see James's shrugging.

'But you're good-looking and charming whereas Cosmo . . . ' Her voice trails off, you can tell she's smiling. 'It doesn't make sense.'

'We go back a long way.' James is smiling too, after all she's just complimented him. 'I need to keep him happy.'

'You mean you're under some sort of obligation?' The question is delivered with a disbelieving little laugh.

'Too right.' He sounds less pleased now; he could be frowning, dark brows angling down on that handsome face.

'Though he's obliged to you too, surely? He gets a fantastic boss and a regular income. What's not to like?'

Ah, she is cleverer than I was, she is weaving in flattery. James is susceptible to compliments, most men are. He laughs for a beat too long. He must have been drinking. Laurel laughs too. I know that laugh, I used to be the one laughing with her. I know exactly what it means as well, she is encouraging him to open up.

'Cosmo's one of the wealthiest artists I know,' James says. 'He's not in it for money.'

'Then he must be a natural teacher.'

'It's more than that. He needs my protection, I need his.' He hiccups.

303

'*I'm intrigued.*' I imagine her moving closer, wide-eyed. '*Do tell.*'

'*Can I trust you never to share this with anyone?*' He is at that watershed moment between sobriety and drunkenness, losing caution, pushed by lust.

'*I'm a therapist, remember? I'm trained to keep secrets. Of course you can trust me.*'

She sounds convincing, she convinced me once, but I have to swallow my anguish and concentrate on what's being said. There's a pause then James's voice again, but this time he sounds angry.

'*You know what? I'm bloody going to. I'm sick and tired of that man lording it over me. He's so fucking arrogant when he should be grateful.*'

The fury is sudden and the voice slightly slurred. James's guard is slipping. He wouldn't swear like this unless he was drunk. '*But you mustn't tell a soul, I could lose my job.*'

'*I give you my word.*'

'*He messed up big time; his job restores his reputation. It gives him credibility.*'

'*Messed up?*'

'*Didn't you read about the trouble he was in a year ago? It was splashed across all the papers.*'

'*I didn't pay it much attention. Those rumours disappeared, didn't they?*'

'*The trouble is, they weren't rumours.*'

'*You mean the things he was accused of were true?*'

304

She sounds interested rather than shocked, and I begin to feel sick.

'*Is this what you do in your sessions?*' James sounds quite drunk now. '*Gradually extract the truth from your clients?*'

'*Admit it feels good to share.*'

His laugh is slower, lazier, his pre-sex laugh. I wonder if she can tell.

'*You were saying? About Cosmo and that girl?*' She sounds interested and seductive at the same time.

'*Cosmo misbehaves, he always has. He can't help himself. He's not the first artist to be seduced by underage girls, remember Gaugin? Eric Gill and Roman Polanski? I turn a blind eye. I have to.*'

Misbehaves? It's still going on and James is covering for him?

'*What happened, exactly?*' She could be asking about a shopping expedition.

'*He went too far.*'

'*You mean he raped her?*' She is nailing him down but why? There is something here, something I'm not seeing. She is playing a game with my drunk husband; does she want power over him in the future? Perhaps she is simply drawn to darkness as so many people are, wanting detail.

'*Technically. I suspect she led him on, the age differ-ence and his position made him vulnerable.*'

'*So you felt you had to protect him?*'

There is a silence, I imagine James nodding.

'*That's very loyal of you,*' Laurel says warmly. '*It's hard to believe you put yourself in so much jeopardy for him.*'

A kiss, a long one.

'*I can't refuse, and he knows that. He's got stuff on me.*' James is breathing heavily now.

'*Stuff?*' Her voice is amused again. '*What kind of stuff?*'

'*I think that's enough for now.*' He's drunk but not that drunk.

The sound of more kissing, of fabric shifting and sliding then a little struggle.

'*No.*' A sharper note. '*If you can't trust me, then frankly, James, I can't trust you. Obviously I can't be with someone I don't trust. I'd better leave.*'

As if on cue, Rasul comes back into the room and stops the machine. Outside the darkness presses close. There are no stars and no moon. The rain hurls against the windows, the storm has picked up.

So Cosmo was guilty of rape and James knew it all along. Angel's face in the paper had been very blank, the face of a victim without justice. Her father had known the truth, he had raged helplessly. There had been a cover up, led by my husband. James had lied to protect his friend and by default, in ignorance and because I believed James, I had too.

What else am I about to find out?

Chapter 37

Cornwall 2023

Julia

'Supper's ready.'

'I have to listen to the rest of this.'

'Eat first, then listen.'

I follow him into the kitchen, this new, authoritative Rasul.

'It's hard to believe what I've just heard.' I don't want to believe it, either of Cosmo or James. I have always despised Cosmo, but I'd never have believed him capable of rape or James of covering for him. 'How has Angel managed to survive what happened?'

'The same way as other victims do, I expect, mostly not well. Girls are changed, destroyed, sometimes hardened. Justice would make a difference, though it's tricky to get.'

He glances at the window. The rain at the glass and the sound of the waves would recall his own memories of horror. His eyes are blank as if somewhere along the journey he lost something, and I recognize that, because so have I. My father took my innocence. He colluded in abuse just as James has done. It's strange that this ugly word should only come to me now, in a Cornish kitchen, twenty years too late. My abuse wasn't like Angel's, but I was fifteen when it started and that's exactly what it was. It's too late for my justice but not too late for Angel's or the other girls'. We have evidence now.

Rasul puts a plate in front of me, a silky tangle of pasta and pesto, so delicious that I eat in spite of myself.

'You have enough to get the police involved, Rasul.'

'There is more than that, worse.' His face is very dark.

'Worse than the rape of a fifteen-year-old?'

'The rape of a thirteen-year-old.'

'What the hell are you saying?'

He pours me coffee then adds a slug of James's whisky. 'You'll need it.' He doesn't smile.

I swallow the coffee, registering the hit of alcohol, then follow him back into the sitting room. He presses play again and James's voice comes into the room, a different, pleading tone.

'Please don't go. I'll tell you whatever you want, whatever it takes.'

I've never heard James beg before, not like this. It makes me shudder. There are light footsteps, getting louder. Laurel is walking away from him towards the fireplace, little dreaming her own Dictaphone is recording every word.

'Trust me with the truth, that's all I want.' There are tears in her voice, they would be glistening on her lashes. She would be looking at him across the room, her hair about her shoulders, her eyelids painted in shades of plum and chocolate, her lips gleaming. She wouldn't look like a therapist now, this wasn't about therapy, this was about sex.

'Don't cry.' James was always a sucker for tears. His voice is louder: he must have joined her by the fire. *'Of course I trust you.'*

'Show me.'

There is a short pause. James will be weighing this up but not for long. He's always been a risk taker; add in alcohol, desire and those tears, he'll be unable to resist.

'You have to promise this will never, ever come out. I could lose everything.'

'I promise.' Her tears are drying already. I can hardly hear them now.

'And you must remember it was years ago. We were a couple of lads miles from home, obsessed by sex like all young boys. We were also pissed.'

'I understand.'

'*Some of the details are hazy but Cosmo remembers everything.*'

'*And that's a problem?*'

'*He kept evidence.*'

'*Evidence?*' That light tone probably feels as if she's stroking him.

'*He took photos on his phone of me with this girl, though he promised he'd destroy them. The family threatened trouble.*'

'*Wait.*' A little laugh. '*What family?*'

'*The girl's, of course.*'

'*So, she was the daughter of a family who were guests along with you?*'

'*Lord no, of course not. I'm talking about the caretaker's family, it was their daughter.*'

'*I see.*' Her tone is cooler. She must be shocked, but James won't have noticed. He won't stop now; having hidden the truth for so long, this is probably a relief. '*Maybe you can retrieve the photos.*' Her voice is serious, she is trying to help.

'*Impossible. They're on the hard drive of Cosmo's private laptop, locked in a cupboard to which he has the only key. As he lets me know, if ever he thinks I'm going to put a stop to his activities.*'

'*Ah, that could be a problem.*'

'*I told you he was clever.*'

'*So where exactly were you back then, all those miles from home?*' Her voice is less serious, a little teasing.

'Abroad, somewhere hot.'

Odd. James maintains he never went abroad until he left home. He hates the heat as much as his parents did, or at least that's always been his story. I was never able to talk to them; they died before we got together.

'Go on.'

'A school friend's father was mates with this rich guy who invited him to his holiday place every year. My friend got dragged along, so he asked if he could bring a couple of pals. I and Cosmo were chosen. On the night in question, we were on our own. It was my sixteenth birthday as a matter of fact.'

My heart begins to beat very fast. There is something horribly familiar about this story.

'What happened?'

'We fooled around with the girl, we thought she was up for it.'

'Up for what?'

'Well, sex obviously.'

'How old was she?' Laurel's voice is gossamer light. *'Exactly?'*

'Thirteen as it turned out. I thought she was older. We taught her swimming; she clearly fancied me. That night we got her drunk. She gave Cosmo a blow job.' He sounds very drunk now, he belches. *'Well, to be honest he forced her. Then . . . '* He stops.

'Then?'

311

'It was my turn.'

'You forced her into oral sex?'

'Anal.'

'So you raped her?'

'I was half out of my mind with alcohol. It was Cosmo's fault. He encouraged me. I had no idea he was taking photos.'

I can't imagine Laurel's face. I can't imagine anything now. I want to turn off the tape. This is worse than anything I could have possibly imagined. James is a rapist, a criminal. No wonder he's subservient to Cosmo, those photos could bring his whole life crashing down.

'What happened then?' Laurel's tone is gently enquiring, but how can she talk to him now? Stay in the same room?

'We were in this shed on the beach. It was night. We were drunk and must have passed out. We woke feeling dire. The girl had managed to get out of the shed and was asleep on the ground. We left her clothes next to her, locked the door behind us, and scarpered.'

'Then what?'

'We got into trouble from her idiot cousins.'

'What kind of trouble?'

'The medieval kind. We needed stitches.'

'And the girl?' Laurel's voice is so soft I can hardly hear her.

'God knows. I'm sure she was fine, tough as old

312

hide, those people. The family left the island later that day; bloody inconvenient for our hosts.'

'What island?'

'Paxos, if you really want to know.'

Rasul is staring at me, he stops the machine, his forehead is wrinkled, his eyes deeply concerned. 'Are you okay?'

I'm staring back, though I'm not seeing Rasul. I'm not even here. I'm back in that decrepit shed behind the beach, the decay and the darkness, the smell of rot and the sound of rats, twenty years too late.

'James and Cosmo were guests at our holiday home, Rasul.' I tell him when I can find my voice. 'This happened on our watch though I'd left the evening before. I was actually told about this a couple of days ago by the policemen who were called to the house the next day but I had no idea who the boys were.'

James must have deceived me from the moment we met or at least, the moment I thought we'd met. No wonder he refused to go to Paxos, he hadn't wanted me to go either. He would have been terrified I'd find out what happened.

'He's about to mention you.' Rasul looks grim. 'Do you want to hear?'

I nod, though I don't. I want to go back. I want to go back to that summer in Paxos. I want the chance

313

to warn that child. I want to put my husband in jail.

Rasul presses play.

'*This obviously goes nowhere.*' James sounds worried. '*Julia could make trouble.*'

'*Julia?*'

'*The place belonged to her father as it happens. We crossed over that summer; an arrogant bitch if ever there was one. She never glanced at me once.*' The fury in his voice surprises me; he must have held on to it for years. '*We met each other years later. I recognized her, she had no idea she'd seen me before.*'

'*How is that possible?*'

Laurel sounds disbelieving, but I could tell her that a half drugged nineteen-year-old with an older lover wouldn't notice a schoolboy. He would have been invisible. The truth is, I don't remember looking at him at all.

'*Thirteen years went by before we met again. I'd transformed myself.*' He sounds triumphant. '*I'd bulked up, my face had widened. The spots had gone, I was a foot taller. I'd even had elocution lessons.*'

'*Why on earth would you do that?*'

'*I come from Northumberland, working class stock though I pretend otherwise. I thought my accent might hold me back, so I changed it.*'

He sounds abashed as if he had just admitted to something shameful, which he had, though it

314

wasn't his background of course, it was the rape of a child. Even if I'd known about the elocution lessons, I wouldn't have connected James to any of the guests. I don't remember hearing those boys speak once. Everything was background except for Paul.

'*Why pursue Julia if you had so much to hide from her?*' Laurel sounds genuinely curious.

'*The challenge, naturally. I was determined to make her notice me this time, plus her old man was stinking rich. He died before we were due to meet luckily, or he might have recognized me. He was very sharp. Her mother was crazy by then, so there was no one left to join the dots.*' James's voice changes, becomes bitter. '*I didn't know she'd been disinherited till after the wedding.*'

'*I see.*'

'*None of this is relevant.*' James sounds anxious. '*We were boys, it doesn't count.*'

'*Cosmo isn't a boy now.*' Laurel's voice is calm, as if stating simple facts. '*You said he misbehaves, in the present. It must be still going on.*'

'*For Christ's sake, forget about Cosmo.*' He sounds edgy. '*This is about us. You said we could be together if I told you everything.*'

'*I meant it, but I want to make it special.*' Her voice has switched back to its most seductive. '*Very special. I have to go to London about my divorce. Give me*

315

three days but tell your secretary to book you time off after that. You deserve this.'

The recording comes to an end.

Chapter 38

Cornwall 2023

Julia

The dawn wakes me, that and the silence. The wind has dropped. Grey light washes over the photographs I'd tipped out on the floor last night. They come from a box that my mother stored in the wardrobe here, out of the way. These photos didn't make it into a frame or even an album. They are rejects, but reject photos tell the truth which is why they get hidden away. I'd been too cold to look properly last night, too tired, too heartsick but the room is warmer this morning, the electricity has been restored. I wrap my dressing gown round me and kneeling on the floor, I leaf through them one by one.

James isn't smiling in the wedding photograph I turn up, but there is triumph in the tilt of his head.

His fingers grip my bare arm. My face is without expression, which could be why my mother rejected this photo; I don't look happy enough, but then I don't remember happiness. I remember relief. I'd secured our future, mine and Lottie's, or so I thought. I had no idea of the price. I push that photo aside, that woman isn't me any more, though I feel sorry for her. She had freed herself from one trap only to walk into another.

As I search through the pile of photos, I hear my mother's voice, dismissing the little girl but it hadn't made sense even then, that shy child making a nuisance of herself? Of course it hadn't made sense, it wasn't true. The subject was dropped. My parents never mentioned the family again; if I'd been less self-obsessed, I might have wondered why.

There isn't a single photo of James and Cosmo in the pile in front of me, though there are several of other guests from that time. James might have destroyed the images of them both in case they gave him away. There are the photos in my parents' room, he wouldn't have thought of those. These days it's a guest room, coldly perfect with its pale floor, ivory blinds, and white curtained four-poster bed. There is a framed photo of the wedding on the windowsill; we are smiling in this one, as if to order. My father often layered photos in the same frame, one on top of another, not bothering to take the old ones out.

I loosen the clasp and, as I hoped, others are jammed in behind. One of the villa; beneath that, the yacht and, lastly, a group of guests around the table: the one that gives me the information I'm looking for. I am present, Paul's head is turned to mine, our shoulders are touching. I remember the heat of that, the sick excitement. Further down the table are a group of three boys. I focus on the skinny one with a mop of dark hair; his eyes are difficult to make out from the angle of the shot, only the slant of the nose is familiar. How could I have guessed that had been James as a boy when I met him as an adult thirteen years later? The fatter, shorter youth next to him has curly ginger hair. With the benefit of hindsight, I can make out Cosmo in embryonic form. The sneer on his face is the same though everything else has changed. All those changes between boy and manhood take place in the late teens and early twenties; both young boys were unrecognizable in the men they'd become.

I search the edges of the photo for the little girl, but I can't see her. My father wouldn't have included a servant's child in any photo. He would never have given her a moment's thought until she was raped by his guests.

I came across her once, sitting under the tree outside the kitchen door. I had been with Paul the night before; we had stayed in his cabin all night. He had deadlines or so he pretended to his wife. The little girl didn't see me returning by the back of the house. She was reading and eating bread and jam, her breakfast probably. She looked calm and happy. I was jealous. The food was incidental to her, and I remember I was jealous of that too; of someone for whom eating was a simple act instead of a guilt-laden battle. Her mother called for help, and she disappeared into the kitchen. My heart had burned; she was needed, loved. Happy. I tried not to look at her again; she reminded me of all the things I didn't have.

What happened to her was my fault almost as much as the boys'. I ignored her. I lost the bracelet she gave me. She brought food to the table as if conveying a gift and waited in the shadows to help, but no one helped her. I have forgotten her name but if I could speak to her now, I might explain that I'd been a victim too; that I'd been sexually exploited, albeit in a much less violent way, but that's hardly an excuse. I was older and more knowing. I'll never be able to tell her how sorry I am.

Beyond the window the gulls are wheeling and calling, fishermen must be about. The sky and the sea are indistinguishable, both white as if all the colour has bled away. Children are still being hurt on my watch. It may be too late to make amends for that little girl, but it's not too late for them.

Chapter 39

Cornwall and London 2023

Julia

In the kitchen Rasul hands me a cup of coffee. He looks worried. 'I've been checking legal websites. Recordings aren't always allowed as evidence. It seems you need consent of the very people you recorded; without that it could be inadmissible.'

My heart sinks. 'Even in a case involving child abuse?'

'It can be allowed if it's within public interest, but that's for the judge to decide.'

'Does this mean we need something else as well, just in case?'

He nods, at the same moment my phone rings.

'Good morning, Mrs Grenville. Sarah Longsdown here.'

'Sarah . . .?' The voice is familiar, so is the name. I scramble to place it.

'Lottie's house mistress.'

'Of course. Is anything wrong?' My mind immediately fills with scenes of disaster: Lottie hit by a car as she ran to a class or found alone and weeping in a cloakroom after one of the boys had hurt her. I can hardly breathe.

'I wanted to check she arrived safely. She told me she was coming to Cornwall to see you yesterday, a family emergency she said, but when I saw Mr Grenville this morning he knew nothing about it, so I thought I'd best double check.'

I actually look around the room as if she might have come in very quietly and was sitting on the sofa or hiding behind the door.

'She isn't here.' I am breathless, struggling to absorb this news while she is silent, probably wondering why my daughter had lied.

'Could you have made a mistake? Perhaps she said she was going to see someone else, a friend with an emergency, rather than family?'

'Definitely not.' She sounds sharp. 'I'd have remembered.'

'We must phone the police then.' My mouth has dried, the words are difficult to say.

'Angel has been calling for her most evenings.' Sarah says evenly. 'They spend a lot of time together, at

Angel's parents' house I believe. She might well have gone there.'

'Angel's house?'

'I thought you knew.' She continues more kindly. 'I would contact her mother as the first port of call. Let me know.'

I've left Grace many messages over the past year, but she hasn't responded to a single one. This time I'm direct.

Hi Grace. Need your help. Lottie left school yesterday apparently to join me in Cornwall but didn't arrive. I thought we should contact the police but the house mistress says she might be at yours with Angel. I'm returning to London now. Can you be in touch?

I send the text and begin to pack. I am zipping my case when the message pings back.

Angel will meet you in London. Text time and place. Don't phone the police.

This means, I choose to believe, that Angel has information and Lottie is all right. Grace would have told me if she knew nothing. She wouldn't have asked me not to phone the police. Rasul looks up trains, I text Grace our arrival time in Paddington and then

Sarah to tell her she was right, Angel may have information and we are meeting as soon as I can get back.

We clean the kitchen, lock windows, turn off the heating. The house is back to its pristine state as we leave. It feels empty, unlike Thalassa, which had been echoing with ghosts.

The fast train from Penzance has few stops, we should be in London by late morning. Rasul checks the status of voice recordings in past trials. I long to be as calmly productive, but my thoughts circle and scream like the gulls on the cliffs. Where the hell is my daughter? Why did she lie to her house mistress? She might be safely with Angel, but what if she'd confronted Cosmo on Angel's behalf? What might that have made him do? She could have gone to James for help, not dreaming the two men were linked and that James would protect his friend. I can't believe James would harm his own step-daughter, but he's harmed a young girl before. His life has been built on a lie; everything he's achieved depends on that lie staying hidden.

The train speeds through the empty fields and dark woods of the November countryside, past church spires and towns, gravel pits and sewage works and, finally the dirt-stained back view of houses in London as we draw into Paddington.

We have decided on our course of action: Rasul will visit the crypt as usual. He will show his network of friends the pictures of Lottie I've sent to his phone; it's possible that rough sleepers in our patch may have glimpsed her if she is hiding out. They are more likely to tell anything useful to him rather than the police. I will find out what I can from Angel, go to the school to talk to Maud in case Lottie confided in her and then see Cosmo. After that Rasul and I will meet up at home and confront James. Rasul will bring Laurel's Dictaphone, useful blackmail should it be needed; if we still have no information about Lottie, we will contact the police. I am comforted by the plan or at least by its making.

Rasul disappears into the crowds at Paddington, and I make my way to the Costa café where Grace told me Angel would meet me. The tables are full. A group of girls sit together, scrolling; a young man with a backpack and a map on the table in front of him is muttering to himself; two women talk loudly at each other. I order coffee, look around and then glimpse Angel outside. I had walked straight past her. She is hunched into a large coat, her hair in tight plaits. She looks smaller than I remember, her features seem pinched, though her eyes are larger. She is watching me. I smile but her expression remains neutral. Angel as the enchanting child she used to be, dances invisibly between us as I walk towards her. This is the girl who spent nights with Lottie, the child I took with us to Cornwall, who jumped over the waves hand in hand with me, someone who had seemed like a second daughter. The girl who's been raped. It's all I can do not to hug her but instead I sit down opposite.

'Hi there, sweetie.'

She doesn't reply, her dark eyes are expressionless.

'How are you?'

She continues to stare at me.

'I'm so sorry.' It seems stupidly late to say this. I can't expect her to understand the choices I was faced with, or that I am besieged with regret that I made the wrong ones. I try all the same.

'Yesterday I found out what happened. I should never have believed my husband. I'm more sorry than I can say. Are you—'

'Mum said Lottie was missing.'

'Has she been in touch?'

Angel is looking across the station, the ghost of a smile hovers over her face. Does she know where Lottie is? She might even be looking at her right now; although when I follow her glance, the swirling crowds fill my vision, and there is no sign of my daughter at all.

'You need to leave her alone,' Angel says quietly but there is no mistaking the hardness in her voice, it used to be full of laughter. Abuse changes people, Rasul said, it hardens or destroys them.

'Is she safe? I can leave her alone if she's safe.'

Angel doesn't reply. She stands to swing her rucksack on her back. I don't notice the exact moment she turns, she is there and then she isn't. I stand up to see where she's gone, but she has disappeared into the crowds.

Did she mean leave Lottie alone in general? Or now? She wouldn't have disappeared like that if Lottie was missing, would she? She didn't seem as worried as she surely would have been if Lottie was in danger. I've been told almost nothing, but my anxiety calms a little.

The lobby of the art department is quiet, the kind of quiet that parents pay money for. Maud is in her office.

'Julia! This is a nice surprise, can I offer you tea?'

'Have you seen Lottie recently?'

'Yesterday but only briefly. She had a tutorial with Cosmo at midday. Why—'

'Is he here?'

'He's in his office, having a clear-out.'

Cosmo is in the middle of his room, a sheaf of papers in his hand. Piles more slide on every surface. Cupboard doors gape. Two computers are balanced on a chair; the shredder is jammed. The room smells fetid.

The same unwashed crockery litters the shelves. His face is dark as if with worry.

'Spring cleaning, Cosmo?'

Or packing up to leave but why now? What have you done?

Cosmo looks up and smiles, his face transforming in the instant into the affable buffoon he presents to the world.

'Something like that. You know how it is.'

'Where is she?'

'Who can you be talking about, my dear?' He shakes his head. 'Or should it be whom, I'm never quite sure.'

He knows I mean my daughter, but it could as easily be Angel or the little girl in Greece, in fact any child since then he has preyed on.

'Lottie's missing. I thought you might know where she was.'

'Should I?' He raises plump shoulders, and his fleshy face adopts a mock bewildered look.

I watch him, feeling shivery with hate. What happens in this squalid place where young girls come with hearts full of hope? What vile bargains has he driven?

'You're her teacher. Maud told me she was here yesterday.'

'For the briefest of moments. Charlotte is not the most attentive of students.'

'What happened?'

'What's with the sleuthing?' He puts a pile of paper by the shredder and reaches into a cupboard, withdrawing more.

'You might have been the last person who saw her.' I should be talking to the police about this pervert, but if he knows where Lottie is, the chance to find out might be lost. Formally accused, he could clam up.

'I doubt it. Have you asked your husband? Oh no, I forgot.'

'Forgot what?'

'He's rather busy right now.'

'What do you mean?' I know exactly what he means but I need to keep him talking, find out what he knows.

'He must have told you about the pretty therapist he's so cosy with?' He is watching my face as he speaks, and he laughs. 'You clearly don't approve. I don't blame you, I don't either. I don't trust her an inch, but James is besotted. Now if you'll excuse me, I need to sort out this mess. I'm in a bit of a hurry.'

Why? Is he planning an escape?

'Okay, Cosmo, sorry to have troubled you.'

I shut the door and hurry back downstairs to Maud's room.

'I've made your tea.' She looks up smiling but her face changes as she catches sight of mine.

'What's happened?'

'Lottie vanished yesterday; the house mistress phoned to tell me. I met Angel earlier today, I had the feeling she knew something.'

'What did Cosmo say?'

'He's not letting anything slip.' I must sound crazy; I know I look it. I haven't showered and my hair is wild. 'I think he's packing up to go.'

'Why now?'

'Maybe Lottie found out something. I know what he did to Angel, perhaps—'

'So do I.'

I am breathless as if winded. 'Why didn't you go to the police?'

'I did,' she says quietly.

'Sorry, of course you did.' I'd forgotten her brave, doomed stance.

'I believed Angel's story,' she continues, 'but the police wouldn't investigate after she withdrew her charges. Cosmo threatened her family, so she had to leave. That drew a line under it as far as the police were concerned. I've looked and looked for evidence, it's one of the reasons I stayed, but Cosmo keeps his computer locked in a cupboard and I don't have the key.'

'I have evidence.'

Maud's cheeks flush pink; it makes her look hopeful, years younger. 'What evidence?'

'Rasul secretly recorded James confirming that Cosmo raped Angel.'

Maud looks bewildered. 'If James knew, why didn't he inform the police?'

'Oh Maud.' I sit down and sip the tea, but it's cold and I put the cup down again unsteadily. 'James is guilty as well; he can't go to the police because Cosmo has evidence on him.'

'What evidence?'

'He admitted to Laurel that he and Cosmo did something terrible years ago. I only know because Laurel promised James she'd sleep with him if he levelled with her about his past. Rasul recorded that conversation too.'

'I'm completely lost. Who are Laurel and Rasul?'

'Sorry. Rasul is a trainee cook who lives with us. Laurel was my therapist.'

'Your therapist is your husband's girlfriend?' She looks astonished.

'Please don't tell Lottie, that's a detail she needn't know. She has enough to cope with already.'

'I'm sorry.'

'Be sorry for Laurel. We're over, James and I, but she must want him so badly that she's prepared to overlook what he's done and the fact he's complicit with Cosmo's crimes.'

'Why on earth should he be?'

'Cosmo has photographic evidence of James raping a child when they were teenagers on holiday; a holiday where my own father was the host.'

The words seem to echo in the silence, broken only by the faint sound of banging coming from upstairs as Cosmo flings stacks of paper to the floor and throws open cupboards.

'Who was the poor child?' Maud asks quietly.

'She was our caretaker's daughter. My father and his guests closed ranks.'

Maud shakes her head, looking sombre. She sips her tea, moments tick by.

'I must go. I'm meeting Rasul and then hopefully, James. After that, if there are no definite leads, I'll have to involve the police.'

'There is one other possibility,' Maud says in her calm voice.

I stare at her, hope flaring.

'You know how much Lottie loves your mother? She could be there.'

'My mother?' My heart sinks 'Lottie won't go near my mother unless I beg her to.'

'She visits often, every week, sometimes more.'

I shake my head. Maud must see the disbelief on my face.

'She doesn't tell you because she thinks it might upset you. She knows things are, well, strained between you and your mother.' She continues carefully, 'She doesn't want to appear to be taking sides.'

'Yet she told you.'

'I'm not her mother,' Maud says gently. 'She doesn't

love me, so she's not worried about hurting my feelings.'

I am on my feet wrapping my coat around me. 'I'll leave my case here. An Uber to Richmond won't take long.'

'And I'll see if I can unearth anything here.' Maud sounds determined, I don't want to tell her it's unlikely she'll get anything more out of Cosmo.

I pause on my way out. 'How did Lottie seem after the meeting with Cosmo yesterday?'

'Excited if anything, in a bit of a hurry. She waved to me from the door and then disappeared.'

'But what did she look like?'

'Exactly the same as usual. You know, a schoolgirl in uniform, with a rucksack on her back.'

Maud's words sound like all those descriptions of missing girls that parents give police before a school jersey is found under a hedge by the roadside or an empty rucksack in woodland somewhere.

Chapter 40

London 2023

Julia

'Mrs Grenville!' The young nurse smiles. I haven't seen her before, she must be new. She has a soft round face and her blonde fringe is squashed into spikes by her cap. 'Your mother's waiting for you. She's so pleased you are coming.'

We both know this is a euphemism.

'Have there been any visitors recently? Her grand-daughter?' The nurse might be new enough not to have read the rules about confidentiality.

'Oh yes. She popped in yesterday afternoon.'

So Maud guessed right; Lottie came here after her meeting with Cosmo, but what has happened since then?

'Do you know where she went when she left?'

She shakes her head, still smiling. 'We don't usually ask our visitors their plans.'

I follow her up the broad staircase with its thick red carpet and along the corridor.

'You have a visitor!'

Mother looks up smiling as the nurse enters but the smile drops when she sees that it's me. Daughter, she might be thinking, not granddaughter. What a pity. Her hair is in the same spun bob as always, a gold cashmere cardigan hangs from her shoulders as if from a coat hanger.

'I'll leave you with your daughter.' The nurse smiles and disappears.

I kiss my mother's cheek, as usual she turns her head away.

'How are you, Mother?'

There is no answer.

'The nurse tells me Lottie was here yesterday, Mother.'

My mother looks about her as if to catch a glimpse of her granddaughter. I look around too, I can't help it.

'Do you know where she went when she left?'

She scans my face silently.

'Please try and remember, it's very important.'

Mother frowns as if irritated, in a minute she will ring the bell and I'll be shown out, it happens often. I lean forward, there's nothing to lose.

'I've just come back from Paxos; something terrible happened just after I left all those years ago. Do you have any idea what it was?'

Her eyes look wary, her mouth tightens.

'Did you know about James and Cosmo and the little girl?'

She shakes her head; she looks extremely old suddenly, very fragile.

'I want to know the child's name, her family name. I want to go back and look for her.'

Mother closes her eyes.

I feel myself being carried away, and grasp her thin arm, as though I'm clinging to a flimsy piece of wood in a flood. 'Did you know who James was when he married me? What he'd done?'

Her other hand reaches for mine; for a moment I think she is being affectionate, but she uses that hand to peel my fingers off her arm. She clutches the bell, ringing it with surprising force.

The nurse comes in and takes the handles of the wheelchair.

'She's very tired.' Her tone is apologetic. 'Her granddaughter kept her busy.'

'Did she?' I stare at my mother, but her eyes are closed as if to guard her secrets.

'They had a grand old time, looking at photos, they were talking away or at least the granddaughter was talking and asking questions.' The nurse smiled down at my mother. 'I'll just settle this one for her nap. I'll be back in a jiffy.'

She wheels my mother into the adjoining room. I am on my feet, scouring the bookcase for the photo albums; a slim volume protrudes from the rest, and I slip it into my bag, just as the nurse comes back into the room.

'I'll show you out,' she says briskly. She might have seen the little theft, but what could she say?

The Uber driver progresses towards Westminster very slowly, rush-hour traffic. My mother has defeated me again, although I know a little more about Lottie's movements, thanks to the nurse. I pull the album from my bag; there are no photos of the little girl but among the many snaps of my father and the flowers and the view, there is one of James and Cosmo swimming in the pool. They would be unrecognizable to anyone who didn't know the story. I doubt my mother has any idea.

I phone Rasul; he tells me no one he's spoken to so far has seen Lottie. I can hear Zoe calling him in the background; he's been held up but promises to meet me at home as soon as he can.

Lottie was all right yesterday afternoon, I whisper to myself. She was fine until then. James might have the answer, especially if threatened with the recordings but what if he claims to have no idea?

My anxiety rises with every mile. We are crawling around Hyde Park Corner behind a bus; I can't wait any more. I begin to tap in 999 but the phone rings. Maud.

'I need to let you know about Cosmo,' she begins carefully.

My mouth dries. What has she found out?

'He's been arrested at Heathrow, about to board a plane. Libby informed the staff by email. It's confidential. I'll let you know more when I have it.'

I sink back stunned; amazement, relief then worry flood into my head. Who told the police about Cosmo? Lottie? If she spooked him yesterday, did he harm her before leaving? Is that why he was attempting to escape? Or did Rasul decide to inform on him? Angel? It couldn't be James, he wouldn't dare.

Big Ben strikes six as I get out of the Uber in our street. It looks as quiet as usual, the brass knockers on the front door shine in the gloom. A large van is making a food delivery to the house at the far end of the road. All seems normal, peaceful even. The house isn't locked or alarmed; James must be here although it's very quiet. He doesn't answer when I call his name.

I dump my things in the kitchen. James's coat is over the back of a chair; he must be about to leave. The curtains are drawn together in the sitting room, there is the remnants of a fire. The cushions on the sofa are dented, I register a brief mental image of them together, talking and kissing as they were when Rasul recorded them.

Upstairs, a case lies open on our bed, the bed we used to share. It's half full, pyjamas and shirts folded neatly. The air feels full of moisture as if someone recently had a shower.

I walk into the bathroom praying I won't find them together, and the world changes.

James is lying in the bath, alone.

James with white skin and a savage stare, naked, in a bath of blood.

Two razors on the floor in a pool of red.

His clothes folded on the chair.

Both wrists have been neatly slit; the borders of the wound gape like the thin edges of an opened purse.

Chapter 41

London 2023

Julia

The bathroom is cold. The window is wide open, but the noise of traffic and birds is faint compared to the beating of the pulse in my head. The iron tang of blood is layered with the stench of alcohol and the scent of soap. An empty bottle of whisky lies on the floor next to the bath, a glass tumbler is next to a brown medicine bottle and scattered tablets.

I look more closely, make myself look. I need to know that James is really dead, in case I should call an ambulance, although it is obvious at first glance that he is.

His pupils are dilated. The stare is empty. There is no pulse at his neck. I touch his hand: the skin is icy. He is gone.

My legs weaken. I want to sit down but the side of the bath is covered with blood.

I kneel on the floor and tip forward. Horror breaks over me, black waves in a storm but I have to weather it for Lottie's sake. I have to protect her from this. I must be the one to tell her, gently, that her stepfather has committed suicide, because it's clear that's what has happened, obvious that it's suicide, not murder. There is the empty whisky bottle and the tablets. The razors, one for each hand. The tidy pile of clothes. A murderer wouldn't leave a tidy pile like that, he would have had to struggle to get James into the bath, but there is no sign of a struggle. The usual bottles and toothbrushes are by the basin, the same towels hanging on the rack. Nothing has been broken or dislodged, nothing is different from usual except for a little tree in a familiar green and yellow pot standing on the bathroom floor. It's Laurel's pot, in fact it's her tree. She must have brought it here as a prelude to moving in, anticipating shared baths amid the calm of green. She won't know what's happened yet, and surprisingly, I feel sorry for her. I find myself wanting to let her know, carefully, that her imagined life is over.

I need to leave this room. I look again at my husband lying in the bath, but this half-submerged body has become a stranger with his face and even that is changing. His nose is sharper as the skin has retracted, the tongue is dry, already darkened. Wet hair is plastered unevenly to the white forehead. His knees protrude above the water, the penis floats like a separate animal, adrift in the blood.

I should say goodbye but my gaze shies from that angry stare and the lifeless body and I look at a leaf instead, floating in the water, blown from Laurel's tree. I grasp the detail as I might a helping hand: the delicate veins, the leathery surface, the scalloped edges; a bright green fragment to set against the red of death.

Then I get up and vomit in the basin.

I rinse it clean, wipe my mouth and walk down the stairs, holding tight to the banisters.

I phone the police. I tell them about the body and about my daughter who is missing. I tell them to look for Lottie first, because it's too late for James. I am passed to another policeman to give her Lottie's details.

As I am texting Rasul, police sirens are getting louder, coming closer. Passers-by will be staring, whispers will be starting and soon the fact of my husband's death will travel through the school. There will be shock, disbelief, and maybe tears. Information will be managed, the children's welfare considered. Some people will be avid for details, they usually are but I need the truth.

* * *

'What do you think happened?' I ask the policeman who has arrived with a team who disperse immediately. We are sitting in the kitchen while others in white hazmat suits walk up and down stairs, sealing rooms and taking photos.

The policeman has downturned eyes the colour of dishwater, fleshy folds by his mouth. A habit of cracking his knuckles. He stares at me impassively.

'I mean, do you think it was suicide or murder?'

He doesn't answer, maybe I sound flippant and it's true, the shock has yet to kick in. We are waiting for a female officer to arrive so she can question me. I wonder how often he comes across scenes like this, people like me. Perhaps he has developed his calm expression to deal with us or maybe it's how he always looks and that's why he was chosen. They will question Cosmo now they have him in custody, but if James was killed, it won't have been by him. A murder would have complicated his escape, it wouldn't have been worth the risk to him.

Angel's father could be hauled in for questioning, though I doubt he would have waited a year for vengeance; he would have struck sooner. In any case, it would be hard to envisage that small man winning a fight against James.

Laurel might have been one of the last to see him alive and therefore a suspect; but why would she kill James? His death would deny her the prizes that had been almost within her grasp: money, prestige, home, companionship. Sex. Everything she worked so hard for has vanished now. Laurel was capable of trickery, God knows, but I can't believe she would be capable of murder. Women rarely are. Even if she was, she would have waited until after their marriage in order to inherit his wealth.

A random burglary gone wrong? A murderer with a grudge against the school? My mind twists and turns but only suicide makes sense. He would have received the email about Cosmo's arrest along with all the other staff, and he would have understood his disgrace was a matter of time.

A woman officer comes in and sits down across the kitchen table from me. She introduces herself as Zahida. She has piled auburn hair, metal framed glasses, and a narrow glance. She doesn't smile which must be something she's learnt; most people can't help smiling when they meet you. She expresses sympathy. Her voice is soft, but the tone is steely.

'I regret I need to ask you a few questions, as the closest to your husband, your answers will be valuable.'

I wasn't the closest, someone else had taken that place, but if they don't know about Laurel, I won't tell them. If I mention my husband's mistress, I might, in their eyes, become a jealous wife. James would have been careful to conceal her from everyone. If they find out about her, they might arrest me. I'll be assumed to have motivation and become a suspect, involved if not actually guilty.

'Was your husband depressed?'

'No.' Angry often, exacting, ambitious. Vain. Image was everything, he couldn't have borne to be exposed as a criminal though that's what he was.

'Were there work worries?'

'I wouldn't say he was preoccupied by worry.' James didn't worry, he relied on others to do the fretting for him.

'Money concerns?'

'No.' There may have been; if there were, he didn't share them with me.

'Did he drink to excess?'

'He liked a drink in the evenings.' He was drunk the last time I heard him on that recording, drunk enough to give all his secrets away.

'And was the marriage a happy one?' Her glance becomes a stare.

'Yes.' He was leaving me, the marriage was over but why would I tell you that?

'Any serious disagreements?'

'We had our differences, most couples do.' Is that what you would call them? The endless corrections, the jibes, the control. The forced sex. The betrayal.

'You had recently been on holiday on your own, why was that?' The eyes glint.

'We have a family property in Paxos, and I went to check on that as the agent will confirm. James was busy.'

If she is hoping to catch me in a lie, she will be disappointed, that was the truth.

'When you came back, you didn't come home.'

How do they know that? Libby?

'My husband met me at the airport. We felt it would be sensible for me to check up on the house in Cornwall, to complete the survey as it were.' Does that sound too neat? Too privileged?

'You were on your own down there?'

'Rasul, our cook, came to bring supplies. We came back by train early today.'

'Why such a brief visit?'

'I attended to what I needed to, and I wanted to see my mother.' Another lie but how would they know?

'And today, can you account for your movements?'

I tell her about the train's arrival into Paddington, where CCTV will have been operational, the visit to the school, and then my mother. Maud will vouch for me and so will the nursing home, who will have a record of my arrival and departure. I tell her about Rasul, who has been at the crypt since our return. Zoe will confirm that. Zahida nods calmly as if she already knows.

They ask me if I have any questions for them.

'My daughter Lottie, Charlotte, left school yesterday,

347

and she was last seen at my mother's nursing home in the afternoon. I waited to discuss it with my husband so I only reported it just now but I'm terrified in case—'

'She is at the station with your cook. They have been there for some hours,' Zahida announces, leafing through the papers in front of her.

'What?' Lottie is safe. Safe! Tears spill. 'What is she doing at the station?'

'We can give you a lift there if you like, she will give you the details herself. I'll get a message to her to let her know you are on the way,' she says, observing my tears calmly.

A large group of people, pupils among them, watch from the end of the road as I climb into the back of a police car. They might think I am being arrested on suspicion of my husband's murder, but I don't care. The only thing I care about is Lottie.

Chapter 42

London 2023

Julia

It doesn't take long to reach Charing Cross police station. The white, colonnaded building looks incongruously grand, like the mansion of a nineteenth-century duke, not a place to process criminals. Lottie and Rasul are waiting on the steps.

Lottie lunges forward and hugs me as I get out of the car. I hug her back and reach my hand to Rasul. He takes it, warm sympathy in his eyes.

'Sorry about James, Mum.' There are tears in her eyes. Could I have thought, fleetingly, crazily, that my daughter could have killed my husband? I hadn't realized I had, until now when the suspicions dissolve in the warmth and the tightness of her hug.

'Are you okay, Lottie?'

'Course.'

'Did they arrest you?'

She draws back and looks at me with scorn in her blue eyes. 'Don't be nuts. I came to tell them about Cosmo. Rasul was on his way to the house, but I asked him to meet me here. I needed a friend but I didn't know about James then, you must have needed a friend too.'

'All I needed was to know you were safe. Thank you for being here, Rasul. Those recordings—'

'Weren't needed.' He nods quietly. That probably means that Laurel is safe from pursuit or questioning, at least for now.

'I desperately need to talk to you,' Lottie says, linking her arm with mine. 'We can't go home. Shall we go to our café?'

The Garden Café has stopped serving meals by the time we arrive, but they let us in. Lottie orders tea.

'Okay, finally I can tell you everything,' she says with an air of relief.

Rasul gets up.

'Wait.' Lottie catches his hand. 'Don't go. You need to listen to this.'

'He might think it's personal, Lottie.'

'Of course it's fucking personal.' The anger in Lottie's voice is stark. 'Everything about this is personal but Rasul's involved, he's helped so much. I want him to know what happened.' She pulls him to sitting, he shrugs and complies. The tea arrives and he pours it; he probably knows my hands will be shaking too much.

Lottie lowers her voice. 'I've been working on Cosmo for months, putting up with his shit so I could get him for what he did to Angel. She wasn't the only one.'

I don't tell her that I know this now, that Rasul's recording implied Cosmo was continuing his abuse. I simply listen, understanding finally why Lottie has been preoccupied for so long, why she's been so much on her own. She needed focus; it must have taken all her courage to carry out her plan.

'I teased him until his tongue was hanging out. He was so frustrated he got careless; it wasn't just girls already in the school. He lit on those coming for interviews. He told them he could secure scholarship funding if they were "prepared to cooperate". Can you believe that?'

I could. He probably tried it on with the girl I saw running down the stairs, the one who told me to fuck off.

'Yesterday morning I took a bottle of wine to one of our tutorials. I'd asked for a discussion about videos as a cover so I could take my video camera along. I put it on his desk, with the recording function switched on. Luckily it's silent and, anyway, he wasn't in the mood to notice. I got him pissed and

351

he dropped his guard. It was as if he was performing on purpose. He told me I was trickier than the other bitches, but I had to do what he wanted, and if I didn't, he'd make the other stuff public. As if I cared.'

'Other stuff?'

'He and James were at Granny's house in Paxos when they were teenagers. Cosmo took photos of James forcing himself on a little girl. I didn't believe him, but now I've seen photos of James and Cosmo in Granny's album, I realise they were there at the time. I think it's probably true.'

I push her cup of tea nearer to her, wishing she hadn't had to hear that. She hardly draws breath.

'I told Cosmo I wouldn't take my clothes off, but that he could have access. I think he found that exciting.'

'Oh, Lottie.' I feel sick at the danger she put herself in, my brave, crazy daughter.

'I lifted my skirt up but kept my boots on and waited till he had his trousers off. I kicked him in the balls with all my strength. He went down so hard I thought I'd killed him. I grabbed my camera, stuffed it in my rucksack and ran out.'

'And went to the police?'

'I went to Granny's first. I wanted to know what had happened in Paxos, so I could tell the police about that too.'

'Granny wouldn't remember about that now, you know how she is.'

'Granny's amazing. She can't remember breakfast, but she knew two of their guests caused trouble with a girl in Paxos. She doesn't know what it was, Grandpa never told her the details, just that it was a secret. She has no idea it was James and I didn't tell her.'

'That was kind, Lottie. Thank you.'

I find I feel sorry for my mother, she was trapped by my father. I know how that felt, he trapped me too.

Lottie is rushing on. 'I was scared about Cosmo tracking me down, so Angel's dad picked me up from the nursing home and I spent the night at hers. By the time I gave the police the video, they'd already arrested Cosmo. Was that because they think he killed James?'

'I don't think anyone killed James. He wasn't a threat to Cosmo; it was the other way around.'

I don't tell her about Laurel. Her presence today would have been fleeting. She would have let herself in, bags packed and hotel booked. She would have called his name and when he didn't answer, would have gone from room to room as I did, and then upstairs. The bathroom might have been the last place she would have looked. Like me, it would have taken her a while to take in what she was seeing. She might have leant against the wall for support. She might have bent over the bath and kissed him, but she wouldn't have lingered. I may not have known her well, but I know she was private; she would have hated the questions she would have had to face.

My phone buzzes. It's Maud. She asks us to supper and to stay the night.

'That's both of you, Rasul too if he wants.'

'Can you fit us in?'

'Come and see.'

Chapter 43

London 2023

Julia

It turns out that I was wrong about Maud's home, which isn't surprising, I've been wrong about everything else. Maud doesn't live in a small flat as I'd imagined, but a large Victorian terraced house in Muswell Hill. She doesn't own a cat but two boisterous spaniels. It's not cold or messy but warm and tidy.

Maud hugs me and then Lottie. Rasul left us at the café; he had friends to catch up with or so he tactfully said. Maud shows us into a large room with deep leather chairs either side of a wood burning stove, a shining wooden floor and antique maps on the wall. There are several tall bookcases, bunches of red chrysanthemums in great jars and a cello in the corner.

An attractive woman of around forty with tortoiseshell-rimmed glasses and long dark hair is working at a computer on a desk by the window. She pushes up her glasses and smiles warmly as if she already knows me.

'This is Prishi.' Maud kisses her. 'She knows what we know.'

Prishi shakes my hand then turns to Lottie. 'Ah, Lottie, I've heard all about you. I need your help, come with me.' They disappear into the kitchen, already chatting.

I accept a glass of wine from Maud and sit opposite her in the armchair.

'How are you?' She watches my face, her expression is warm, a little anxious.

'Better than I was, at least for now. I probably haven't taken it in yet but Lottie's very calm which helps, especially as she's been through so much.'

'Prishi will take care of her this evening. We thought she might like doing something ordinary like cooking.'

'Prishi seems lovely.'

'We've been together for fourteen years. She's an anthropologist at King's.'

It's hard to imagine fourteen years with anyone. I'd had five with Anthony, seven with James. I raise my glass in acknowledgement.

'What happened to your therapist?' Maud asks quietly.

'She's disappeared. The police don't know about

her, and it's probably best left that way. She could be a suspect in their eyes.'

'Rightly so, I can't help thinking.' She looks at me, a level Maud glance.

'It can't be her; why kill the fatted goose? For what purpose? It doesn't make sense.'

'If you say so.' Maud refills my glass. 'Now about Cosmo's arrest—'

'That's a puzzle too. Rasul hadn't given them the recordings by then. Lottie had compromising video footage but hadn't shown it to the police by the time he was arrested. I have no idea how they knew—'

Maud is listening, a faint smile on her face.

'My God, Maud, it was you! You told the police!'

The smile broadens. 'When Cosmo first arrived, he asked me to order him a case for his private laptop. I unpacked it for him when it arrived. It was solid with a good lock, so I ordered one for myself. I didn't tell him, men like Cosmo need to think themselves unique.' She fondles one of the spaniel's ears. 'After you left today, I informed him I was having a clear-out, and he could help himself to any paintings he wanted. I knew he'd be unable to resist.' The other spaniel noses his way forward and she strokes him too. 'I said I was going upstairs to clean the top studio. Soon after that I heard him clattering downstairs. He'd locked his room, but I had the master key ready. His laptop case was in the cupboard but for once he'd neglected to lock that door, just as I'd hoped. Greed makes people careless.' She chuckles, allowing herself a mouthful of wine. 'I took the case out of the cupboard, it was heavy, so I knew his laptop must be inside. I substituted my case which also contained my laptop, the two cases weighed about the same. I locked the door to his room and met him coming back up the stairs. His arms were full of the pictures he'd taken from the walls of my study and he didn't so much as glance at me.'

'Clever Maud. I could never have kept my cool like that.'

'Long years of teaching practice. I took Cosmo's computer to the police straight away. They found a receipt for a ticket to Indonesia along with all the images on his hard drive. They were waiting for him by the steps to the plane. He hadn't even noticed my computer was in the case, not his.'

Chapter 44

London 2023

Julia

'Are you all right?' Lottie asks as I leave Maud's flat the next morning. 'Really?'

She has chosen to stay behind with Prishi today, out of the way of reporters. Calls to Sarah Longsdown have been made, explanations given. Lottie remains calm, relieved if anything. The burden has been passed. Angel has been vindicated, the wheels of justice have begun to turn. Lottie is an acknowledged star.

I don't know how to answer her question, I'm not sure how I am. A bomb had been dropped into my life, several bombs, and in the aftermath, my head still rings with noise. Unexpectedly, the person I most want to see is Laurel. I need her warmth and her wisdom, it can't all have been an act. She gave me more than she took away, I'd like to tell her that.

The white house in Pimlico looks the same, but there is no label by the second bell and no answering buzzer. I try all of them, one by one. I give up with an ache in my throat and am walking away when the door opens and a young woman stands on the doorstep, a sleeping baby on her hip. She is barefoot in ripped jeans, with diamond earrings and blonde hair falling in waves, a welcoming smile on her face.

'Hi there, can I help?' A warm Irish accent. She looks pleased to see me, and I remember the days when I was on my own with a baby, glad to talk to anyone who rang the bell.

'I was looking for the therapist on the second floor.'

'You mean Laurel? Oh sorry, she's gone.'

'Gone?'

I am bereft although I'd suspected as much; Cosmo knew about her, he might tell the police, and she'd know that the only way to escape their intrusion would be to disappear.

She hitches the baby up. 'She left yesterday. Family stuff, she said.'

'You knew her?'

'A bit.' She leans against the wall, settling in for a chat. 'I met her a while ago. She came up first because she'd heard the baby crying. I thought she was going to complain but she came to help. She stayed with me till he went to sleep. She came back a few times after that, though she was so busy.'

'Busy?' I'm doing it again, Laurel's technique.

'God, yes. I used to pass her clients on the stairs all the time. Women, men, young girls. She must have been good at what she did. She was good to me anyway.'

'Did she leave a forwarding address?'

She shook her head. 'I have a feeling she was going abroad.'

The baby wakes and begins to cry. I thank her and turn to go.

'She was kind, I'm going to miss her.' She sounds sad and I know how she feels. Laurel has gone, disappearing as mysteriously and suddenly as she arrived.

I look back again when I reach the corner. The young woman is still standing there; despite the baby clasped close, her figure looks lonely. I wave and she waves back. She was right. Laurel was kind. I'm going to miss her too.

Chapter 45

London 2023

Julia

James's death is pronounced unsuspicious.

His post-mortem showed high levels of alcohol and diazepam; in the absence of any other evidence, it was assumed by the coroner he'd taken his own life, the precipitating factor being Cosmo's arrest, spelling his own disgrace. The media concluded he had taken the easy way out. Cosmo has said nothing so far.

Can it ever be easy to end your life? A warm bath, whisky, a handful of sleeping tablets, a deep slice across both wrists with a razor; it might sound simple but the moments before would have been difficult as well as the moments after. I wondered what images would have flickered in front of his eyes and if any had been of me.

Loose ends tie up, circles close.

The headmaster's house reverts to the school, the deputy takes over: a middle-aged historian with a dry sense of humour and a ferocious work ethic. It is agreed the school will be in safe hands while the fallout from the scandal is repaired.

Angel returns. Counselling is made available for her and for Cosmo's other victims, young girls whose identity is protected. Not everyone has come forward yet. Lottie doesn't consider herself a victim but submits to counselling, which she enjoys.

James's savings are made available to me, a modest sum; regular payments had apparently been made into Cosmo's account. I bank all that's left for school fees. Lottie wants to carry on at the school, it's where her friends are, though she decides not to board any more. Angel is a day girl again; they'll hang out more easily this way.

A maternity leave vacancy for a French teacher at the school becomes available, my application is successful. The school governors offer me a small flat in Kennington, kept for visiting teachers or ones who find themselves in need and I am considered to be in need, a new widow. It's a small top-floor flat in a red brick building close to a gasometer. There is no garden but there is a balcony and a room for Lottie. I can't hear any bells from here. I accept gratefully. My life is different, but it's mine, which may be why my anxiety has ebbed almost completely. I make the most of everything: Lottie of course, Lottie most of all, but also my pupils, my colleagues at school and the changing colours of the Thames which I cross every day. I left behind all the furnishings in our Westminster house, but I took the tree that Laurel left in the bathroom. It just fits on the balcony. There were trees like that in the garden at Thalassa; it reminds me of Laurel, of our sessions, of Paxos.

Rasul is taken on as assistant catering manager in my old team and finds a flat in Finsbury Park. The house in Zennor is up for sale but I hesitate over Thalassa.

A month later, a thick package arrives to the school and addressed to me, it's from Greece. Lefcothea's promised photos of Thalassa, which will be useful as I plan to rent it until I decide what to do. I take the packet home. Unwrapped, the package contains a book and photos, but not from Lefcothea, in fact there is no accompanying note.

I haven't seen these photos before. They are old family snaps taken at Thalassa but not of our family. The Greek mother smiles from the back door, the father sleeps in a chair. Their boy is playing with something on the ground, and the little girl is sitting under the olive tree. My eyes fill with tears, so I can't see her properly at first, but I drink her in.

She has a book in her hands and a black and white

cat on her lap. Her necklace glints in the sun. I look closer, stare, find my magnifying glass. Look again. A pretty gold necklace.

Gold necklaces are common. Anyone could have a necklace like that, a glamorous therapist just as easily as a little girl in Paxos, but all the same my hands tremble when I pick up the book, a cracked leather-bound edition of *The Legends of Greece and Rome*.

A spray of dried leaves has been placed inside, marking the story of Daphne, the nymph who was chased by Apollo and who was changed into a tree, a laurel tree. One of my favourites. I read it, as much to calm my heart as anything, then I turn to the first page, inscribed in pencil with a name that calls to me over the years. I remember now how it sounded in her mother's voice, or in her brother's when they played hide and seek among the olive trees.

Sofie! Sofie!

I take the spray of leaves to the potted tree on the balcony because, as I have already guessed, the leaves will be the same, both laurel leaves. I stand on the small balcony above the busy street, the morning sun on my face, amazed that it has taken me this long. I thought I was determined but nothing compares to Sofie's determination, her courage. I imagine the anger incubating for years, becoming purpose, transforming that shy child into a powerful woman who called herself Laurel, capable of executing justice on her own terms.

The dried leaves crumble in my hand, but the leaves on the tree are smooth and leathery under my fingertips. I see her carefully placing the tree in the bathroom, calling to James to admire her present. I see her running his bath, folding his clothes, stooping over him as he lay grinning up at her lapped in warm water. I see her handing him whisky generously laced with sleeping tablets, refilling the glass again and again, smiling. After a while, she might have started to undress. Distracted, intoxicated, increasingly drowsy, he wouldn't notice that the whisky tasted bitter until it was too late. I wonder if she waited until he slipped into unconsciousness before she started cutting. I imagine her whispering her real name to him and watching him realize the truth as the light dimmed from his eyes. I see her placing a leaf in the bath, just before she left, a private message to me that I only now understand.

She must have known she took a risk in sending me the book, but she trusted me; we have things in common after all, we are both victims, both survivors. My father wronged us both and so did my husband. My wounds are far less severe, but she has avenged me too.

When I pick up the wrappings the book came in,

a small bundle falls out, tissue paper around a little bracelet of shells with fine blue letters that spell my name. It slips over my wrist. The tears come then.

Six months later, the teacher whose maternity leave I was covering becomes pregnant again and decides not to come back. The post becomes permanent, with time off for a part-time MA in Arabic Studies at King's.

Rasul comes round to cook supper to celebrate. He and Lottie go to the pub afterwards and, in the rush, he leaves his new sunglasses on the table, on top of the pile of post he'd collected from his pigeonhole in the staff room on his way. I pick them up as I clear things away, and the glasses slip. At the top of the pile, there's a postcard of a beach so familiar it could have been our cove. I turn the card over. I shouldn't have done but I can't resist and anyway it's in Greek. I can only read two words: the one at the bottom is 'Sofie'. The one at the top, 'Nico'.

Jakob's words come back to me: '. . . *the little boy survived if that's what you mean. Nico. Odd that I remember his name and not the girl's, that's vanished.*'

When Rasul returns with Lottie, he sees that I know. Nico not Rasul.

I don't let him apologize. He won't accept my apologies either. He feels guilty but relieved that I know. He felt guilty for years; he had been present

368

as a child on the night of his sister's ordeal, hiding and terrified, as she was brutalized.

'We stayed with cousins on Corfu after that, our parents died soon after. Sofie thought everything that happened was her fault. I blamed myself.'

There is a silence. Lottie puts her hand on Nico's.

'In time she was helped by my aunt's friend, transformed really. She wanted to give something back. She studied psychology in Italy, then trained as a therapist. She was good, the word spread. And all the time, we followed the media for news of your father, though it was the boys she was tracking. About a year ago, she spotted Cosmo's picture in the press along with James's at the time of that investigation. Cosmo was cleared but we guessed what had really happened, what was probably still happening. We moved to England. Sofie started counselling again, as Laurel Rossi. I became Rasul, the refugee cook. It allowed me to meet you. We wanted all the information we could gather for our plan, though I wasn't expecting such kindness.' He bows his head then carries on. 'Cosmo and James having refused therapy, she adapted her plan and turned to you. When she understood what you'd been through, she almost withdrew. In the end, we decided if you knew the whole story, you'd want us to continue. She thought you'd want justice too.'

If by justice, he means James's death he doesn't

clarify; there's no need to. I know what happened. Sofie's leaf and her tree have told me already.

I hadn't imagined being followed on Paxos, it had been real. Nico tells me Dimitrios was the man filling the pool with his son and it was the son who had followed me. I am part of the family legend it seems, someone regarded with suspicion though not hate.

I have Thalassa's deeds sent to me by my mother's lawyer, and I've discussed my plans with Nico.

Dimitrios and Roxana are settled now, besides she has arthritis. It would be too big a place for them. The other cousin, Christos, is head of a large engineering company in Boston, Nico tells me, all his dreams worked out. Nico doesn't want to leave his job either. He's fond of us; it seems we are also family now.

'Sofie.' I say her name for the very first time and it sounds soft, like forgiveness.

'Give it to Sofie.'

Chapter 46

Paxos 2023

Sofie

The blue is deeper than she remembers, so is the silence.

She stands as they used to do, her face to the sun, her body filling with warmth and light. She can feel her fingertips swell, her skin relax, her heart unfold.

She can smell herbs. She can smell the sea.

Tomorrow Gabriella is coming with her girls. They will sit on the beach. They will talk and watch the children together.

Dimitrios has burnt the shed to the ground.

His son made a sign for the gate, with flowing script below a carved laurel tree, its boughs lifted like arms, the oval leaves evenly spaced.

Thalassa – healing centre.

There are bookings already, from Paxos, from Greece, from London.

There is much to do but she stands where she is for a little longer. She closes her eyes.

Athena is here and so is Babas. She can feel them both.

She is home.

Acknowledgements

I would like to thank my superlative publishing teams at HarperCollins on both sides of the Atlantic, with special gratitude to Rachel Kahan, my editor at William Morrow, New York and Phoebe Morgan at HarperFiction in the UK. Their peerless editing and generous support made *All Her Secrets* the very best it could be. Martha Ashby expertly piloted it onwards at HarperFiction and Belinda Toor is now guiding the process with great skill. Jo Kite and Maud Davies are in charge of marketing and publicity respectively and I thank them both for their inspired work. I am so grateful to these expert professionals for all their dedicated help.

I owe so much to the cover design teams at both William Morrow and HarperFiction for their outstanding artwork.

Thanks as always to Eve White and Ludo Cinelli

and Steven Evans at Eve White Agency for their endless support, advice and friendship, and to Rebecca Winfield and Nick Walters of David Luxton Associates.

A special thank you to Scott Gill, my brother-in-law, with whom I explored the beautiful Greek island of Paxos, a key setting in the book. Together we discovered remote villages and deserted beaches, many of which have found themselves in the pages of *All Her Secrets*. I was grateful for Scott's company and marvellous spirit of adventure.

Many grateful thanks are due to Rachel Melville-Thomas, neighbour and child and adolescent psychotherapist, for her valuable advice on trauma and childhood.

Susan Barrett, whose own book *The Garden of the Grandfather* is a fascinating record of her life in Greece, kindly provided insights into the Greek language and suggested words that I was able to incorporate into the text. Thank you, Susie.

I am lucky enough to belong to two writing groups and we meet regularly for friendship, inspiration and writing.

My children contribute the sparkle and the music of my life and I am extremely lucky that my husband Steve works from home as I do. His presence is the calm backdrop of my writing days.